PRAISE FOR KATE CARLISLE'S
FIXER-UPPER MYSTERIES

"An immensely satisfying page-turner of mystery."
—*New York Times* bestselling author Jenn McKinlay

"I fell for this feisty, take-charge heroine, and readers will, too."
—*New York Times* bestselling author Leslie Meier

"Carlisle's second contractor cozy continues to please with its smart, humorous heroine and plot. Fans of Sarah Graves's Home Repair Is Homicide series will appreciate this title as a solid read-alike."   —*Library Journal*

"Highly entertaining. . . . Quick, clever, and somewhat edgy. . . . Shannon's not a stereotype—she's a person, and an interesting, intelligent, likable one at that, which makes it easy to become invested in her tale."
—Smitten by Books

"An engaging cozy, including a complicated mystery woven throughout."   —Mystery Suspense Reviews

"A great read, and I recommend it to both cozy and other mystery readers alike."   —Open Book Society

"The Fixer-Upper series is a fan favorite and for good reason. The characters are the kind of people many of us would love to have as friends and neighbors, as well as coworkers and family."   —The Cozy Review

OTHER BOOKS BY KATE CARLISLE

BIBLIOPHILE MYSTERIES

Homicide in Hardcover
If Books Could Kill
The Lies That Bind
Murder Under Cover
Pages of Sin
(novella ebook)
One Book in the Grave
Peril in Paperback
A Cookbook Conspiracy
The Book Stops Here
Ripped from the Pages
Books of a Feather
Once upon a Spine
Buried in Books
The Book Supremacy
The Grim Reader
Little Black Book

FIXER-UPPER MYSTERIES

A High-End Finish
This Old Homicide
Crowned and Moldering
Deck the Hallways
Eaves of Destruction
A Wrench in the Works
Shot Through the Hearth
Premeditated Mortar

ABSENCE OF MALLETS

A Fixer-Upper Mystery

Kate Carlisle

BERKLEY PRIME CRIME
New York

BERKLEY PRIME CRIME
Published by Berkley
An imprint of Penguin Random House LLC
penguinrandomhouse.com

ISBN: 9780593201336

First Edition: December 2021

Printed in the United States of America
1   3   5   7   9   10   8   6   4   2

I am grateful to Linda Smith Rutledge, who, in late 2020, opened her heart and her wallet and contributed to a cause that was vitally important to both of us. For her overwhelming generosity and fun-loving spirit, I happily dedicate this book to her.

Chapter One

Coffee. The aroma was calling my name and nudging me out of a deep, dreamless sleep. Still, I lingered under the covers for a moment, wishing I could stay for another hour and savor the quiet warmth. Through the fog, though, I managed to remember that my day was going to be insanely busy. I had to get up.

Besides, there was coffee.

And there was Mac.

That did it. I threw back the covers and stumbled to the bathroom to splash cold water on my face.

After brushing my teeth and taming my wild mop of red hair back into a single braid, I dabbed on some moisturizer and lip balm, then stared at my image in the mirror. For a few wonderful seconds, I reflected on how much my life had changed over the past eight months. That was how long it had been since Mac Sullivan and I had been living together. I wasn't sure I'd ever be able to wipe that happy smile off my face.

I dressed quickly and rushed downstairs to the

kitchen, where I was greeted with ecstatic barking from Robbie, my West Highland terrier, and an affectionate head bop from Tiger, my orange marmalade cat.

"Good morning, creatures," I said, and bent down to give Robbie a brisk belly rub. Mac's silky black cat, Luke, sauntered into the room just then, looking like a tiny panther on the prowl. "I didn't forget you," I murmured, and gave the newcomer a light scratch under the chin.

I stood up and there was Mac. He was leaning against the counter by the coffeemaker, holding a fresh cup of coffee and grinning at me.

He seemed pretty darned happy these days, too. Setting the cup down, he walked over and pulled me into his arms. "Good morning, beautiful."

I wrapped my arms around him and held on, breathing him in. After a long moment, I leaned back to smile at him. "Good morning yourself. And bless you for making coffee."

He reached for the cup and handed it to me. "You're welcome, sleepyhead."

I took a big, life-affirming gulp of strong coffee, then checked the clock on the stove. "It's barely six o'clock. How long have you been up?"

"About two hours." He grabbed his own cup and took a sip. "I woke up with this crazy idea for a turning point and needed to get it written down while it was still in my head."

Mac, also known as MacKintyre Sullivan, was the author of a hugely successful thriller series starring the dangerous and hunky former Navy SEAL, Jake Slater. That was a description I could easily ascribe to Mac as well: dangerous, hunky, and a former Navy SEAL. He had recently started his twelfth book in the series, and this one featured an elaborate plot to kidnap the woman Jake had fallen in love with and ransom her for the American nuclear codes.

Together, we gathered up the makings for a quick breakfast—granola, yogurt, and berries—while he told me his crazy idea, which included a bombing and a car chase. I thought it was brilliant and exciting and not crazy at all. We each had another cup of coffee and then talked about our plans for the day.

"You've got your new writers' group arriving today, right?"

He grinned. "Yeah."

When Mac moved in with me all those months ago, he'd made the decision to turn his own home, the historic lighthouse mansion three miles up the coast, into a writers' retreat. The venerable Victorian mansion had been lovingly restored by me and my crew. My name is Shannon Hammer, and I'm a contractor specializing in the Victorian style that our town was famous for. Mac's mansion was a particularly beautiful example, comfortably furnished, with six bedrooms and an idyllic location right on the beach by the old lighthouse. It had a wide front porch with a stunning view of the ocean and was perfect for a quiet getaway for serious writers.

In anticipation of groups of curious writers visiting every week, Mac had asked me to start refurbishing the famous old lighthouse next door to his home. It had been decommissioned last year by the coast guard. Since Mac owned the property, he was told that he could do whatever he wanted to do with it, but he wasn't about to paint it pink or something. Not after all he'd been through with the town's planning commission and the historical society. No, he was determined to keep the lighthouse looking as gleaming white and as beautifully tall and dignified as it always had been.

But the fact was, the old structure needed some serious rehab work.

My foreman Wade and I had gone through every inch of the space with Mac and had made a lengthy list of the repairs and changes we would need to make before the lighthouse could be reopened safely.

I planned to bring the lantern and lens room back to its original rustic style, and rebuild and reinforce the main gallery—otherwise known as the catwalk—that circled the very top of the structure. Mac wanted to have the interior circular stairway walls painted. The stairs themselves had to be reinforced and retreaded. The concrete exterior was pitted in spots from years of salt air and moisture. It needed to be resurfaced and repainted. The old windows, many of which were cracked or broken and permanently fogged over, needed to be replaced.

We had yellow "Caution" tape draped across the main entrance to alert people to keep out. But because the lighthouse had always been an attractive nuisance— we had already caught a few of the local kids sneaking around—I had installed a simple audio-video alarm system that would alert my cell phone if anyone ignored the warning signs and ventured inside.

Meanwhile, Mac's writers' retreat plan had been an instant success. As soon as he started putting feelers out on social media, the reservation requests began to pour in. He had hired Frank and Irma, a local couple, to manage the retreat operation, including scheduling, cooking, and housekeeping. They lived on the property in the gorgeous attic suite in the mansion my crew had renovated for that purpose.

Needless to say, Mac and I had a lot going on. But we liked it that way.

I gazed at him. "Did you check out this latest group?"

"You bet I did," he said decisively.

I smiled. Mac never asked our police chief to run the names of the people in his groups through the various law enforcement systems. No, these days it was easier to simply look up their names on social media, check out their websites, and google them. Social media tended to reveal a lot about a person. And Mac didn't like to be surprised, especially when these people would be living unfettered in his home for a week or two, sometimes longer.

So far, the visiting writers had been completely respectful of Mac and his property. They had been friendly to our townspeople, and they spent their money in our shops and restaurants, which made the entire enterprise a win-win for everyone. Every single one of the writers had seemed interested in anything Mac suggested in terms of places to eat or things to do around town.

It made sense that they would hang on Mac's every word. After all, he was a bestselling novelist whose books had been turned into blockbuster films. He was often a guest speaker at conferences, where he would teach workshops or give seminars on writing. So it figured that any visiting writer would be smart to follow his recommendations. Besides that, Mac was simply a good guy. He was smart and funny and generally made himself available to the groups for writing advice on any subject they could come up with.

As I loaded dishes into the dishwasher, I turned to study his expression. "You don't have to hang here with me. I can tell you're itching to get back to the book."

He grinned. "Am I that transparent?"

I had to laugh. "You're the most *non*transparent person I've ever met. But I know you."

"Yeah, guess you do," he murmured.

The first time I'd ever seen Mac deep in the writing zone, I had decided to put together a lovely basket of snacks and goodies and brought it over to him while he was working. It was a shock I wasn't prepared for. His hair was sticking up in every direction. His beard had grown out. His clothes were so wrinkled, I was pretty sure he had slept in them, and he stared at me as though he'd never seen another human being before. Then suddenly, he grinned wildly, grabbed the basket, and closed the door in my face.

So that was Mac on a deadline. We could laugh about it now, but I wouldn't make the mistake of climbing into that cage again.

He gathered up our pets' water bowls and took them to the sink to clean and refill them. Robbie scurried over to check things out, and Mac leaned down and gave him an affectionate scratch behind his ears.

When he was done with the task, he said, "Guess I'd better get back to blowing up stuff so I can be ready when the group arrives."

I wiped off the counter. "What time do they get here?"

"They should be here by two o'clock. They left early to drive up here from San Francisco."

"How many are coming?"

"There's six in this group. They're here for two weeks."

I raised my eyebrows. It was unusual for a group that size to stay for two weeks since most people, including writers, had day jobs.

Mac noticed my reaction. "Yeah, kind of different, right? But maybe they're all independently wealthy."

"Nice for them."

He chuckled. "Anyway, I'm going to show them around town and then bring them over to Homefront this afternoon. That way, they'll be able to navigate their way back to the writing workshop tonight."

"Then I'll see you there." I leaned in close and gave him a kiss. "Can't wait."

He touched my cheek and kissed me back. "Likewise."

I drove into the parking lot of Homefront and found an empty space in front of the community center. Looking around, I had to marvel at how all of this had come together in such a short time.

It had been a dream of Mac's for as long as I'd known him, and probably years before that, too. He had heard about veterans' villages in his travels and when he got together with old friends. Every time he went on a book tour, he would take time to visit a local veterans' group.

Mac brought the best ideas home to Lighthouse Cove, and finally last year, he and a few of his local Navy SEAL buddies purchased five acres of land on the outskirts of town. This marked the beginning of the veterans' project they had been planning for years.

When our police chief and former marine, Eric Jensen, got wind of Mac's plans, he asked to join the team.

It was always a good thing to have the chief of police on your team.

The plan was to create a village of fifty tiny homes for the benefit of veterans in the area who needed housing and other kinds of help. Mac and his pals had teamed up with a national veterans' group who would guide them through the process and help them manage the property and the numerous services to be provided. The national group also advised our guys on legalities such as zoning issues and security.

I was thrilled when my construction company won the bid to build the tiny homes for local veterans in need. It didn't hurt that I already had several veterans on my crew, and we had years of experience building custom tiny homes. However, we had never built more than one home at a time—until now.

After numerous meetings with the town council and the planning commission, we had brought in various experts for advice on utility placement, land grading, and water management. Once sewer lines were dug and utilities were run, we began construction on a contemporary-style, three-thousand-square-foot community center that promised to become the heart of the development. It would provide a gathering place and would house an industrial kitchen, a dining room, and a gymnasium, along with offices and meeting rooms for all the various services they planned to offer: a visiting nurse and a dentist, a legal aid advisor, a veterans' benefits expert, mental health professionals, a vocational counselor, even a unisex barber shop. These services would also be made available to any veteran in the area, not just the residents of Homefront.

Then we started building the homes themselves. It was going to be amazing. I was so proud of Mac.

Glancing around at the brand-new blacktop parking lot in front of the center, the sidewalks, the landscaping, and the twenty-five homes that had already been completed and were now occupied, I had to admit that I was also proud of myself and my team.

I might've mentioned it before, but Mac and I seemed to thrive on keeping busy. He had set in motion the veterans' village project long before he ever decided to invest in the Gables development. But then, when he found out last year that I had signed on to turn one wing of the old insane asylum—now known as the Gables—into a small, elegant hotel for my friend Jane, Mac had decided to make that investment, too.

Both the Gables job and this veterans' project were long-term commitments that would keep us busy for the next year or so. I couldn't complain. Not when it would keep my crew employed and happy.

I climbed out of the truck and locked the door. After pulling my tool chest out of the truck bed, I walked toward our work site.

The rapid-fire blast of a nail gun suddenly ripped through the air. Despite the constant mini explosive bursts, I had to smile. This was the sound of stuff getting built, and in my world, nothing was better than that. I moved along the sidewalk, past a dozen tiny homes that were already built. Each was unique in design and embellishments and paint color.

Rounding a corner, I spotted a ladder leaning against

the frame of house number thirty-one. I climbed twelve feet up to the roof to watch Sean Brogan, my head carpenter, nailing thick layers of plywood sheathing to the rafters of the tiny house.

He finished a row and stopped nailing. The abrupt silence was almost shocking.

"Hey, boss," he said when he noticed me.

"Didn't want to interrupt," I said. "Just wanted to see how it's going."

"It's going great. This is the second roof of the day."

"No kidding? What time did you start?"

"I got here about six thirty."

I smiled. "I'm impressed."

He glanced around the property, then shrugged. "I get a good feeling working here."

"I know what you mean. I'll let you get back to it." I climbed down the ladder, and the nail gun blasts started up before I reached the ground.

"Hey, Shannon."

I turned and saw Johnny Schmidt walking toward me, hauling a thick roll of waterproof black underlayment.

Both Sean and Johnny had been on my crew since I'd first taken over the company from my father about seven years ago. That was when Dad had a mild heart attack and decided to step back. Of course, he couldn't quit altogether, and I expected to see him show up here one of these days.

"Hi, Johnny. You need help with that?"

"Nah. I'm good." He leaned the thick roll against the heavy, exposed plywood wall. "These homes are so small, it doesn't take much of this stuff to cover the roofs."

"Good point."

Once Sean and his nail gun were finished, Johnny would take over, carefully rolling out the water-resistant underlayment and using a staple gun to affix it to the plywood layer that Sean had just laid down. Once those two layers were completed, Billy, the third man on the roofing team, would climb up and complete the job by nailing composite shingles to the underlayment. The job also entailed installing flashing along the edges of the roof and around the kitchen and bathroom vents. "Flashing" was a thin metal strip that was necessary to redirect water and prevent leaks from occurring.

Early on, faced with the prospect of completing fifty tiny homes over a six-month period, I'd had to sit down and figure out a way to streamline the system. Together with my two foremen, Wade Chambers and Carla Harrison, we had devised an assembly line of sorts and settled on a plan to work on five houses at a time. One newly paved road—dubbed the Parkway—ran from the community center to the end of the property. Five short lanes branched off of the Parkway in opposite directions and five houses would be built on each lane. Eventually we'd have fifty homes.

Our assembly line started with a team of four working to lay down each concrete slab foundation. Wade supervised because he was a genius when it came to pouring the perfect slab.

Once five slabs were poured, another team moved in to begin framing the houses and adding the rafters. A team of three worked on the roofs. At the same time, our electrical and plumbing teams began running pipe and wiring through the frame and into the different parts of the house.

I had another team working on the interiors, first insulating the walls and hanging drywall, laying down subflooring, tiling the main rooms, bathrooms and kitchens, installing sinks and appliances, and painting. Another group was taking care of business on the exteriors, first applying the oriented strand board, or OSB, to the frame. OSB was like plywood, only stronger and cheaper, and it contained resins and wax that made it water-resistant. The outside team also installed the siding and finally the paint. And still another team of three handled the windows, doors, and vents for heating and air-conditioning.

While those five houses were being completed, the slab foundation team would start on five more. And so on. Occasionally, a team would switch a member or an assignment in order to keep from getting bored—or worse, developing a repetitive strain injury.

So far, I was thrilled that things were running like a well-oiled machine. *So far.*

The nail gun went abruptly silent. I looked up and saw Sean pulling off his safety glasses. He grinned down at me and Johnny. "Is this the best job in the world or what?"

"The best, for sure," I said with a laugh, feeling lucky to have crew members who loved the work as much as I did. It helped that they also appreciated the importance of this massive project. "And you rock that nail gun."

He smiled coyly. "I do, don't I?"

I laughed again.

Setting down the nail gun, Sean descended down the ladder.

Billy arrived in his pickup truck and parked on the

new sidewalk in front of the house where we were working. He jumped out and slammed the door shut. "Morning, guys."

Sean joined Billy, and together, they hoisted an extension ladder from the back of his truck. This particular ladder had an electrical lift attachment that would carry heavy bags of shingles up to the roof.

For most jobs, we used a conveyor belt to move shingles from a larger truck straight onto a roof, but these houses were compact enough that the electric ladder lift was easier to manipulate in and around the village.

I glanced up and saw that Johnny was standing on the roof now. He had rolled out one panel of the waterproof underlayment and begun to attach the material to the OSB with his staple gun.

"The man's a machine," Sean said, following my gaze.

All of them were amazing, I thought, then said, "Let's get going on the next roof."

"For sure, boss," Billy said, and the two of them walked ahead of me to the next house in line.

"Hey, girl."

I whipped around and saw my friend Julia Barton walking toward me with another woman.

"Hi, Julia." I smiled at the older woman.

"I don't know if you remember Linda Rutledge," Julia said. "She was in my class in high school."

"I don't think we've met," I said, smiling as we shook hands. "But you look familiar."

Linda grinned. "I remember you, Shannon. You were always so friendly and helpful."

I was pleasantly taken aback. I'd been on the hospitality committee back in high school and figured I should be warm and welcoming to everybody. It was nice to know that some people noticed. "Thanks."

"We were seniors when you were a freshman," Julia said with a grin aimed at me. "So you're forgiven if you don't remember us."

Linda patted Julia on the shoulder. "It's been a long time since high school. And yet, you still look fabulous."

"You can see why I'm friends with her," Julia said.

At first glance, the two women couldn't have been more different. Linda was lovely, tall and blond with a classic peaches-and-cream complexion and big blue eyes. She wore a loosely woven fuchsia sweater over a long skirt in a rainbow tie-dyed pattern with pretty sandals. When I looked at her, the first word that came to mind was *serene*. She came across as someone who would listen and care very much about your life and struggles.

Julia was short and curvy, with curly dark hair and a dynamic personality. Today she was in total boss mode, wearing a sharp-looking black pinstriped pantsuit with a crisp white shirt and three-inch heels. Despite the business attire, she always came across as the life of the party. She was cute, perky, and fun.

"The funny thing is," Julia continued. "We barely even spoke to each other in high school. It wasn't until we met up in the army that we got to be good friends."

"In the military, you find out quickly who you can count on," Linda explained. "I could always count on Julia."

Julia leaned her head on Linda's shoulder. "Back at you, sweetie." She straightened, and with tongue in cheek, she added, "Although I have to admit, it was lowering to realize that every guy I ever liked always developed a crush on Linda."

"That's not true," Linda insisted. "They all fell for you because you were so much fun."

They smiled at each other and I could tell that their teasing was done with love.

"Anyway, Shannon," Julia said, "I wanted to introduce you two because Linda would like to take your class."

"Oh," I said. "That's great."

The class she was referring to was a construction skills class that I had volunteered to teach as part of the Homefront occupational program. Their mission was to provide courses for the residents and other local vets in the hope that the knowledge and skills they gained might lead to jobs and income. So far, the courses included cooking, writing, auto mechanics, retail skills, and construction basics. They would be adding others as time went on.

Julia ran a nonprofit organization that was partly underwriting the construction class. Her aim was to inspire more women to train for careers in construction. Her father had been a carpenter who had occasionally worked with my dad. And Julia had been trained in carpentry by her father, who always believed that women were as talented as men when it came to working with wood. Supporting this class was one way for Julia to pay it forward.

I turned to Linda. "Have you done any construction work before?"

"Not exactly," Linda admitted. "I'm a mosaic artist, so I do a lot of work with tiles and glass. I'm hoping to be able to use my artwork in a more constructive way."

"You should see her work," Julia said. "She's an artistic genius."

Linda beamed. "And now you see why *I'm* friends with *her*."

"I do," I said, smiling at them both. "I'm happy to add you to the class, and I'd love to see some of your work sometime."

"The first class is tomorrow night, right, Shannon?" Julia said.

"That's right. Seven o'clock in the meeting room. We'll start with a conversation about tools and rules and go from there."

"Tools and rules." Julia grinned. "I like it."

"I'll be there," Linda said enthusiastically. "And I can bring some of my work with me, if you have any time to look at it."

I brightened. "That would be great."

"Okay, this is working out," Julia said, clapping her hands together. "I promised Linda a tour of the center now, so we'll see you later, Shannon."

"Sounds good."

"Nice to meet you, Shannon," Linda said, and waved goodbye.

I watched them stroll down the new sidewalk toward the center. Then I jogged over to the next house on the schedule to see how my crew was doing.

A few hours later, I was up on the roof of house number thirty-two, rolling out a sheet of heavy black underlayment and quickly tacking it down with my pneumatic staple gun. I had offered to take on the job because, why should my guys have all the fun?

It was the stapler that made me want to do the work.

I could take out all my deep-seated aggressions with a simple click of my finger. *Not* that I had all that many deep-seated aggressions, but whenever I did, I grabbed that staple gun and went to work.

I supposed a nail gun was good for that, too, but a nail gun was way too serious. And much heavier. You didn't want to get caught daydreaming while using a nail gun—not that I ever daydreamed on the job! But seriously, you could kill someone with a nail gun. Plus, it was a lot louder. But a stapler was . . . friendlier. Don't get me wrong; it was a serious tool and it could definitely leave a mark. But it probably wouldn't kill you.

In between staple shots, I heard someone shout, "Hey, Irish."

I looked up, then gazed down at Mac and smiled. "Hi, Mac." He had called me "Irish" from the first day we met. It had something to do with all this red hair of mine.

He was surrounded by six people I'd never seen before. They had to be the new writers' retreat group. There were four men and two women, and they looked up at me with polite interest.

"Everyone," Mac said, glancing around the group. "This is Shannon Hammer, the contractor in charge of the Homefront construction."

"You're a contractor?" a tall, well-dressed guy asked, sounding incredulous.

"Yeah."

I still got that reaction a lot, which was another reason why I had gladly signed on to teach the construction class. We could use more women in this business.

"Shannon," Mac continued, "these are the members

of the writing group that just moved into the lighthouse mansion."

I waved. "Hi, everyone. Welcome to Lighthouse Cove."

"Thanks," a few of them murmured.

"It looks like a cool little town," one of the women said.

I smiled. "We like it."

"How's your day going?" Mac asked.

I took a quick look at my wristwatch. It was one-thirty. "Pretty well. I have to finish the underlayment on this roof and start another. I should be done around four-thirty."

"Good. I'm going to show these guys around the plaza and then head on home to do some work," Mac explained. "They'll check out the shops and the pub and then come back here to sit in on my writing workshop."

"That should be interesting," I said.

"Are you kidding?" one of the guys said. "It'll be awesome." He gazed at Mac with such reverence that I had to smile. It wasn't every day that young writers like these could hang out with someone as famous and talented as MacKintyre Sullivan.

"Okay," Mac said to the group. "I'll walk you guys over to the parking lot and give you directions back to the town square. It's just a few blocks away and the pub is right on Main Street."

"That's really nice of you," one guy said. "Thanks, Mac." He seemed to be the most outgoing of the group, as well as being the tallest and the best looking, with wavy blond hair like the classic surfers wore. He was dressed conservatively in a blue-and-white-striped shirt with a button-down collar and—wait. Were those *pressed* blue jeans he wore? Yes, they were.

I was being judgmental and silently smacked myself. It came from hanging out with construction workers my whole life, guys who would no more iron their jeans than dance the *Lambada* on top of the bar at the local pub.

"We'll try not to get lost," the dark-haired woman said with a smile.

"You won't. Let's go." Mac glanced back at me and winked. "Be back in a while."

"I'll be here."

I watched the group walk away, but then the tall blond guy turned back around. He held up his cell phone, aimed it at me, and clicked it. Then he grinned.

What the—? He was taking a picture of me? That was just weird. But then he wiggled his eyebrows and winked at me.

One of the other guys turned and saw what was going on. This guy was pale and thin with rounded shoulders and dark eyes. "Lewis," he said as he strode back and grabbed the taller fellow's arm. "Time to go."

Lewis looked ready to argue, but his shorter friend simply narrowed his eyes. It took a few seconds, but then Lewis grinned at me. "See you around."

The two of them turned and walked quickly to catch up with Mac and the others.

I was honestly flummoxed. Had the blond guy been flirting with me? Or was he mocking Mac? Whatever he was doing, he was a fool to be doing it to MacKintyre Sullivan's girlfriend. The very same girlfriend who was currently gripping a powerful pneumatic staple gun in her hand. I could hurt him with that.

And what about his friend, the guy who had pulled him away? I assumed they were friends, but it was almost as if he had some kind of control over Lewis. That moment of confrontation between them left me wondering.

And what was with the picture taking? It was sort of like an invasion of privacy. But maybe I was being overly sensitive. Either way, I wasn't happy with the idea that some stranger staying in Mac's home would act like a jerk behind Mac's back.

I sighed. I was probably overreacting. And to be honest, Mac would probably laugh it off if I told him about it. So I mentally shoved the pressed-blue-jeans bleached-blond clown out of my head, picked up my staple gun, and got back to work.

Chapter Two

It was the end of the day, and I was packing up my tools when Police Chief Eric Jensen walked up. "Hey, Shannon."

I had to smile. Here was another tall, cute guy, I thought. But unlike the button-down photo-taking guy from earlier, Eric's attitude was mainly serious. And it didn't hurt that he was built like a linebacker. After meeting him for the first time a few years ago, I had thought of him as Thor. He did bear a strong resemblance to a particularly hunky Viking god.

"Hi, Chief." I latched my toolbox closed, then stood. "What's going on?"

"Not much," he said. "I had a meeting with the project manager. He thinks things are going pretty smoothly around here."

"Good. I think so, too."

Before I could lift my toolbox up off the ground, Eric grabbed it and began to walk with me to my truck.

"Thanks," I said.

"No problem. I talked to Mac a little while ago. If you don't mind, I'm going to grab Travis and join you for dinner."

"That sounds great."

Travis Sutter was an old friend of Eric's from their days in the Marine Corps. Eric had been trying to get him to move to Lighthouse Cove for years, and now that Homefront was up and running, Travis had jumped at the chance to move into one of the tiny homes. He had worked on dozens of different jobs all over the world, including construction, so Eric had convinced me to hire him. I was glad I did. The man was a tireless worker, and everyone on the crew liked him.

"I was hoping we'd see Chloe sometime this week," I said. "Have you heard from her?"

I supposed it was a silly question. My sister, Chloe, had met and fallen in love with the police chief last year, and since then, the two of them probably talked on the phone at least once every day. Now they were engaged, and I couldn't be happier. Chloe was the star of *Makeover Madness*, the popular home improvement show on the Home Builders Network. She lived in Los Angeles, and because of a mysterious incident that happened to her in high school, there was a long period of time when she didn't visit. But the mystery was all straightened out now, and she was happy to get back to Lighthouse Cove every few weeks to visit her family and friends and her fiancé.

"Yeah, I've heard from her, and I'm about to spoil her surprise," Eric said, chuckling. "She's going to join us for dinner."

"Oh." I brightened. "That's an excellent surprise."

We got to my truck, and Eric easily hefted the tool-box over the side and onto the truck bed.

"Thanks, Eric."

"You bet. I'm going to run over to Travis's place and get him. We'll meet you guys at the pub."

"See you there."

But before Eric could take a step, Mac drove up. He parked his black SUV in front of the community center and jumped out.

"You ready?" he asked Eric.

"I'm on my way to get Travis," Eric said. "It might take a few minutes. How about if we meet you at the pub?"

"Mind if we go to the wine bar instead?" Mac asked. "My new group of writers will be at the pub, and I don't want to cramp their style."

Eric raised an eyebrow. "Where's the fun in that?"

I choked on a laugh. "Wow, Chief."

Mac stared at him for a moment, then chuckled. "Hell, you're right. So we'll meet you at the pub."

"See you there," Eric said, and jogged off toward Travis's new home a few hundred yards away.

Mac wrapped his arm around my shoulder and leaned in to kiss me. "How'd the rest of your day go?"

"It was good. Busy. We're almost halfway through the next five houses. I spent the rest of the afternoon doing what you saw me doing, stapling my little heart out."

He grinned. "Get all those aggressions out of your system?"

"Works like a charm every time." I laughed. "Nothing can bother me now."

"Glad to hear it." He rested his head against mine.

"Did the writers get settled into the mansion?"

"Yeah. Interesting group." He frowned for an instant, then his expression cleared. "Anyway, from here, they followed me to the town square. I gave them a quick tour, showed them the pub, the bookshop, Emily's place, all the hot spots. Then they decided to walk to the pier, and I went home to work."

"Did your writing go well?" I asked, after deciding I would bring up his "interesting group" comment later.

"It went great," he said, with an evil grin. "I blew up a criminal arsenal and killed four bad guys."

I frowned. "Only four?"

With a quick laugh, he said, "Sorry, babe. I'll do better tomorrow." He kissed me once more, and then we each got into our vehicles and drove to the pub.

My sister, Chloe, was holding the corner booth for us, and I waved from the doorway.

"I'll go say hello to the writers," Mac said. "Meet you at the table."

"Okay." I walked quickly across the pub and grabbed my sister in a tight hug.

"How can you look so gorgeous after working all day?" she wondered.

"And you're such a hag," I said, laughing as I leaned back to look at her.

"I really do hate you," she insisted.

"I know, sweetie. I feel the same way about you." I pulled her back for another hug. We had been talking smack to each other for as long as I could remember. "I'm so glad you're here."

She scowled. "Did Eric blow the surprise?"

"Of course."

"Men." She shook her head in mock derision. "How do we tolerate them?"

I took a long look at Mac on the other side of the room and smiled. "It's not easy."

She gave me another hug. "I've only been gone a month, but I've missed you."

"I've missed you, too," I said, as we both slid into the booth. "How long are you here for?"

"Two weeks. And I brought my video camera. I want to tape some shorts of you guys working on your tiny houses. We're going to use them on the show."

"Really? That's great."

"Well, it's just such an amazing story. I'm thinking I could turn it into a weekly segment. You know, so everyone can watch your progress."

"I'd love that."

Chloe already had a glass of wine, so I quickly ordered my own. Then I said, "We've finished fifteen more houses since you were here last month."

"That's amazing. Eric said they've opened the community center, and they're starting to give classes on stuff."

"Yeah, occupational workshops and classes. In fact, Mac's teaching one tonight, so we'll have to eat fast."

"Are you going with him?"

"Yes. I really want to watch him teach. I've seen him do a few short workshops and such, but this is something new."

"He'll be great."

"Oh, absolutely. And frankly, I want to get some pointers since I'll be teaching my own class tomorrow night."

She gazed at me. "Nervous?"

"I shouldn't be, but yeah."

"No, you shouldn't be," she agreed. "You're the boss of a few dozen people, mostly men. Just pretend you're talking to your crew. Telling them what to do."

"That might work. I'll be fine once I get going. It's just the idea of starting something new. I want it to go really well."

"It will."

The waitress brought my glass of Pinot Noir and dashed away. I took a quick sip, then said, "Hey, you should come tomorrow night. You can be my special guest star."

She held up her hand. "Sorry. You're on your own."

"Why? Are you afraid?"

"Me, afraid?" She gave a mocking laugh. "My television show is watched by millions. I'm not afraid of anything." She shrugged. "I just don't want to steal your thunder."

Now it was my turn to laugh. "Okay, Hollywood. But let's just remember, I taught you everything you know."

"Uh, that was Dad."

"Okay. Maybe. But hey, I did teach you how to use a stud finder."

She glanced at the front door just as Eric walked in. "I guess I owe you for that."

I laughed and bumped her shoulder. "That's right. Look, you don't have to participate if you don't want to, but I would love you to be there. And afterward, you can tell me everything I did wrong."

"Now that sweetens the deal." She tapped her temple, pretending to consider it. "Okay, I'll be there."

I fondly leaned against her. "You're my favorite sister."

"And you're mine," she said, and gave my cheek a sisterly smooch.

"Here they are," Eric said to Travis, who followed behind him. Then Eric sat down next to Chloe.

"And there you are," Chloe said softly, and kissed him. And there was nothing sisterly about it.

Travis glanced from me to Chloe, clearly fascinated. "I've never seen you two together. It's a sight to behold."

"That's nice to hear," Chloe said.

At a superficial glance, Chloe and I didn't look like sisters. When she moved to LA, she had changed her hair color to blond and wore it straight and sleek. I'd kept to my original color of dark auburn and done almost nothing to alter the long, thick, wavy style. But our eyes were the same shape, and we smiled and laughed the same, among other similarities.

Mac walked up behind Travis. "Hey, how's it going, man?"

"Couldn't be better," Travis said. "Looking forward to the workshop."

"Me, too." Mac slid in next to me, and Travis took the chair at the open end of the booth. "I hope you'll read some of your stuff tonight."

Travis looked uncomfortable. "Uh, I'm bringing something, but I'm not sure it's any good."

"Everything I've read of yours is great," Mac said easily.

Eric pointed at Travis. "That goes double for me, man."

Travis was saved from answering by our waitress, who hurried over. Since Mac had to get to class, we all gave our orders right then. "You guys make it easy," she said with a smile, and rushed off.

"Are the writers settling in okay?" I asked Mac.

He gave a quick glance at the six writers sitting in a booth at the opposite side of the pub. "Yeah. They're looking forward to my workshop. I'll officially introduce everyone there."

"Looking forward to it," Eric said.

"You mean you've got six *real* writers showing up tonight?" Travis looked even paler than a minute ago. "Not sure I'm up for that kind of scrutiny."

He was a fascinating character, I thought. Good-looking in a kickass cowboy kind of way, with clear blue eyes that actually twinkled when he smiled. He was strong and burly, with a thick red beard and a gruff voice. When I first met him, I secretly thought that if his beard had been white and his stomach more rounded, he'd make a perfect Santa Claus. He was a little rough around the edges, but I didn't mind that.

Mac chuckled softly. "I happen to consider *you* a real writer, Travis."

He was obviously embarrassed by the praise, because now his cheeks took on a pink tinge.

"Mac says you've got real storytelling talent," I said. "I'm looking forward to hearing you read your work."

He waved my words away. "Aw, it's just a bunch of scribblings from too many years on the road."

"Not true," Eric said firmly.

"Don't you start," Travis grumbled.

Eric grinned as he held up his arms in surrender. "You know how I feel about your stuff, but we'll let it go for now." Turning to Mac, he said, "Tell us about this new group."

"I'll have to keep my voice down because they're sitting across the room."

"It's too loud in here for them to overhear us," Eric said.

But we all leaned closer as Mac spoke softly. "They're all good friends, part of a long-standing plot group. They're all around the same age, thirtyish. Five of them are published, all within two years of each other, and that's unusual. Two of them are more successful than the others, but they all seem pretty generous with their time and advice. Well, except for one guy."

"Let me guess which one," I said warily. "The cute blond guy with the button-down collar."

"How do you know?" Chloe asked. "Have you met them?"

"Not exactly," I whispered, casting another glance at the writers' table. "But it's got to be him. He irons his blue jeans."

"What the hell?" Travis said irately.

I laughed. "Right? Who does that?"

"Okay, wait," Chloe said. "Some of the guys on my construction crew happen to iron their blue jeans."

"That's because they're actors," I said. "Not real construction workers."

She grimaced. "That's mostly true, but it still seems unfair to judge this guy for that reason."

"There's more." And I explained what happened when the guy took my picture and then winked at me.

"That's kind of creepy," Chloe admitted.

"I might be making too big a deal out of it," I hedged.

"You're not," Eric said flatly.

"I trust your instincts," Mac said. "But look, I'm going to try to keep an open mind. These people are living in my house for two weeks, so I want to hope for the best."

"You're right." I winced. "I'm sorry I mentioned it."

"I'm not," Mac said, and squeezed my hand. "If he does anything else to creep you out, I want to know."

"Okay."

After a long moment, Eric said, "So? Tell us more about the group."

"Oh yeah." Mac shook his head ruefully. "Got off track there." He took a sip of beer. "So, this is the first group that's ever booked the retreat for two weeks, and that's not cheap. I think they decided to go for it because they're all struggling with their second or third book and need to shake things up to get them all back on track. They're looking to be inspired."

Chloe smiled. "Lighthouse Cove should definitely inspire them."

"I think so." Mac nodded. "They're right there on the beach next to the old lighthouse. They can drive along the coast or come into town or go up to the Gables. Trust me, there's plenty of creative motivation out there."

Eric leaned in closer. "So why do you think that one guy is such a tool?"

"I didn't say that," Mac said, then gave up. "But yeah, he seems to be."

"You think I should keep an eye on him?"

"No," Mac said, waving away the chief's concerns. "He's just got a lot of attitude, probably because his first book was so huge. It's like it hit the cultural zeitgeist and just took off. Topped all the bestseller lists for weeks. So not only is he the current darling of the industry, but the fact that he achieved such instant success means that he's become the central focus of their writers' group. So he gets all the attention."

"So he acts like a tool," Eric finished.

Mac sighed. "As you say."

"How'd you find all that out about this guy?" I asked.

"The dark-haired woman, Sheri. She told me."

"If one of them is dishing the dirt," Chloe said, "then the group isn't as close as they seem."

"Of course not." Mac grinned. "According to Sheri, the button-down guy—his name is Lewis, by the way— Lewis acts like he's better than the rest of them, he knows more than everyone, and he's always bragging. You know the type."

"Sheri seems awfully willing to share all the tawdry details about the guy," I said.

"She does, and I'm not sure why."

"Because she wants to get close to you," Chloe said simply.

"That would be my guess," I said, then frowned. "And this is beginning to sound like middle-school melodrama."

Mac nodded. "The weird thing is that Sheri got real defensive of Lewis when the other woman, Annabelle, joined us and started ripping into the guy. Sheri shut her down on the spot."

"So they're all just a little bit crazy," Chloe said cheerfully.

"Tell us about the others," Eric said. As chief of police, he liked to know who was hanging around his town.

"There's Brian," Mac continued. "He's the dark-haired skinny one with the stooped shoulders. He's super quiet, a little bit awkward, seems like a nice guy. From what I can tell, he's Lewis's biggest fan. Sheri says they've known each other since kindergarten, and they're still best friends."

"Has he published anything?" I asked.

"Not yet," Mac said, and frowned. "I'm not even sure what kind of stuff he writes."

"He the one who looks like he forgot his pocket protector?" Eric asked.

Mac chuckled. "Yeah, he's kind of a nerd."

"Nothing wrong with being a nerd," Travis admitted.

"True," Mac said. "Let's just say that he seems very shy."

"His shyness probably works out well for Lewis," Travis said. "He wouldn't want to share the limelight."

"That's what I was thinking," Mac said.

"He was the one who stepped in and pulled Lewis away from taking another picture of me."

"Then I'm grateful to him." Mac patted my leg.

"Lewis seems to be the alpha male of the group," Chloe said. "But if Brian was the one who pulled Lewis away from you, maybe Brian's got more power and control than it appears on the surface."

"Nerds will rule the world," Travis said philosophically.

"According to Sheri," Mac said, "the rest of the group thinks Brian is okay, but they also suspect that he's simply riding Lewis's coattails, and that'll get old for both of them eventually."

"Riding his coattails where?" Travis asked.

Mac chuckled. "To publishing nirvana, I suppose."

"Wherever that is," Eric said with a smirk.

Chloe jumped in. "It means that Lewis can introduce him to the right agents and editors, get him included in book signings and other events, that kind of thing."

"You should know," I said, very proud that my little

sister had published her own beautiful home style book last year, which was a big success.

Our dinner arrived, and I paused to appreciate the intoxicating aroma of the fish and chips.

"This looks fantastic," Chloe said, gazing lustily at her cheeseburger and crispy fries.

Eric stole a fry, then looked at Mac. "Tell us about the others."

"Okay, I'll be quick. Sheri is a librarian who's recently published her first romantic suspense and is contracted to write two more. She's smart, and just a bit devious, I think. She told me she thinks the idea of riding Lewis's coattails is a fine way to get ahead."

Chloe looked horrified. "Was she talking about Brian or herself?"

"Good question," Mac murmured.

Travis shook his head. "Weird."

"Oh yeah, it's weird," Mac said. "Then there's Annabelle, the other woman in the group. She didn't have much to say, but I know she writes women's fiction. She just signed another two-book deal and she seems to be doing well so far."

"Who's left?" Chloe asked.

Mac chuckled. "The big guy with the elbow patches is Kingsley. He sold a book of horror short stories. More literary than genre, I'm told. I haven't read any of them, but I'll probably check them out."

Besides the elbow patches, Kingsley wore wire-rimmed glasses. He was starting to go bald, which might've explained why he wore his curly black hair in a thick ponytail halfway down his back.

"Who names their kid Kingsley?" Travis mused.

Eric nudged him. "Good question."

"He's too young to be wearing a cardigan with elbow patches," Chloe said. "But then, maybe he fancies himself writing for *Masterpiece Theater.*"

Mac grinned. He took a quick bite of fish, then a sip of his beer. "And finally, there's Hugh. He's the short, baby-faced fellow sitting on the end. He writes techno-thrillers. Not sure how well he's doing, but hey, he just sold a fourth book. So, good for him."

"So you've got competition," Eric said with a grin.

"My books aren't as techno-heavy as Hugh's, but yeah." Mac chuckled. "Competition is good for me, right?"

"You can take it," Travis said.

Chloe was staring across the room.

"Stop staring," I whispered. "They're going to know we're talking about them."

"That guy's got a thing about his phone," she said. "Have you noticed he hasn't put it down? He took a selfie with the group, then a couple of himself. Then he took pictures of everyone's food. And now I think he's recording their conversation, because he keeps angling the phone toward whoever's talking."

"I noticed that, too," Eric said, his eyes narrowed.

Travis shook his head. "Hope he doesn't try that in the workshop tonight. I get into some personal stuff about PTSD in my story, and I'd rather not have the whole social media world listening in on my problems."

"I won't let that happen," Mac said fiercely.

When Travis first moved to town, Eric had confided to Mac and me that his friend suffered from PTSD. It was one more reason why Travis had chosen to move into the village. He wasn't always sure of himself living among civilians, but more importantly, he would be able to get all the services he would need at the community center. When I hired him for my crew, he was open and honest about the disorder.

"You know, Mac?" Eric began. "I think I'll check out your writing class."

Travis held up both hands. "Don't do it on my account."

"I'm not," Eric said easily. "Just like to keep my finger on the pulse of my town."

Chloe looked around the table, then turned to me. "And you'll be there, too. Right?"

"I wouldn't miss it."

She sighed. "I was looking forward to a quiet night at home watching TV, but since you're all going to be there, I can't stay away. You have room for one more in your class, Mac?"

"For you? Always."

The meeting room inside the Homefront community center had been arranged to accommodate a relatively small group tonight, with ten chairs in a semicircle facing a tall director's chair. Next to the director's chair was a side table and a whiteboard.

With fifteen minutes left until the workshop began, there were already sixteen people standing around the coffee machines or talking together in small groups. And that didn't include the six writers from the retreat group who hadn't shown up yet.

"You've got a good crowd here, Mac," Eric said.

"There are more people here than the number that signed up, but this is great. The more the merrier, right?"

"I'll get more chairs," Travis said.

"Thanks, Travis." Mac turned and gave my arm a squeeze. "Guess I'll start greeting people."

"You go ahead," I said. "They'll want to talk to you."

I watched him approach a group of three men and introduce himself. I didn't know why I'd been holding my breath, but I let it out slowly as the group welcomed Mac heartily.

I turned and headed across the room to help Travis with the chairs.

The doors of the paneled wall units were folded back accordion style to reveal several tall stacks of chairs. "I can help," I told him, and we began carrying chairs over to the semicircle.

"I can help, too," Chloe said, and grabbed a couple of chairs.

"Where'd Eric go?" I asked.

"He saw the light on in the program director's office, so he's down there talking to him."

I nodded and set out two more chairs.

"Hey, Parks," Travis called. "Give us a hand here."

An older man, grizzled and slightly stooped, came shuffling across the room and took a few more chairs from the stack.

Chloe and I supervised the arrangement of a second larger semicircle of chairs behind the first one.

"Think twenty-five will be enough?" Travis asked.

I glanced around, did a quick head count. "Maybe a few more, just to be safe."

"I got 'em," Parks said, and set three more chairs down to complete the circle. "That should do it."

"By the way, ladies," Travis said. "This is my buddy, Parks."

"Hi, Parks," Chloe said, shaking his hand. "Thanks for your help."

"A pleasure." The older man nodded his head and said with a gravelly voice, "Parker Bellingham Jones the fourth, at your service."

Parks looked to be in his fifties, I thought. And despite his fancy upper-class name, he must've had some hard times along the way.

Travis snorted. "He's got a way about him."

"Not sure why," Parks said, chuckling. "And still not sure how I earned such a highfalutin moniker like that when I grew up in a trailer park."

"I have a good friend who lives with her parents in a trailer park," Chloe said. "Only they call it a manufactured housing community."

Parks smiled. "That's a nice turn of phrase, isn't it?"

"She loves it there," Chloe continued. "They have a pool and a restaurant, and there's golf and all sorts of fun things to do."

"We mostly had a bunch of kids to play with," Parks said. "And when I was a kid, that's all I really wanted."

Chloe glanced around. "Do you live here now?"

"I do. Four doors down from my buddy Travis."

I glanced from one man to the other. "Did you know each other before you moved here?"

"Nope," Travis said. "I met Parks the day I moved in. He brought me a loaf of bread as a welcome gift."

Chloe beamed at Parks. "That's awesome."

"Who can't use a loaf of bread?" Parks said with a shrug.

"Man." Travis blew out a breath. "That is some genius-level philosophy right there."

Parks chuckled. "More like trailer-park philosophy."

"One and the same," Travis murmured.

Eric walked back into the hall and joined our little group. Chloe introduced him to Parks, and the two men shook hands.

"Pleased to meet you, Chief," Parks said.

"You too, Parks," he said. "Are you settling in okay?"

"Sure am," Parks said, then sobered. "What you fellows have built here, it's something I never thought I would see in my lifetime. It's a dream come true just to be here."

"It's something we all needed," Eric said quietly.

"True that," Travis said solemnly.

Mac walked over and greeted Parks. "Thanks for helping with the chairs."

Parks nodded. "Always glad to help."

"Let's go sit down," Travis said, nudging Parks. The two men walked over to the semicircle and took seats in the front.

I looked up at Mac. "Did you meet everyone?"

"Yeah. They're all psyched. I think it'll be a good workshop."

Chloe leaned in next to me. "I'm going to go save us three seats in the back row."

"Good idea," I said.

Eric checked his watch. "You about ready to start this thing?"

"Almost." Mac glanced up at the wall clock. "Waiting for a few more folks to join us."

As if on cue, there was a commotion by the double doors. We all turned to see the six writers walk in, chatting and laughing. A few of them waved at Mac as they crossed the room and made their way over to the circle of chairs. Once there, they had a quiet debate about where to sit. The two women suggested that they all sit in the back row because they weren't actually participating. Two of the guys agreed, but—big surprise—Lewis wanted to sit up front. His good friend, the one Mac had identified as Brian, joined him.

Lewis wore a vintage jacket over his button-down shirt. It was suede with fringe along the sleeves and the hem and across the back. Some of the fringe was beaded, and I had to admit, it was fabulous.

"He's going for the cowboy rock-star look," Chloe whispered.

I almost giggled out loud. Despite the fabulousness of the jacket, it just didn't suit his otherwise preppy style.

Lewis skirted around the group and made his way to the front row, and seeing him sit there so close to Mac made me wonder if Lewis had some mischief in mind. I didn't say anything to Mac, but I knew he was more than capable of handling any disruption that came his way. I focused on Chloe as she grabbed three seats at the end of the second row.

"I'm going to join Chloe," I said, and gave Mac's arm an encouraging squeeze. "Knock 'em dead. Or alive."

He grinned. "Alive is better."

"Looks like the gang's all here," Eric murmured.

Mac nodded. "Then let's get started."

Chapter Three

Mac welcomed everyone and then introduced Police Chief Eric Jensen to the attendees.

Eric stood and glanced around at all the faces. "Thanks, Mac. I want to thank you all for participating in this first of many workshops at Homefront. We're trying to do some good things here, and we all appreciate your support." He glanced at Mac. "Back to you."

"Thanks, Chief." Mac gazed at a piece of paper in his hand. "I also want to point out that we've got a few visitors tonight who won't be a regular part of the group. You probably recognize Shannon Hammer, who's heading the construction crew working on the houses. Her sister, Chloe, sitting next to her, is also a contractor."

We both waved at the group, and Mac continued. "We've also got six visitors who are all writers. They know the ups and downs of writing a book and trying to navigate the publishing industry. So during the break, they've offered to answer questions and talk about their books with you. Raise your hands, guys."

The authors raised their hands, and everyone else turned to get a good look at them.

When the hubbub died down, Mac began the workshop. He asked some questions, then gave some ground rules. "No one is obligated to do the work or turn in assignments. You don't have to read your work out loud. You can do as much or as little writing as you want. You can just come and listen if that's what suits you."

There was an audible sigh of relief.

Mac flashed a quick grin. "Yeah, I get it. But let me add that if you *do* participate and take a chance and write something and then read it out loud, you're going to get more out of it than you ever imagined. Think about it." I watched Mac glance around at the faces of the veterans. So many of these men and women had been through so much, and that didn't just refer to their time on the battlefield. Some had experienced even more trouble once they came back home.

I knew Mac didn't expect to impart any sort of wisdom or higher understanding in here. He just wanted them to enjoy themselves in the few hours they would spend in his workshop.

"Okay, lecture over," he said, and moved on to the idea of setting a story in a particular place and using sense memory to make it come alive. The smells, the colors, the heat and the cold, the buzz of insects, or the taste of salt air. He asked for questions and gave amazing answers, and I found myself fascinated by his voice and the way he phrased certain words. There was always a hint of humor in his tone. He found life interesting and fun, and he was never bored or listless, but always enthusiastic, even when it came to deciding what to have for dinner. He made me laugh, made me happy, and I felt so lucky to have him in my life. And it was always a thrill to know that he felt the exact same way about me.

I was shaken out of my happy little daydream when Mac's tone suddenly changed. "Are you recording this?"

Mac was pointing at Lewis. The writer was taken aback, and I had to wonder. Did he think Mac wouldn't see him holding up his phone the way he did?

"Yes," Lewis said. "I like to have a record of everything."

Mac sat back in his chair, looking perfectly relaxed. "I prefer that you not record this workshop."

"But—"

"In a few minutes, some of us will be reading our work out loud. You must realize that for many beginning writers, it takes a lot of courage to stand up and read your own words to an audience. I'd like you to respect their privacy and put your phone away."

Lewis looked at Brian for support. "But I always record our writers' meetings. It's not like I'm going to play it to the whole world. It's just for my personal use."

"Lewis," Mac said succinctly. "I'm asking you to put your phone away."

"Maybe we could take a vote," Lewis said brightly.

"In this workshop, my vote is the only one that counts."

"Wow." He frowned and his lower lip stuck out. He was pouting! "That doesn't seem fair."

In a casual move, Mac stood and folded his arms.

"What's fair is that you consider the feelings of the other people in the room. Now please, put the phone away."

I had to admire Mac's patience. I would've drop-kicked that jerk right out of the room.

Lewis gave an ill-tempered shrug. "Didn't think it was that big of a deal." He glanced around as though he might be able to rally some of us to his side, but it wouldn't work with this crowd. He reminded me of a popular football player back in high school who most of us secretly hated, but because he was such an arrogant bully, none of us had the courage to tell him to buzz off.

Mac was not one to be intimidated. He sat down and blithely moved on to the subject of dialogue.

I glanced over at Lewis and Brian in the front row and noticed Brian ignoring his friend as he stared at the doorway. He elbowed Lewis, and because I was watching him, I could tell what he was whispering. *Wow, she's pretty.*

Lewis rolled his eyes in disgust but turned and looked. I couldn't help but peek over my shoulder and see Julia and Linda looking in. Glancing back at the two men, I saw Lewis wiggle his eyebrows. *Oh, hey. She's hot.* Then he whispered loudly to Brian, "Dream on, dude. They're both above your pay grade."

Brian scowled, clearly in disagreement with Lewis's assessment. He turned back to listen to Mac, but Lewis continued staring across the room at the two women. As I watched, he pulled out his cell phone, and sure enough, he aimed and clicked a photo.

He wasn't even trying to be discreet. The guy was too obsessed with recording the moment.

I glanced at Mac, and for a brief second, we made

eye contact. I knew that he'd seen the entire byplay between the two men. And I knew we'd be talking about it later.

Halfway through the workshop, Mac gave everyone a ten-minute break. I stood and stretched, then turned to Chloe. "Are you going to stick around?"

"Heck yeah," Chloe said. "I want to see what those knuckleheads do next."

"That guy has no shame," I said.

"You're right," she said. "But I'm staying anyway because Mac is an amazing teacher."

"He sure is," I said. "I'm more impressed than ever."

"And how about that reading from Travis?" She shook her head in awe. "Wow."

"It was beautiful," I said.

Travis had read a short story he'd written about wrestling a bear to rescue a baby. It was both brutal and very touching. I'd never imagined a wilderness adventure story could be so lyrical.

"It made me cry," Chloe admitted. "And laugh."

"Uh-oh," I whispered.

She gave me a look. "Oh, come on. I heard you sniffling, too."

"It's not that. It's that." I jerked my chin toward the other side of the room, where Lewis was deep in conversation with Linda. And now Julia was heading my way, looking annoyed.

"Now what has he done?" Chloe wondered.

Julia came right up to me. "Who is that guy?"

"He's one of the retreat writers."

"He's an obnoxious idiot. He just told Linda he's never met anyone so beautiful in his entire life."

"She is very pretty," Chloe admitted. "Who is she?"

"Linda Rutledge," I explained. "She grew up here."

"I don't remember her," Chloe said, frowning as she gazed over at Linda.

"She was a few years ahead of us in school." I looked from Chloe to Julia. "You remember Julia, don't you?"

"Sure." She grinned at Julia. "Your dad was a really good carpenter. He worked with our father sometimes, right?"

"That's right," Julia said.

"And now she's in charge of the nonprofit foundation that's underwriting the supplies and equipment for my construction skills class."

"That's fantastic," Chloe said. "Paying it forward, right?"

I almost laughed since I'd thought the very same thing.

"That's right," Julia said. "Trying to get more women into the business."

"I would love to see that happen," Chloe murmured.

I nodded. "You and me both."

"But listen, you guys," Julia said. "I want to tell you what else that clown said to Linda."

"Tell us," Chloe said.

"After he told her she's beautiful, he asked if she was a natural blonde."

"He did not!" I said.

"Was he joking?" Chloe asked.

"No. And then he took a bunch of selfies with her, like they're friends or something. He'll probably show them to people and try to convince them that she's his girlfriend. He's a presumptuous jerk."

"Yeah, I'm betting he hears that a lot," I said.

"And Linda's so nice, she wouldn't think of stomping on his instep."

"Not like any of us," Chloe said with a laugh.

I had to laugh, too. According to one of our high school gym teachers, stomping on someone's instep was one of the primary ways of fending off an attack.

I patted Julia's shoulder. "Don't worry, he's only here for two weeks."

"Two whole weeks?" Julia said, and pressed her hand to her forehead. "Just kill me now."

After the workshop, Mac agreed to stick around for coffee with some of the attendees. I went on home to feed the animals and get started on payroll for my crew.

By the time Mac got home, I was finishing a glass of wine and watching TV.

"I'll have some of that," he said, pointing to my wineglass. "Give me just a minute to put my stuff away."

"Okay." I walked into the kitchen and pulled the bottle of Chardonnay out of the refrigerator. I grabbed a glass and filled it for Mac, then poured myself another half glass.

I waited for Robbie and the cats to smother him in welcome barks and head bumps, then handed him the glass. "Here you go."

"Bless you." He took it, but before he took a sip, he leaned in and kissed me. "You didn't miss much after you left."

"Oh, thank goodness. I would hate to miss another neurotic scene starring Lewis." I led the way back to the living room, and we sat on opposite ends of the couch with our feet touching.

"I'm afraid every scene with Lewis will be neurotic," Mac said. "The guy sucks the air out of the room."

"I know. He demands attention by being a jackass." I pondered the idea. "My dad had a friend who used to say, 'Any attention is good attention.' He was talking about his teenager who acted out sometimes to get noticed. And even if it earned him a smack on his arm, the kid was happy because at least someone was paying attention to him."

"That's exactly what's happening here." Mac sipped his wine, then shook his head in frustration. "And I really hate to keep talking about these people. It sucks the air out of *our* room."

"Then let's not talk about him anymore."

"Hey, that's a good idea." He set his glass down on the coffee table. "You're pretty smart."

"Yes, I am." I swirled my wine, then sighed. "Look, I'm not about to tell you what to do."

He smiled. *"But?"*

"But if I were you, I wouldn't hang around them. Their energy is just too toxic."

"Another good idea. And that won't be a problem because after tonight, they're on their own." But then he winced. "Except I already promised to lead them in a writing exercise in a few days."

"I'll bet you made that promise before you got to know Lewis."

"Yeah." He took a deep breath and exhaled. "The rest of the group is okay. I liked them all. Except, well, Brian hangs on Lewis's every word, so that's hard to watch sometimes. But otherwise, they're not bad people. They're smart. And they're good writers, all in all."

As usual, he would try to make the best of a weird situation. But I'd seen the look of concern on his face. The writers' retreat had been a labor of love for him, and I didn't like to know that he was so worried about it. I reached for my wineglass and took a last sip. "When are you doing the writing exercise with them?"

"In three days. I plan to do it on the beach at sunset."

"I should come with you."

"To protect me?" he asked wryly.

"If I have to."

Now he smiled broadly. "I would love that."

I moved over to his side of the couch and wrapped my arms around him. "Then I'll be there."

I was up early the next day and joined Mac in the kitchen, where he had already fed our little creatures and made the coffee.

"You're becoming an early riser with this book," I said, and poured myself a cup of coffee.

"For some reason, this story's been waking me up at four o'clock every morning. But it's a good thing. I can get the work done early and then hang out with you all afternoon."

"I like that idea."

Because Mac was one of the founders of Homefront, he spent a lot of time with the project manager, setting up interviews on different news programs around the country. His fame as an author helped with their fundraising efforts, and he helped with his hands, too. He had planted gardens, moved furniture, painted houses, and pitched in with various administrative stuff. The best part about that was that he was able to spend his days at Homefront, which meant that we could see each other throughout the day.

I sat down at the kitchen table, and Robbie immediately barked for more attention. I patted my lap and he leapt up. "Good morning, sweetie," I said, giving him a hug and then rubbing his belly.

Mac poured himself a second cup of coffee. "So tonight's the night, right?"

I had to exhale slowly. "Yeah. I don't know why I'm nervous."

"I don't, either. You're the absolute best choice to teach this class. And it's really going to help a lot of people."

"Your workshop helps, too."

"My workshop is fun and interesting and semieducational," he said. "But yours is more than that. You're teaching people the actual skills that will help get them good-paying jobs."

I sipped my coffee. "Maybe that's why I'm nervous. There's a lot riding on this."

He took a couple of eggs from the refrigerator. "Scrambled eggs and English muffins okay?"

"Sounds great."

He cracked the eggs into a bowl and began to whisk them. "Did you convince Chloe to join your class?"

"I think so." I smiled. "I told her she could criticize my performance afterward."

He grinned. "She won't be able to pass that up."

"Who could?" I took charge of the English muffins, separating them with a fork and popping them into the toaster oven.

After adding some fresh chopped herbs to the egg

mixture, Mac poured it into a frying pan. He topped the eggs with a few crumbles of goat cheese—our latest obsession—and covered the pan. In a few minutes, it would become a tasty open-faced omelet.

As we sat down to eat a few minutes later, he frowned. "I forgot to tell you something that happened last night."

"What is it?" I felt the brush of soft fur against my leg and knew that the cats had come to join us. Robbie was already sitting next to my feet, as usual.

"You know that I stayed afterward to talk to everyone."

"Yeah."

"Well, the writers ended up staying, too. While we chatted, Travis and Parks put all the chairs away. And when they were done, they joined us. And the first thing Sheri did was compliment Travis on his short story."

"That's nice," I said. "These eggs are delicious, by the way. They're so creamy and light."

"Thanks." He grinned. "I'm getting pretty good at that."

"Yeah, you are. Oh, but finish what you were saying. Sorry to interrupt."

"No problem. So right after Sheri spoke, Annabelle jumped in, and she raved about Travis's story, too."

"It was a really good story," I said.

"Absolutely. I'd love the chance to get it published, but that's a conversation for another day. Anyway, as soon as Annabelle finished talking, the little guy, Hugh, told Travis that, yeah, he liked the story, but something was a little off. He called the whole thing anachronistic."

"What?"

"Basically, it means the language is inconsistent with the time frame or the setting. Hugh said it was old-fashioned."

I frowned at him. "But that's part of Travis's charm. He's an old-fashioned guy. It's what makes the story uniquely his."

"Exactly," Mac said. "So right after that, Kingsley tells Travis that he noticed there were two places where he used the passive voice. He says, 'You might want to watch that in the future.'"

"You've got to be kidding," I said with a scowl. "Did you want to punch him?"

"As much as I wanted to take my next breath. I was about to tell them all to shut up, but before I could say a word, Lewis had to jump in with his two cents. He says, 'If you'd like to see a good example of a strong active voice, I would recommend that you read my book.'"

"Oh my God." I buried my face in my hands. "They're all horrible."

"Yeah. And at this point, Travis was looking completely dejected."

"But why? He must know their opinions are worthless."

Mac sighed. "He may be a kickass ex-marine, but he's understandably insecure about his writing. And he's not the only one."

"Well, despite his insecurities, he was brave enough to read it out loud."

Mac frowned. "Which gave everyone a chance to take potshots."

"Poor guy." I took a bite of my English muffin. "He's tough on the outside, but he has a fragile heart."

Mac reached over and squeezed my hand. "I probably shouldn't have told you."

"I'm glad you did. Because when I see Travis today, I'm going to give him a big hug and tell him how awesome his short story was."

He smiled. "Coming from you, that'll make his day."

I made good on my promise to give Travis a hug when I found him helping our electrician run conduit within the frame of house number thirty.

"Morning, boss," he said.

"I don't want to interrupt the work, but I had to tell you how amazing your story was last night."

"Aw, thanks, Shannon."

"My guys are always going on and on about the stories you tell at lunch, but I've never had the chance to hear any of them until last night. You are really talented."

He shrugged self-consciously. "That's nice of you to say."

"Well, I mean it, and I wanted you to know. I'll see you later." I walked away before his cheeks could turn any pinker.

It was all true. Travis had become quite a hit with my crew members, who had begun to gather around him at lunch to listen to his adventures.

According to my crew guys, Travis had done some traveling after he left the Marines. He mainly paid his way by working on construction sites wherever he landed next. He'd spent time working on the Alaska pipelines and had helped build irrigation systems in Africa. When he couldn't find a job, he surfed and played guitar for anyone who would listen.

He was a remarkable guy, a real character. And most importantly, he was strong and willing to work hard. I was lucky to have him on my crew.

At the end of the day, I grabbed Sean and Johnny, and got them to help me set things up for my class. In the main meeting room, we fashioned three wide tables using sturdy sawhorses and thick plywood boards. I placed two of my tool chests, along with my power drill and pneumatic staple gun, on top of the sideboard, giving me easy access to everything once I began to give my tools and rules talk. The larger tool chest held many of my pink tools and I thought the women would get a kick out of that.

I wouldn't be demonstrating any power saws for the first few weeks, so Sean and Johnny had carried in enough precut lumber for the women to make the first project I'd be showing them.

A few minutes after the guys took off, Julia came in carrying several large shopping bags. "I'm glad you're here. You look all set up and ready to go."

"I think I am," I said. "How are you?"

"I'm great. And I have a surprise." She set the bags down and pulled a few things out.

"What is that?"

She held one of them up. "Aren't these great?"

I blinked, then laughed. "You brought everyone a tool belt?"

"Well, yeah." She smiled. "And they're pretty nice, too."

I picked one up. "They really are. I like the camo style."

"I figured since everyone's ex-military, they would

approve. I had to choose between these or a pink belt, like the one you use."

"Don't scoff. There's a very good reason why I use pink tools."

"What is it?"

"My guys don't steal them."

Her mouth gaped open. "Oh, that's brilliant."

"Works for me." I examined the camouflage tool belt more carefully. It was well made with a two-inch-wide belt and a sturdy buckle. There were four main pockets, eight smaller pockets, plus a couple of sleeves and two hammer loops. "This will do the job."

"You probably have a bunch of these, but I did bring one for you."

"Really?" It might've been a simple tool belt, but I was touched by her thoughtfulness. "Thanks. I can use it to show everyone what to put in the pockets and the best way to wear it so you don't get dragged down."

"That's a good idea." She chuckled. "My dad gave me my first tool belt when I was six years old. He loaded it with tools, and I just about fell over from the weight."

I laughed. "Chloe and I had a few of those moments, too."

"Hey, will she be here tonight?"

"Yes. She may not stay for the whole class, but she'll be here."

"Great!"

"Are you staying for the whole two hours?" I said.

She grinned. "Of course."

"I'm glad. The more women we have who actually know construction, the better it will be for the newbies."

"I absolutely agree." She tucked her shopping bags

under the sideboard. "Linda should be here in a few minutes with her mosaics. I've got to run down the hall for a quick meeting, but I'll be back before the class starts."

"See you then."

Julia got as far as the doorway and turned. "Here's Linda now." She stopped to say hello to her friend, then took off. Linda Rutledge approached carrying a small toolbox and an artist's portfolio tucked under one arm.

"Hi, Shannon," she said cheerfully. "I was hoping to get here early enough to show you some of my work."

"We have time," I said. "How are you doing?"

"Great. I'm so excited about your class."

"Me, too," I said. "I think it'll be fun."

"Where would you like me to set up?" she asked.

"How about right here?" I indicated the nearest ply-wood table.

"Perfect." She set down her toolbox and opened her portfolio case, spreading a dozen color photographs out for me to see.

"Oh wow," I said. "These are beautiful."

"Thanks. The photographs are easier to carry around," she explained. "But I also brought a few actual samples of some things I worked on recently." She pulled out two pieces of unframed artwork mounted on backer board.

"These colors are amazing," I said. "Like something from Van Gogh's sunflowers."

"I did a whole series of Van Gogh–inspired pieces. I love working with bright colors."

"You've managed to duplicate his brushstrokes with the placement of your glass and tile pieces."

"Yeah." She smiled. "That was fun."

"And this one is completely different." I switched my attention to her second project. "It looks like an underwater world with all those shades of blue and green, and the seagrass wafting in the waves and the tortoise swimming by. It's beautiful. Like a painting." I looked at her. "You're really good at this."

"Thanks. Coming from you, that means a lot."

"I have a stonemason on my crew who does stuff like this on a larger scale. You know, stone walls and patios and driveways and such, with lots of design elements, curlicues, whimsical creatures."

"Is that Niall?" she asked.

"Yes, Niall Rose. You know him?"

"We've met. His sister, Emily, introduced us after she found out about my mosaics."

"Emily's one of my dearest friends, and Niall is engaged to another friend."

"Jane," she said.

I had to laugh. "I feel like we're just a few degrees of separation from each other."

"Life in a small town. It's amazing, isn't it?"

"It really is." I stared at the artwork as an idea began to form.

"Well, I'll get this out of your way." She stacked the photographs and the mosaic boards, ready to slip them back into the portfolio case.

"Linda, I wonder if you'd be interested in working with us. Now, it's not exactly the Louvre, but I was thinking that your mosaic art would be fabulous as the backsplash in some of the kitchens we're working on."

She blinked. "What do you mean?"

"Well, so far we've just been using run-of-the-mill tile work for the backsplashes. But we'd really like to give each house a unique touch, something that sets them apart. You've seen the different Victorian flourishes we've added to the outside, right?"

"Yes. I was just telling Julia that I love the miniature widow's walks on some of the houses."

"I do, too. Some of them have scalloped shingles on the gables instead of the plain siding." I smiled. "And here and there, you'll even see a touch of gingerbread around the front door. We want to make sure these little houses are in line with the town's Victorian history and style."

"I would love to work with you." But she began to frown.

"What's wrong? Are you working somewhere else?"

"No, no. It's just that I always picture Victorian mosaic art as being pretty rigid. Straight lines and repetitive patterns, you know?"

"I do. They're not exactly abstract expressionism, right?"

She laughed. "Not at all."

"Well, I agree that Victorian floors and walkways were fairly rigid. But what about Tiffany lamps? They're from the Victorian era, but their glasswork was pretty avant-garde for the time."

"Oh, of course." She smacked her forehead lightly. "I wasn't thinking." She stared at one of her photographs, then nodded. "Yes, I would love to work on your backsplashes."

"Wonderful."

"I'm already getting ideas." She laughed again. "I can't wait. Thank you. It'll be a real honor to participate."

"You're sweet, but don't be too honored. We're going to put you to work."

"I won't complain." She packed everything up in her portfolio and leaned it against the wall, out of the way. "Um, should I start tomorrow?"

"If you can. Do you have your own materials, or would you like to work with what we have?"

"If it's okay, I'll bring my own materials."

"Good. We want your personal touch on all of this. And of course, we'll be glad to reimburse you."

"That's nice. If I could have the use of a utility table, I can bring my things and get started in the morning."

"We'll get you all set up."

"Wow, this is great." She gave a short laugh. "Thank you."

I smiled. "No, thank *you*."

Julia dashed in just minutes before I was about to start the class. She came right up to me and whispered, "Those two guys are hanging around out in the hall, waiting for Linda."

"What guys?"

"Those writers," she said, scowling. "The ones that were here last night."

"Huh. Well, I don't need any distractions, so let's see if we can close the door." I walked across the room to do just that and saw Parks come out of the café.

The powers that be had decided early on that the dining room in the community center was to be called the café. It sounded less institutional and more casual, which everyone agreed was a good thing.

Parks strolled over to Lewis and Brian. Lewis was wearing his fringed suede jacket, and while it was beautiful, I still didn't think it suited him. Brian wore a sweater vest over a white shirt, and they both wore pressed jeans. I had a fleeting thought that maybe Brian ironed Lewis's jeans for him. They seemed to have an odd relationship.

And where had that thought come from? I wondered, feeling very catty.

"You fellas thinking of joining the military?" Parks asked.

Lewis looked horrified. "What?"

"Homefront is a place where veterans live and thrive. Would you like a tour of the facilities?"

Lewis looked at him as though he had three heads. "No, we don't want a tour. We're waiting for someone."

"Someone in the meeting room?"

"Yeah."

"Well, son," Parks said, his voice more gruff than usual. "There's a class going on right now, and our vets take their studies seriously. It'll be over in about two hours, so maybe you ought to text your lady friend and let her know where you'll meet her."

"How do you know we're waiting for a lady?"

"Because I'm not stupid."

"Oh." Brian frowned.

"Regardless," Parks continued, "we'd rather you didn't loiter out here for the next two hours."

I wasn't surprised to see Lewis straighten his shoulders in an obvious move to confront Parks.

I was about to intervene and back up Parks's edict when Brian shrugged and said, "Doesn't matter. We'll see her later at the pub."

Lewis scowled at him. Brian smiled back, but it wasn't a particularly pleasant look.

"Okay, fine," Lewis said. "I'll text her." And he and Brian headed out the door to the parking lot.

And once again, I had to wonder who the alpha male was in that relationship. Then I shook my head. Why did it matter?

Parks turned to me and grinned, then gave a quick salute.

"Thanks," I whispered.

As I walked back to my spot at the front of the room, it occurred to me that if Brian and Lewis had been allowed to remain by the door, Lewis might've tried to record my class. It wasn't the worst thing that could ever happen to me, but it was rude and invasive, and I was grateful to Parks for intervening. I thought of Mac's words of warning to Lewis last evening. Clearly those words had bounced right off of the guy's hard head.

And that's when I realized that it was his clear disrespect for Mac that had me so irritated with him. I would rarely want to wish ill on anyone, but I could admit, I'd be perfectly happy if Lewis caught some icky, short-term digestive disorder and left our town for good.

Chapter Four

"Thank you all for signing up for the class," I began. "I think we'll have a good time. You all know Julia Barton, whose foundation is responsible for all of us being here tonight."

"Hi, Julia," everyone said.

"Hi, gang," Julia said, pushing her chair back to stand and wave. "I'm thrilled to see all of you here, and I have a little something for each of you." She pulled out the shopping bags and walked around, handing each of the women one of the camo tool belts.

"These are cool," one woman said. "Thanks."

"I thought you'd appreciate the camo design."

"Absolutely," several of them said at the same time. A few of them buckled the belt around their waists.

"Thanks, Julia," I said. "So in a little while, I'll give some suggestions on how to wear the belt and what to carry so you're not so weighted down that you can't walk."

"Oh good," a short blond woman said. "Because I don't have a clue."

"You will, don't worry," I assured her. "Okay, we should get started."

The group settled in.

I took a deep breath and began. "I'm hoping that most of you will find this class personally empowering. Not only because it might help get you a good-paying job, but also because the simple act of building something with your own hands can be truly uplifting. Even something as unpretentious as a bookshelf can give you the most amazing feeling." I chuckled. "Of course, I'm looking at a group of women who can shoot a rifle with incredible accuracy and climb over twenty-foot walls."

The entire group laughed, thank goodness.

"Still," I said, "it's pretty cool to know that by the end of this ten-week class, you will have acquired many of the skills you'll need to build a house."

"A house?" Linda said.

"A *house*," I repeated. "But more about that later. Tonight we'll spend the first hour going over tools and rules. I'll begin with hand tools, then graduate to a few of the power tools you'll need to use. And we'll discuss some commonsense rules for using the tools the right way."

"So I don't hit myself in the head with a hammer?" a blonde said. Her name was Heather, and she had been a MedTech—a medical technician—in the navy, and I doubted she would ever hit herself with a hammer.

"That's rule number one," I said, with a laugh. "We'll learn the difference between an impact driver and a power drill, and you'll all get to use my beloved pneumatic staple gun. No table saws or circular saws for a few weeks yet."

"What about the second half of tonight?" a women

named Sari asked. She had been an Army Ranger, still a rare accomplishment for a woman, but confessed that once she left the service, she couldn't find a job and was later diagnosed with PTSD. She had been on a VA waiting list for two years before discovering Home-front. It was like a miracle for her.

"I'm glad you asked," I said with a grin. "In the second half, we'll use our newly gained knowledge of tools to build something simple. A bench."

"A bench?"

"Yes. A picnic bench. It'll go with the other bench and small picnic table that each of you will be con-structing over the next few weeks."

"What in the world are we going to do with a picnic table?" a woman asked. Her name was Becca, but in my head, I'd started calling her "the doubting one."

"You have a couple of choices," I said quickly. "I checked, and you're all allowed to have patio furniture on the side lawn outside your house. But if it's not something you'd care to have on your property, you can either give it to another veteran or a friend or family member who wants it, or you can donate it to the town park."

"It's good to have options," said Amy, who'd told me she'd been a fighter pilot in the air force.

"The point is to learn how to build a simple piece of furniture that has a practical purpose. It's rewarding and fun. And of course," I added, "if you move away, you can take it with you."

"I like that part," someone said.

"In our third week," I said, "we'll go on a field trip to the lumber yard and the hardware store. I talk to so many women—and plenty of men, too—who are baffled by all the mysterious and intimidating gadgets and doohickeys that are necessary to complete everyday projects. For instance, there are dozens of different fasteners and a hundred different screw sizes and a million other gadgets and thingamabobs you absolutely must know about. So we'll go through and decode some of that stuff so you won't ever feel intimidated again."

"I love that," Amy murmured.

"And then our fourth week, you'll each use your new skills to build something. Anything. But this time, it's your choice. It can be a bookshelf, or a frame for a couch or a bed, or a table, a desk, a birdhouse, or whatever you'd like to try."

I took a deep breath and let it out. "From the fifth to the tenth week, you're all going to help me build one of the tiny houses here in the village."

"What?" Sari said.

Amy gaped. "You're kidding."

"Nope. We'll build the frame together. And we'll insulate the walls, we'll add the subfloor, and we'll hang drywall. We'll work on the heating and air vents, we'll help run the electrical and plumbing lines, we'll nail down the external sheathing and the underlayment, then hang the vinyl siding. We'll get up on the roof and lay down plywood, then another type of underlayment, and then shingles. We'll hang the front door and install windows. And we'll paint. In the interior, we'll plumb the kitchen and bathroom, build the closet, and organize the rest of the space. And by week ten, you'll all have built a real house."

"That's crazy," Amy said to the woman sitting next to her.

Linda looked at me in disbelief. "You really expect us to build a house?"

"I sure do," I said with a grin. "And I expect you to do a great job because another veteran will live in that house someday soon. Pretty cool, right?"

"Kind of scary," Sari admitted.

"But totally awesome," Amy said.

"You'll supervise, right?" the doubting one asked.

"Oh yeah, I'll supervise, my entire crew will supervise, and by the time we're finished with the class, you'll all have the skills to build a house."

"Woo hoo!" Sari said, and everyone joined in.

Suddenly, the doors flew opened and Chloe walked in. I had to laugh. My sister was dressed in what I liked to call her Contractor Barbie outfit. Her clothes and makeup were perfect, and she looked like she was ready for her close-up.

I rolled my eyes, but she just grinned. "Hi, ladies. I'm Chloe."

Becca gasped. "Oh my God, I watch your show every week."

"That's so nice to hear," Chloe said, and set down a heavy canvas bag on top of the plywood table.

"Everybody," I said loudly. "This is my sister, Chloe. And it looks like she brought presents with her."

"Of course I did." She pulled out a big, thick book. "An autographed copy of my book for each of you."

I threw my arm around her shoulder. "You're a class act, kiddo."

"You're not so bad yourself. Help me hand these out."

I grabbed several books and took them to the four women sitting at one of the other tables. "Here you go.

It's a really good book on home decorating, and there's a lot of info on carpentry, too."

"And lots of DIY projects you can do at home," Chloe added.

"Thank you," Amy said.

"Wow, this is great," Sari said, stroking the cover of the book. "Thanks."

When the excitement died down, Chloe asked, "How many of you have worked in carpentry or construction?"

Only Julia raised her hand.

I glanced around. "So Julia, Chloe, and I have spent our entire lives in the carpentry and construction field. Obviously we're not the norm."

Chloe made a face. "Speak for yourself."

I elbowed her. "I didn't say we're not normal. But it's a sad fact that in our world, there are a lot more men working in the field than women. But Julia and Chloe and I are proof positive that, given the opportunity, women can be just as awesome as men when it comes to building."

"More awesome," Chloe added.

"Yeah," Julia said. "I really want to see more women on the job."

"So let's make that happen," I said, and held up a hammer. "Starting right now."

At the end of the class, each of the women carried their bench project down the hall to a small office that we'd be using as a temporary storeroom. I made sure that everyone who lived in town had a ride, and we watched the women who lived on the Homefront campus walk to their homes. Then Chloe, Julia, Linda, and I stood in the parking lot and talked about the class.

"It went so smoothly," Julia said. "You're such a good teacher."

"Thank you," I said. "But I'm not even sure what makes a good teacher."

"Lots of patience and a good sense of humor."

I nodded slowly. "Okay. I can see that."

Chloe grinned. "And it helps to know your subject matter."

"And you do," Julia assured me.

"You were great," Linda said. "I'm so impressed and really excited about building the house."

"It's going to be fun."

A black Audi pulled into the parking lot, and we all watched to see who was driving and where they were going. When Lewis got out, I almost groaned out loud.

"What is he doing here?" Julia asked quietly, but I could tell she was irritated.

"Oh, it's Lewis," Linda said brightly. "I told him we might go to the pub after class, but it's later than I thought we'd be. He must've gotten worried."

"You have a date with him?" Julia asked, incredulous.

"It's not a date, silly," Linda said, waving away that idea. "We just talked about meeting there."

"Looks like he thinks it's a date," Chloe murmured, for my ears only.

Julia put her hand on Linda's arm. "He's not a very nice guy."

Linda patted her hand. "Oh, he's not so bad."

Lewis crossed the parking lot. "Linda? I wasn't sure if you remembered our date."

Julia made an annoyed *humph* sound, but said nothing.

"Our class just ended," Linda explained. "I can follow you to the pub."

"Okay." He frowned at the rest of us, as if he thought we'd all be coming along. And maybe that wasn't such a bad idea.

Linda gave Julia a quick hug. "Nighty night."

Then she hugged me as well. "The class was just super. And I can't wait to start on the mosaics tomorrow. See you then! Bye, Chloe!"

She walked quickly across the parking lot to her car.

Lewis pulled his jacket close as he sat down in his car, then raced out of the parking lot. Another car engine started up on the far side of the lot, and that car drove out as well. It was a small white SUV, I noticed, and thought it might be one of the kitchen staff leaving for the night.

"Well, that's disappointing," Julia said when both cars were gone. "Linda's a smart woman, but she's just too nice for her own good."

"Try not to worry too much," I said gently. "She'll be fine."

She gritted her teeth. "I don't know why he bugs me so much."

"Because he's a player," Chloe said with certainty. "I've never even met him, but I've seen his type in action."

"I guess that's it."

"And you're Linda's good friend," I said. "You're naturally protective."

"True. She's so open and friendly, I worry that a guy like that will take advantage." Julia sighed. "Well, I'd better be going. I've got another meeting here tomorrow morning, so I'll probably see you at some point."

"I'll be around," I assured her.

"I'll be here, too," Chloe said. "I'm taking videos for my show."

"That sounds like fun." She waved as she crossed the parking lot. "Good night."

When I got home, Mac and Robbie were on the couch, watching a basketball game. The cats were curled up in different parts of the room apparently uninterested in the big game.

I stood in the doorway gazing at them all and thought how happy I was to be home.

"How did it go?" Mac asked as he stood and gave me a kiss, then walked with me into the kitchen.

"Really well. It's a good group. Five of the women live in Homefront houses, and the other seven are from town." I chuckled. "Chloe made a grand entrance, and everyone fell in love with her."

He wrapped his arms around me. "I'm going to bet that they fell in love with you, too."

"I think they really enjoyed it. And the fact that I'm gearing it all toward a career in the business made it even more interesting. At least, for most of them."

"Did you tell them they're going to build a house?"

"Yes, and they all freaked out. In a good way." I grinned. "I think they're all pretty psyched."

"So no pests in your class?"

"Just one woman who questions everything I say. She's not too bad, just a little fearful, I guess. And I get that."

"Any injuries?"

I laughed. "Not yet. And I don't expect any. These women have fought in wars. I can't imagine they'll fall apart when faced with a power drill."

"Good point."

"There was one weird moment," I confessed. "And it had to do with Lewis."

He frowned. "Lewis? The writer?"

"Yes."

He held up his hand. "Wait. I'm going to get my beer. And you probably need a glass of wine."

"What a good idea."

Mac retrieved his beer and then poured a glass of wine for me. We sat down, and I told him the story about Parks shooing Lewis and Brian out of the community center before the class, and then later, how Lewis showed up for his "date" with Linda.

"You're kidding me."

"No. And Julia was really concerned." I relayed that conversation to him.

"Maybe I'd better have a talk with him," Mac said.

"I hate the idea that you've got to deal with him. Like you're a chaperone or something. They're not kids."

"No, and neither is Linda," he said.

I sighed. "Linda is a lovely, friendly woman, and Lewis is a player." I glanced up. "That was Chloe's word for him."

"That about sums it up."

"Oh, and she starts working for me tomorrow."

"Who? Chloe?"

"No." I laughed. "Linda."

"Is that right?"

"She's an incredible mosaic artist, and I got the

bright idea to ask if she would do some of the back-splashes in the houses."

Mac nodded approvingly. "That's a great idea. It'll give some of them that unique touch you're looking for."

"Exactly." I took a sip of wine and sat down at the table. "I thought she might be insulted at the idea of doing backsplashes, but she's not working right now, so she can use the money, and she's happy to help the cause."

"Good. Another win-win for Homefront."

"Yes. Oh, and Chloe will be working at the village tomorrow, too. Taking videos of our work for her show."

"She mentioned that." He sipped his beer. "That'll be nice for you."

"It will." I smiled. "You should've seen her walk into the meeting room. She was in full Contractor Barbie mode. She looked fabulous. And she brought a copy of her book for everyone in the class."

"That's pretty nice."

"It was awesome. And she stayed to the very end. She helped some of the women with the bench project. Answered questions. Talked about her show. She was great."

"It sounds like your first class was a hit."

"Totally," I said, and yawned. "And wow, I'm really tired. I feel like I'm about to fall on my face."

He wrapped his arm around my shoulders. "Let's go to bed."

The next morning, I placed my coffee cup in the dish-washer and was about to leave for Homefront when a loud alarm rang through the house. The sound was so shrill that I thought my car alarm had gone off and ran to the back door to go outside and turn it off.

"Is that your phone?" Mac asked before I'd taken two steps out the door.

I stopped and listened to the high-pitched tone. "Is it?" It took me another second or two to recognize the sound. "It *is* my phone."

I ran back to the kitchen table, where I'd left my cellphone sitting on top of my purse.

I grabbed the phone and switched off the noise, then stared at Mac. "It's the lighthouse alarm."

"I was afraid of that," Mac said. "We'd better get out there."

"Wait. Let's look at the video before we take the drive. It could've been birds or something harmless setting off the alarm."

"You think birds could've unlocked the door?"

I smiled ruefully. "No, but let's check first anyway." I replayed the video to see what had set off the alarm. It was dark inside the stairwell, but the morning sunlight managed to cast its hazy light into the space. I could just make out the images.

"Oh hell," Mac muttered when he got a look at the intruders. "They're worse than teenagers."

We could see Lewis, Brian, Sheri, and Annabelle tiptoeing carefully up the stairs, giggling and chattering as they went.

Lewis led the way. He held up his phone, and a bright light suddenly flashed when he turned on his flashlight app.

"The view from up there is going to be spectacular," he said excitedly.

"Perfect for a romantic tryst," Sheri said.

"Or a murder," Lewis said, causing the others to laugh.

We listened to them talk for another few seconds, until they climbed out of sight and the audio could no longer be heard.

I glared at the phone, then looked at Mac. "What's up with these writers? Aren't they supposed to be writing?"

"I don't know what the hell they're doing."

"We should call Eric and report them," I grumbled.

Mac's eyes were flat and cold. "That's exactly what I'm going to do."

I arrived at Homefront a few minutes late, after taking the time to report the lighthouse break-in. Mac had told Eric to give those idiots something to think about. Eric promised he would send a patrol car over there to bring them down to the police station for a "stern lecture." That worked for us.

Now I had to think about today's work. I had already texted Sean and Johnny to ask them to bring one of the utility tables and a couple of chairs over to house number thirty-three for Linda. I wanted her work area to be close by where I was working, just in case she had questions for me. Plus, I really wanted to see what she was doing.

I was stopped at a traffic signal, so I reviewed my to-do list, then quickly texted Linda to let her know where we'd be setting up her work area. She replied with a thumbs-up, and I tossed the phone on the passenger seat as the light turned green.

It was Wednesday, so the gardeners would be arriving around ten thirty. I always made a point of adding that detail to my to-do list because I wanted to make sure that we moved any of our equipment and supplies out of their way.

I knew Chloe would show up at some point, but she wouldn't require any coddling. She'd go wherever she wanted to go and videotape whatever she thought was interesting. I was okay with that, and yeah, I had to admit that I'd spruced up a little, just in case she insisted on catching me on camera. I could never aspire to the Contractor Barbie level that she had reached, but I did okay with some lip gloss, a touch of blush, and a quick swish of mascara.

Also noted on my list was the arrival of all the window glass for houses twenty-six through thirty. We had purchased the windows already framed, from the panes and the sash to the window sill and the outer molding. My windows team could basically slide the whole piece into place, which cut down on breakage and made our jobs easier. Once each window was in place, one of us would level the frame, then caulk it, drive in the screws, and touch up the paint. Then rinse and repeat that procedure for eight windows on five houses.

Three weeks later, the glass man would return with the exact same order for the next five houses.

All of our windows were double-paned, which meant they had two layers of glass, which gave more protection from both cold and hot weather. And they were double-hung, meaning that they could be opened from both the top and the bottom. We had made that choice for the comfort and security of the vets.

I expected the glass man to show up sometime in the late morning, so I would have plenty of time to get some work done before he arrived.

I grabbed my tool chest and headed for house number thirty-three. The houses fanned out from the community center and were arranged in blocks of five to seven houses on each side of the Parkway, the winding blacktop drive that led from one end of the property to the other. Each house had its own individual style, and each of the vets who'd moved in had added their own touches. Trees that had been planted early on were growing taller, and their leaves shimmered in the light sea breeze. Colorful flowers lined the sidewalks, making the whole place feel friendly and welcoming.

I spotted Linda sitting at the utility table next to house number thirty-three, already at work. At this point in the development of the community, the houses were unfinished, and although they were surrounded by grass, there were no flowers or trees planted yet.

"Good morning," I said. "I'm impressed that you got here so early."

Linda smiled a greeting. "Some of your crew were already here, so I figured I was right on time."

"Most of the guys like to get an early start, and so do I."

"Me, too," she said. She wore her hair in a simple ponytail today, and her outfit of jeans, cotton pullover, and work boots was construction-site approved. Not that it mattered to me, but I had a feeling that Julia had schooled her on what to wear. Her long pretty skirts and loose sweaters might be damaged if they came in contact with the jagged edge of a plywood board or some other hazard around here.

"I like your outfit," I said. "You fit right in with the rest of the crew."

She grinned. "That's the look I was going for."

"How was your date last night?" I asked, then immediately wanted to bite my tongue. It was none of my business. But when had that ever stopped me? Besides, I'd just seen that video of Lewis breaking into the lighthouse, and I wanted to try and give Linda some warning.

Linda gave me a patient look. "Now, you know it wasn't a date. He's just a nice young man, and I think he's lonely. We had a very nice time."

"Um, good. I'm glad." *A nice young man?* I shook my head. Linda made Lewis sound like a high school kid and she was his teacher. In reality, he was probably in his early to mid-thirties while she was close to forty, which was not that much older. And despite her protests the night before, Lewis had considered it a date. Not that it was any of my business.

I distracted myself by checking out the myriad boxes of glass fragments and pottery shards that were carefully arranged by size, shape, and color. It was a little bit of artwork in and of itself.

"Were any of the other writers there?" I asked. I couldn't help myself.

"No, just Lewis." She sighed. "He's been so successful with his first book that he's afraid the others are jealous."

"Really? Is that why you think he might be lonely?"

"Yes. And what the others don't understand is that he's really struggling with this second book he's supposed to write."

"I didn't know that."

"It's true. There's a lot of pressure on him to produce something equally impressive this time around, and the poor guy doesn't know what to write yet."

"But isn't the second book due in a few weeks?" I

asked. Living with Mac, I'd begun to get a sense of publishing schedules and deadlines and such. Wouldn't Lewis's publisher want him to send in his next book pretty soon?

"It's due next month," she said. "He's really beside himself with worry. He admitted that he has nothing inside him, not even a germ of a story. It's so sad. He actually said his well had run dry. It broke my heart."

"Can't his writer friends help him out? I don't mean help him write the book, but maybe they could all help with plotting or with keeping to a schedule or helping him avoid distractions."

"They won't," Linda said, and she sounded so sad and so full of empathy, it was painful to listen to her. Don't get me wrong; I didn't feel sorry for Lewis. I felt sorry for Linda! I was pretty sure that if Lewis weren't such a giant pain in the neck, he would probably get more sympathy from his writing group.

The weird thing was, the other writers seemed to worship Lewis. They doted on him. Admired him. So why wouldn't they help him out? Maybe Lewis was pulling a number on Linda, telling her lies to drum up sympathy that wasn't deserved.

"What about Brian?" I asked. "The two of them seem like really good friends."

"Oh, they are," Linda said. "They grew up together, and now they support each other in every way."

In every way? I wondered. Just what did that mean? Was it possible that Brian had written . . . no. As soon as I thought it, I stopped. I was grasping at straws.

With my mind on Lewis and Brian, I stared blindly at the table, then blinked in surprise at what was right in front of me.

"Wow," I whispered, and focused in on the neat line of at least ten or twelve different mallets laid out at one end. Some were no-nonsense tools, one looked more like a gnarly chunk of wood than a tool, and a few of them were obviously so old, they might've been antiques. They all were arranged in order from the very smallest mallet, about six inches, to the largest at almost two feet long. I went ahead and counted them and mentally confirmed that there were twelve of them.

"Wow," I said again. As a tool fanatic, I instantly coveted her collection. "What a fabulous assortment of mallets. I assume you use them for your mosaic work."

"Yes. Aren't they great?" She beamed. "Some of these were my grandfather's. The ones on that end are antiques."

"I thought so. The wood is really beautiful."

She picked one up. The wood was bloodred and as smooth as glass. "Look at this one."

"It's so . . . primitive," I said, imagining the multitude of hands that had worked and worn down the handle over hundreds of years.

"That's the perfect description," Linda said. "I just love the feel of in in my hand. But as old as it is, it still gets the job done."

"I believe it." I reached for the biggest antique mallet and weighed it in my hands. The handle was almost two feet long, and the head of the tool came to a rounded point on one side. "This feels a lot lighter than I thought it would be."

"That one is a few hundred years old. The wood has become porous over the years, so it's not as heavy as it once was. But it's still reliable for cracking glass."

"I believe it," I said. "Did your grandfather work with mosaics?"

"Oh yes. He's fairly well known in the esoteric world of mosaic art." I could hear the pride in her voice. "In fact, some of his pieces are on permanent display in the American Folk Art Museum in New York City, among other places."

"That's so impressive. Is that how you got into it?"

"Yes." She smiled. "Grandpa wanted my father to follow in his footsteps, but Dad was tired of living the artsy-fartsy lifestyle—as he put it. So he sold out, as my grandpa would say. He went off and became a high-priced lawyer."

I grinned. "But you wanted to learn the art."

"Yes. Grandpa was thrilled to teach me, but my father was furious. In fact, he threw a fit, which made me angry enough to run off and join the army."

"Ah. I wondered how you wound up in the military."

"Yes, running away from dear old Dad. Things are much better between us now that I'm back home, but he still talks about me going off to law school one of these days." She rolled her eyes. "Not in this lifetime."

"Well, you seem to be doing what you love, and that's important." I picked up another mallet. "Now this one is heavy."

It was big and obviously handmade, with a large rectangular head about eight inches long and four inches thick. The thick handle was a gorgeous piece of wood, about ten inches long.

"Yes, that's quite a serious tool."

I lifted it again. "It's beautiful. And wow, I'm amazed how heavy it is for a wooden mallet."

"I agree, it's beautiful. My grandfather made it from white ash and black walnut. And there's a reason why it's so heavy."

I studied the smooth wood grain. "Why is that?"

"Because it's filled with lead."

I blinked. "What?"

"Yeah, lead." She grinned. "He'd made a big, beautiful mallet and then decided that he wanted to add some weight to it. So he melted down some chunks of lead, then drilled a hole in each side of the head, carefully filled the holes with the melted lead, and let them dry. Then he sealed it all up with another slab piece of wood, and voilà. He added almost two pounds to the head."

I studied the mallet. "He was an artist in wood as well as mosaics."

"He was. I'm lucky to have inherited his tools."

"You could sure break some bones with it," I muttered.

"Oh, for sure."

"Do you mind if I take a picture of this? I really want to look into getting something like this for my very own."

"I don't blame you. Sure, snap away."

I pulled out my phone and took pictures of the mallet from every angle. I couldn't wait to show them to Niall Rose, my stonemason. Of course, he probably had something similar in his own tool collection, but nothing as beautiful as this.

I slipped my phone back into the pocket of my tool belt.

Linda's tools were so interesting and unique, I could've spent all day talking about each one of them. It was tool talk, so I wasn't wasting time, right?

I knew a little something about mosaic tools from working with Niall, so I recognized the *hardie* that was sticking out of the large wooden block on her table. A hardie was a type of chisel, but not the kind you held in your hand. Instead, it was driven into a heavy block of wood so that only the sharp edge stuck out a few inches. When the mosaic artist balanced a chunk of marble or glass or stone onto the hardie's edge and pounded it lightly with a mallet, the glass or stone broke neatly in half.

If you ever took a mosaic art class, you would spend plenty of days learning the proper way to work with the hammer and the hardie.

I picked up something that looked like a miniature pickax, about twelve inches long. The business end of this tool was made of heavy steel with an arced head. "Now this looks like it could hurt you."

"The two ends are pretty sharp." She pointed. "If you look at this side of the hammer end, you'll see a little rectangle of a different material along the sharp edge. That's carbide, and it's only used to cut glass. The other side is all steel, and it can be used to cut slate or marble or other pieces of stone."

"What happens if you use the wrong side?"

"If you try to cut stone with the carbide end, you'll damage the stone."

"Interesting. I didn't know that."

"This is my everyday mallet. It works best with the hardie, unless I need a softer touch. Then I use one of the wood mallets."

Finally, I reached for Linda's rubber mallet. "Now this one looks familiar."

"I imagine you have one just like it."

"I do," I said. "Except mine's got a pink handle."

"Oh, yeah," she said with a smile. "Julia told me about your pink tools theory. Very smart."

"What can I say?" I tested the mallet, pounding it lightly against the palm of my hand. This was a useful tool when you required a softer, more nuanced impact than a steel-headed hammer. I wasn't exactly the queen of nuance, given that I had a complete tool chest filled with pink tools. But what the heck? Pink had always worked for me.

Chapter Five

When I saw Sean and Johnny walking toward me, I handed the rubber mallet back to Linda and prepared to get to work.

She set the mallet down with the others. "What are you all working on today?"

I tapped the exterior wall of the house right next to us. "We're finishing the roof on this house, and then we've got some windows arriving today. They're being installed on those five houses over on the north side of the Parkway." I glanced at my watch. "Which reminds me, have you seen the insides of any of the houses yet?"

"Julia took me on a quick tour of one of them last week. But I'd love to get a closer look at the backsplashes, now that I know I'll be doing some of them."

"That's a good idea. I need fifteen minutes to talk to my guys, and then I'll come back and we'll take a tour."

"Perfect," she said brightly. "I'll be here when you're ready."

                    *   *   *

Linda and I walked through three houses that were almost finished, but not quite ready to be occupied. In each house, Linda studied the room for a few minutes.

"This is really well designed. And that's a generous kitchen counter space for what's basically a single apartment."

"My crew and I have been building tiny homes for the last few years," I explained. "We usually add a bonus touch or two, like a loft or a deck or a back porch or an atrium kitchen window. But for these houses, we needed to make them superefficient without making them so small that the vets felt claustrophobic."

"That's a thoughtful approach to take."

"The houses were always going to be one room," I said, "but why not divide it up a little? Give them both a bedroom space and a small living room space. And then we added a little more area to the kitchen, and this is the design we came up with. So far, everyone's pretty happy with it."

"The vets I've talked to are very pleased to be here." She pulled out her measuring tape. "Okay, let's do this."

"Let me know if you need me to hold down the tape measure."

"I will, thanks." She stared for a minute, then went about measuring across the counter and up the wall. "The main counter area, with the sink, is twelve feet long, and the backsplash extends up the wall eighteen inches." She wrote it down in a notebook, then murmured, "I should find something heat resistant for the backsplash over the stove."

"It's up to you. Most glass or tile backsplashes will work in the stove area in terms of heat resistance."

She took another measurement and calculated under her breath. "You don't have a hood or a microwave over the stove, so I'll keep the same eighteen inches there."

"We're willing to add a hood, but most of our residents end up dining in the community center café for their meals. I mean, if they want to stay home, they're more liable to open up a can of soup or scramble some eggs or heat up some chili rather than cook a big gourmet meal. But we're giving everyone who moves in a choice of a fancy designer hood if they'd like one. If they're more inclined to hit the café every day, then we'll install a simple exhaust vent in the ceiling over the stove. It's up to the vets."

"That's a really nice deal," she said, holding her tape measure and jotting down the numbers.

"We were able to get such a good discount on the hoods, we can afford to make the offer."

"Okay, I've got my measurements," she said, then dropped her tape measure into the pocket of her camo tool belt.

I nodded approvingly. "You appear to know what you're doing."

"I think I do," she said with a smile.

"Great. I'll walk you back to your work area."

"The sun's coming out," she said, gazing up at the sky as we strolled across the Parkway. "I might move my table to the other side of the house in a little while so I can continue working in the shade."

"I'll help you move it."

"Thanks."

"And I'll try to find you a more permanent space to work in. Maybe one of the empty offices inside the community center."

"One of the offices would be fine, until I'm ready to start gluing. Then I'll need to work outdoors. The glue can be caustic."

"Oh yeah, glad you mentioned that. Well, as long as the weather cooperates, you're welcome to work outside."

"That sounds just fine," she said with a smile.

I laughed. "You're too easy."

"I'm just happy to be working on this project."

"That's how we all feel. It's a good place to be."

"Linda!" Someone shouted her name.

We both turned, and I wanted to groan out loud. It was Lewis.

Why wasn't he in jail? That was my first thought, and I had to take a few deep breaths to calm down. This guy had really gotten under my skin! But honestly, what was he doing here? Didn't he have a life? A book to write?

I wondered if the cops had been too late to catch them inside the lighthouse. I'd have to ask Eric later.

"Hello, Lewis," Linda said sweetly. "We were just talking about you."

"Were you?" He raised a cocky eyebrow, and his smile was so smug, I wanted to smack him. Honestly, Linda was the dearest person in the world, but she didn't have a clue about guys like Lewis.

I cleared my throat and said loudly, "Good talking to you, Linda." Then I made a big deal about checking my watch. "Wow, it's late. Guess we'd better get back to work."

"Gosh, I guess so," she said.

I waited for a moment to see if Lewis would take the hint and leave, but he didn't. He just stared at me, clearly waiting for *me* to leave. I realized that he was actually trying to intimidate me, and that wasn't going to happen.

"Lewis," I said finally. "I'm sorry I didn't mention it sooner, but since this is a construction site, nobody is allowed here without authorization and a hard hat."

"Linda isn't wearing one," he said, challenging me.

"Linda only started working here today, and I was just on my way to get her a hard hat." A tiny lie, but it worked for me. I stood where I was, gazing at him.

He stared back, and his lips tightened into a thin line. Finally, he huffed out a breath and turned to Linda. "Linda, I really need to talk to you. It's important."

"Why don't you call me later?" she suggested.

He gritted his teeth in frustration. "Fine. I'll call you later." Then he strolled away slowly, ambling along the walkway as though he didn't have a care in the world. But I knew he was angry. He didn't like being told what to do.

I watched him until he reached the front parking lot and got into his car.

I turned to Linda. "I'm sorry I had to make him leave. I know he's your friend, but he's been kind of a pest to me."

She wrung her hands, clearly uncomfortable with conflict. "I know he shouldn't be coming here. And Julia doesn't seem to like him, either, but I think she's just being protective."

"She's a good friend," I said, keeping it simple.

"When I see him next time, I'll tell him to stay away."

But she wouldn't, I thought. It wasn't in her DNA to do anything that might hurt someone's feelings.

"Don't worry about it." I smiled. "I know it's hard to be the bad guy when it comes to friends."

"I hate it," she confessed. "Confrontation has always been hard for me. Probably goes back to my father issues."

I had to smile at her explanation. "If he comes around again, I'll be happy to handle it."

If he came around again, I thought, I would ban Lewis from the property. I wouldn't mind that confrontation at all.

I was standing outside house number twenty-six, going over this week's schedule with Wade, when I heard the heavy downshifting of a powerful truck engine. I glanced toward the main driveway in the distance and saw the glass transport trailer driving onto the property.

"He's early," I said. "I've got to run down there and direct him where to go."

"You want me to go?" Wade asked.

"Thanks, but I'd rather have you wrangle the guys to move the equipment out of the gardeners' way."

"Oh yeah," he said. "It's Wednesday. Duh. I'm losing track of the days."

"It's good to be busy," I said brightly.

He snorted. "That's what I keep telling my wife."

I laughed and took off. Wade was a fanatic when it came to scheduling, and he was permanently attached to his tablet. But we were all super busy these days.

I jogged the few hundred yards to the parking lot where the driver was waiting. As soon as he saw me, he honked his horn and waved. I waved back and indicated that he should drive toward me. I led him back across the property to the five houses that would be getting windows today, and he brought the truck to a stop on the Parkway in front of house number twenty-six.

He shut off the engine and climbed down from the cab. "Hey, Shannon, how's it going?"

"Great, Eddie. How are you doing?" I had known the man for years, since I was a teenager working for my father.

"Couldn't be better." He pointed to the row of houses in front of us. "These are the five?"

"Yes. And my window guys will be here in just a minute."

"Very good." He circled to take in all the changes. "Boy, you're whipping through this project. You'll be finished in no time."

"It's going pretty well," I said. "We're right on schedule, so that's a good thing."

"Speaking of schedules," Eddie said, "I was able to bring you that special glass you ordered last month."

My eyes widened. "The beveled glass window?"

"Yeah. It's on the truck."

"That's awesome. But you know it's going to another site."

"Sure," he said. "The Cranberry Lane site, right?"

"That's right. Carla's supervising over there."

"It'll be nice to see her. When we're through here, I'll deliver it to her."

"Thanks, Eddie. I'll let her know you're coming. The owner's going to be thrilled. And so am I."

"That's what I like to hear."

Wade walked over. "Hey, Eddie. Good to see you."

"Good to be seen," the glass man replied with a grin.

"Eddie brought the beveled glass picture window for the Cranberry Lane house," I said.

"Oh, that's fantastic," Wade said. "When we're done here, I'll follow you over there."

"Good enough," Eddie said. "You two want to take a look at it?"

"Absolutely," Wade said, and we followed Eddie over to the truck.

The thick, beveled glass was eight feet square, and it would look stunning in the classic Queen Anne Victorian home that overlooked the ocean.

"That is beautiful, Eddie," I said. "Man, you do good work."

"Thanks, Shannon," he said. "It was a challenge, but I think it turned out really nice."

At that moment, I heard the husky sound of the lawnmower starting up. Checking my watch, I saw that it was ten thirty.

"Like clockwork," I murmured, and in the distance, I saw the big lawnmower chug into view down by the community center. The head gardener, Mario, was riding it, and I smiled. The man had once confided that he liked to imagine he was on a horse riding the range. And why not?

"Hey there, Shannon."

I glanced up. "Parks. Hey, thank you again for taking care of business last night."

The older man squinted at me. "What're you talking about?"

"You got those two guys to leave the center."

"Oh, yeah." He tightened his jaw. "Troublemakers. I didn't like them hanging around. They were at Mac's workshop the night before, and I wasn't impressed. So I told them to skedaddle."

I chuckled at his language. "Well, I appreciate it."

He gave me a salute. "No problemo."

"You on your way to the center?" I asked.

"Yeah," the older man said. "Thought I'd see what they're serving for lunch and maybe get a haircut while I'm there."

"Well, enjoy yourself," I said, impressed all over again at the many services the center provided for their veterans.

"Always do," he assured me.

My crew and I had been working on the windows for an hour when Linda and Travis walked over to see how it was going. I knew that Travis was installing siding on the current row of houses over by Linda's work space.

I noticed that Linda was now wearing the hard hat I'd given her earlier. "That hat looks good on you, but I can bring you a different color tomorrow if you'd like."

"No, I love the pink."

"I'm glad," I said. "Because none of my guys will go near the pink ones."

Travis smothered a laugh. "I don't know why. I think the pink looks good on everybody."

"I think so, too," I said. "It's cheerful, right?"

Linda giggled. "I just love working here."

"We're all glad you're here," Travis said shyly.

Linda glanced at someone in the distance. "Shannon, isn't that your sister?"

I turned and watched Chloe approach. "Sure is."

She had the camera in her hand and was taking video as she walked up to the group. "Hi, y'all."

"Hi, Chloe," Linda said.

I pointed to Travis. "You met Travis the other night."

"I remember," Chloe said. "We all had dinner together."

"That's right," he said. "Good to see you."

"You, too." Then she looked at the guys working on the nearest house.

"So they're doing windows?" she asked.

"Yeah." I pointed down the line of small homes. "These five houses are getting windows today."

She nodded. "Okay if I get closer? I want to get a good look at the process."

"Sure. Just let them know what you're doing so they don't knock you over."

"Okay. Thanks." She walked up to Wade, who was supervising the operation. He gave her a hug, then pointed toward the front of the house so she could get a view from the inside. She disappeared inside the house, and after ten minutes, she walked out and approached the guys doing the exterior work. She held the camera up so she could get the whole view of the window being installed. I could see her zooming in to catch the exciting application of the caulk. I would tease her about that later.

I heard the drone of the lawnmower engine coming closer, and I moved in to warn Chloe. "Your video is going to get drowned out by the lawnmower."

She shrugged. "I'll probably do a voice-over in this section so you won't hear the background noises."

"Good plan," I said.

I backed away from Chloe and the window installers, and began to walk across the Parkway toward Linda and Travis, who stood next to Linda's table. They were still chatting, and I had a brief moment of doubt about hiring Linda. It wasn't that she couldn't do the work. It was just that she was so nice that people would be interrupting her constantly, and she wouldn't be able to say no.

I quickly let that go. The bottom line was that her talent and artistry was worth it. Besides, I liked her and was probably just as guilty as anyone for interrupting her work.

Gazing off toward the community center, I was surprised to see that Assistant Police Chief Tommy Gallagher and his snooty wife, Whitney, were walking this way. I use the term "walking" advisedly, since Whitney was tiptoeing on six-inch strappy stilettos. On a construction site. I rolled my eyes but then reminded myself that this was Whitney. What else would she be wearing with black leatherette leggings and a tight sparkly sweater that drooped teasingly off the shoulder? Strappy stilettos, of course.

Not to be dramatic, but Whitney Reid Gallagher was the bane of my existence. What the heck was she doing here? It was a question I had asked myself for years.

At that very moment, the lawnmower came by, and I was happily distracted by the movement. I watched the gardener maneuver it carefully over the curb and begin to cross the Parkway.

And that's when all hell broke loose.

The beveled glass window that was strapped to the wide side panel of the glass truck suddenly shattered into a million pieces.

The noise was ear-piercing. Glass showered the ground, and small shards bounced and flew every which way. Some of my crew shouted warnings. All of them shielded their faces.

Linda screamed and covered her eyes.

"Take cover!" Travis bellowed.

A few people dove to the ground.

Travis yanked Linda into his arms. He fell with her onto the grass and shielded her completely, using one arm to cover the top of her head. From where I stood, I could see his body shaking. All the noise of the glass shattering had freaked him out.

Taking a careful glance around, though, I saw that no one had been hurt. "Thank goodness," I murmured.

I spoke too soon, I realized, when I caught sight of Whitney trying to run in those treacherous heels toward Travis and Linda. Before anyone could stop her, she bent over and gave Travis a sharp smack on his shoulder.

"Let go of her!" she screamed. "Get off of her! Leave her alone!"

What the heck?

She turned and shouted to her husband. "Tommy! Arrest him!"

I rushed forward, grabbed Whitney's arm, and managed to drag her a few feet away from where Travis was still on the ground. "What do you think you're doing?"

"He attacked that woman!" she cried. "I saw him."

"No, he didn't," I insisted. "What's wrong with you?"

"Me?" She was outraged. "What's wrong with *you*?"

I stared at her, wondering why she suddenly sounded like Pee-wee Herman. *I know you are but what am I?* I shook the thought away and looked around for

Tommy. He was moving from group to group, checking that everyone was okay. He stopped in the middle of the Parkway and motioned for Wade to join him. It was obvious that Tommy was busy, but I was furious, and he was the only one who could help.

"Tommy," I barked. "You need to get her out of here."

Whitney teetered on her heels but managed to straighten up her shoulders. "Don't you tell my husband what to do!" It was her best royal-to-servant tone.

I rolled my eyes. I'd known Tommy my whole life. He was my friend. But I wasn't about to put up with his wife's nonsense for one more minute. "This is my construction site," I said, shaking my finger at Whitney. "And you're not welcome here."

Her eyes twitched, and she sputtered in shock and disgust. I didn't care.

"Tommy!" This time I shouted his name. "I suggest that you get her out of here before someone gets hurt."

Tommy was an experienced law enforcement officer. More importantly, he knew his wife and was smart enough to heed my words. With one arm, he steered Whitney around and pulled her in the opposite direction.

I stared at them. Tommy had always been an easy-going guy, but I still had to wonder how in the world he'd put up with her toxic idiocy for so many years.

I knelt down and patted Travis's back. "Everything's cool, Travis. You and Linda are okay. You're safe."

"Yeah," he murmured, stirring. "We're okay. Thanks."

Through the chaos, I realized that Chloe had been filming the whole thing. And then I saw Eric running from the community center to see what all the commotion was.

I ignored him and joined Wade in the center of the Parkway. It was distressing to feel and hear the glass crunching under my boots.

"What the hell?" he said, looking shell-shocked.

Before I could respond, the gardener jumped off his mower and dashed over to us. "I'm sorry, you guys. I must've picked up a rock when I drove over the dirt along the curb. I heard it rattle around under the deck cover for a few seconds, and then it shot out of the grass chute." He scraped his hair back from his forehead, and his expression was desolate as he pointed toward the glass truck. "It went straight for the truck. That's what broke the window."

I was pretty sure he was right. It made sense.

"It's okay, Mario," I said, trying to calm him. "We'll get it all taken care of." The thought of replacing that gorgeous beveled window made me a little queasy, but it still wasn't Mario's fault. He and the glass truck, as well as Travis and Linda and Whitney and the rest of us, had been in the wrong place at the wrong time, resulting in chaos.

Travis, meanwhile, was standing now. He had one arm around Linda and was still shaking.

I walked over and stood with them. "You guys are okay?"

"Yeah," he muttered, and sucked in some air. "Just trying to breathe."

I glanced at Linda. "How are you doing?"

"I'm fine. I'm worried about . . ." She didn't finish the sentence but just aimed her big blue eyes at Travis.

"He'll be okay." I touched his arm. "Right, Travis?"

"Oh man," Travis muttered, obviously mortified. He

managed to straighten up and take one step away from Linda. "I'm sorry."

"Don't be sorry," Linda said. "It was very frightening. You protected me and I appreciate that."

"Travis," Eric said, walking toward us. He could see that Travis was still shaky and trying to catch his breath.

"Yeah?" Travis glanced at him, then shook his head. "Man, it sounded like Fallujah there for a minute."

"I hear you, man," Eric said, then gave his arm a mild thump. "Let's take a walk."

Travis gave a brief nod, and the two men walked off toward the community center.

Linda gazed at me. "He's never said anything to me, but I can guess he's got PTSD."

I saw no reason to avoid the issue. "Yeah."

She nodded, then said softly, "I have a mild case of it myself. Nightmares mostly. If you've been to war, you almost can't help but come home with some form of it."

"I believe it."

"All that shattering glass," she said. "Who knew what was happening? It could've been a bullet. Travis probably thought so." Linda rubbed her arms. "Who was that woman that came over here?"

"That was Whitney Gallagher. She's married to Tommy."

"Tommy, the assistant police chief?"

"Yes."

"That's his wife?" She looked appalled. "But he's so nice."

I just smiled. "Yes, he is."

Linda frowned. "She looked vaguely familiar to me."

I nodded. "She went to high school here."

"I don't remember her from high school. Some-where else." She reached for a pottery shard and rubbed it between her thumb and fingers like a touch-stone. "I didn't like the way she was slapping at Travis. I'm glad you made her leave."

"It was my pleasure," I said flatly.

"I hope she doesn't make trouble for him."

"She won't," I said firmly. "I won't let her. But just for your information, she was one of several townspeo-ple who threw a big fit when Mac and Eric first pro-posed the idea of Homefront."

"There'll always be detractors," Linda said. "It's too bad she was here to witness that little ruckus."

"I was thinking the same thing," I said. "It'll give her more fuel to fan the flames."

"I don't like hearing that anyone might be against our veterans' community."

"Me either."

"I wonder if I can change her mind." Linda frowned thoughtfully. "What was her name again?"

"Whitney Reid Gallagher."

Her eyes narrowed. "Okay, I know why she looks familiar. Her father is Forest Reid, the property de-veloper?"

I nodded. "That's right."

"Hmm. He and my father are friends." She smiled. "Business friends. They belong to the same yacht club."

"Is that right?" I said, and grinned. "That's life in a small town."

She thought about it some more. "Maybe I'll ap-proach her on that level."

Intrigued, I stared at her for a moment. "You're sneaky, Linda. I like that about you."

She laughed lightly. "I just want everyone to be happy. Even Whitney."

I would gladly wish Whitney to perdition, but didn't say so. "I'll just wish you good luck with that."

My crew and I spent an hour cleaning up the glass.

Eddie worked right along with us. "I've been working in glass all my life," he said, and shrugged. "You break a few."

"This one is breaking my heart," I confessed, as I swept another small pile into the heavy-duty trash bag Eddie had provided. He'd clearly had plenty of experience with broken glass throughout his years in the business, because he was totally prepared to deal with the mess.

"I don't blame you," he said. "It was a beauty, if I do say so myself. But we'll make you another just like it and put a rush on it."

"Thanks, Eddie. I'll mail you a check as soon as possible."

He held up a hand. "Oh now, just forget about it. It was nobody's fault. Just a quirk of fate. Besides, your Homefront project has given me more steady work than I've had in the last five years. So let's call it even."

"Are you kidding?" I was ridiculously touched. "Thank you. It's always a pleasure to work with you."

"You're a good girl," he said. "You do your father proud."

"Thank you. That means a lot."

"Shannon," Wade called from the second house. "We need some expertise over here."

I exchanged a look with Eddie and laughed. "Like nobody else has expertise around here?"

"He wants to hear it from the boss."

"I guess that's me." I smiled. "I'll be back to help with the cleanup."

"I'll be here," he said, and continued sweeping up the glass.

It was Linda's idea to go to the pub that night, and she enlisted Eric's help to convince Travis to come along. She didn't think they should leave Travis alone after what he'd been through earlier in the day. Naturally, Chloe and I invited ourselves. I called Mac, and we agreed to meet at home so we could walk to the pub a block away.

On our walk, I told Mac what Linda had divulged that morning. "Lewis told her that his second book is due in one month, and he hasn't started it yet."

Mac stopped. "Are you kidding?"

"No. Linda said that he has no idea what to write. He's struggling, and his friends won't help him. He was so successful with his first book that they're jealous. And he's very lonely."

"What?" Mac started to laugh but then sobered. "Oh no. She believes him."

"Yes, she does. She feels so sorry for him because there's so much pressure on him to produce a second brilliant work."

"Wow."

"Yeah." We continued walking. "Linda said he's got nothing inside him, not even a germ of a story. His well is dry."

"Good grief," Mac muttered. "He's got to be pulling her leg. He must be writing something."

"I've got mixed feelings," I confessed. "I hope he's pulling her leg because it's just sad if he can't come up with another story. But if he *is* lying to her, then it's even worse. She's the most empathetic person I've ever met, and she honestly feels his pain. So if he's faking it, he's an even bigger jerk than we thought. If that's even possible."

Mac shook his head. "It just gets better and better, doesn't it?"

"Or worse and worse," I said.

The six of us were enjoying our first round of drinks when the writers walked into the pub.

Sheri saw us and waved. Mac and I waved back, but Lewis took one look at Travis sitting next to Linda and scowled. He didn't move forward, just stood nearby staring daggers at Travis until Annabelle finally came over and nudged him along. They followed the rest of the group to a corner booth.

Chloe's gaze met mine. "Did you see his face? That guy is a little too revved up for my taste."

"For sure," I murmured. And that's when I remembered the lighthouse incident from the morning. With everything that had been going on all day, I had completely forgotten to ask Eric what happened.

"Eric," I began. "Did your people find those trespassers inside the lighthouse?"

"Sorry, Shannon." He grimaced. "They were gone by the time my officers arrived."

"Rats," I said.

"I guess you didn't hear about the traffic pileup out by the interstate," he said.

"No." I was taken aback. "What happened?"

"Six cars managed to careen into one another," he explained. "It took my guys a while to get back to town, and by the time they made it up to the lighthouse, there was nothing to see."

"Were any people hurt?" I asked.

"Only minor injuries, thank God."

"They're all pretty lucky," Chloe said.

"Absolutely," Eric said. "But look, Shannon. You still have your video from the lighthouse, right?"

"Yeah. It's on my phone."

"We can confront them with the evidence. Make them pay a fine if you want."

I glanced at Mac. He was thinking about it and so was I. "I'd rather not reveal that we've got the camera inside the lighthouse. You know they'll do it again because they got away with it this time. And next time, we'll catch them in the act."

Mac nodded. "I'm in total agreement. I'd much rather sneak up on them."

"Okay," Eric said. "We'll catch 'em next time."

"I'd like to hope there won't be a next time, but that's just wishful thinking."

Travis started to slide out of the booth. "Just realized I left my wallet in my car. I'll be right back."

"I'll walk with you," Linda said.

"You still watching out for me?" he said, his voice teasing.

"Maybe I just want to take a little walk," she said.

Despite his playful tone, I could tell Travis was grateful.

I stared at them for a few seconds, then turned my gaze toward the writers' table. Lewis and Brian were gone. I spotted them standing at the bar. Lewis was staring at Travis and Linda, watching them like a mama hawk.

He was obviously seething. He couldn't hide his emotions well at all. Brian stood next to him whispering something. He looked angry, too. I was dying to know what they were talking about.

I'd never been very good at reading lips, unfortunately.

I suddenly noticed that Chloe was watching something going on behind my back and practically snarling. "What is it, Chloe?"

She jerked her chin toward the other end of the bar.

I turned casually, as though I were checking out the room, and saw Whitney standing at the bar with her bestie Jennifer Bailey. The two had their heads together, and I figured they were plotting or gossiping about somebody.

The two women had been the epitome of mean girls in high school and had done their level best to make my life miserable. Despite them, I'd had a pretty great time in high school—until our senior year, when Whitney decided it would be fun to steal my boyfriend away. She began dating Tommy behind my back and ended up pregnant. She'd delighted in rubbing it in my face ever since.

I once asked Whitney why she'd been such a jerk to me, and she said, "You were just too nice."

I recognized that while Tommy wasn't exactly innocent, it was Whitney who had orchestrated the whole thing. Even so, Tommy's betrayal had really hurt. It took me a few years, but I finally got over it when I realized that he would have to spend the rest of his life with Whitney, and that was big-time payback in my book.

These days, I was good friends with Tommy. Whitney absolutely hated that, so naturally, I was happy to rub *her* nose in it. I was fine with being petty when it came to Whitney.

"There's Tommy," Eric said. "I've got to have a word with him."

"I'll go with you," Chloe said, and with a look at me, she followed him over to the bar.

"Alone at last," Mac said, leaning over to kiss me.

"The pub is no place to go to be alone," I said with a laugh.

"Especially with all the intrigue going on around us."

We talked for a few minutes about our plans for the weekend. He told me about the latest scene in his book, and I told him about the broken glass and how Travis had reacted.

"I thought Travis seemed a little quiet tonight," Mac said. "Guess that's why."

"Yeah."

"I'll come by tomorrow and talk to him."

"Good idea."

We both sipped our drinks for a few moments.

"Something's going on," Mac said, watching the bar area.

I frowned. "I picked the wrong spot to watch the action. Do you want to tell me what's happening, or should I turn around?"

"Don't turn around just yet," he murmured. "Lewis and Brian have now moved to the other end of the bar and are chatting up Whitney and her friend."

"Jennifer," I said, baring my teeth. Just saying her name could annoy me.

"Yeah. The blonde," he said. "Meanwhile, on the

other side of the bar, Chloe and Eric are talking to Tommy and another officer."

"Oh, shoot," I said, frustrated. "That means Chloe can't overhear Whitney's conversation with Lewis."

Mac grinned. "Ahh. That's why she went with Eric."

"Of course," I said with a smile. "But she won't give up easily."

After a few seconds, he nodded. "You may be right. Chloe is now taking a casual walk around the bar. Wait for it."

"Okay." I hated not seeing what was happening. "But don't keep me in suspense too long."

"She's good," Mac murmured. "She's really good. She's talking to the blonde while Whitney is chatting with Lewis."

"Oh, that's smart."

A minute later, Chloe returned to our table, sliding into the Naugahyde booth, looking as cool as a chrysanthemum.

"Tell me everything," I demanded.

"Tell her," Mac said, squeezing my hand, "before she goes crazy."

Chloe grinned at Mac. "You know her so well."

"Talk," I hissed.

"Okay. I didn't get to hear too much, but I did hear Whitney tell the writer guy—it's Lewis, right?—that he attacked her."

"Meaning Travis attacked Linda? She actually told him that?" I don't know why I sounded so incredulous. It was right out of the Whitney playbook.

"Yup," Chloe said.

Chloe leaned in closer. "So then she said something

about her husband being the police chief and how he's going to shut down the village if these are the kinds of troublemakers who are going to live there."

Troublemakers, I thought angrily. If there was a troublemaker in town, it was Whitney Reid Gallagher.

Mac frowned. "So she's lying about Tommy being the police chief?"

"She's a piece of work," Chloe grumbled.

"She thinks it makes her more important," I said. "She doesn't even know Lewis, but she'll still lie to impress him."

"The woman is twisted," Chloe said.

"The lie won't do any good, because Lewis knows that Eric is the police chief," Mac said. "I introduced him in my workshop the other night."

Chloe laughed. "That's right. Thank you for reminding me."

I sighed. "That whole broken-glass incident fell right into her lap. Now she can use it as a cautionary tale that the vets are dangerous."

"Unfortunately, I'll bet you're right," Mac agreed.

"What was she even doing at Homefront?" I wondered.

"She's probably checking things out," Chloe suggested. "Seeing if there's some way she can stir up trouble."

I sighed. "Mac, I'm only going to say this to you and Chloe, but I'm absolutely certain that her main motivation for trying to get the village shut down is to get back at me."

"Of course," Chloe said matter-of-factly. "First of all, you've always been the biggest thorn in her side. And second, you were involved with Homefront from the start, and your construction company is in charge of building the whole place. Which makes you very important to the project and to the town."

Mac shook his head. "Doesn't she know that Travis is one of Eric's closest friends?"

Chloe and I stared at each other.

"I'm not sure she does," I admitted.

"Well, she's going to find out real soon," Chloe said. "Because I'm going to tell her."

"No. I don't want you to get involved," I said. "You know how she is. She might try to retaliate."

Chloe raised her chin imperiously. "You seem to have forgotten that her husband is my fiancé's *underling*."

I blinked. "Oh my God."

Mac's grin lit up his eyes. "You're scary."

"When I have to be," she said airily.

I shook my head. "I'm embarrassed to say that I totally forgot that minor detail."

Chloe rubbed my arm in sympathy. "You've been a little discombobulated lately."

I thought about the constant work it took to keep the massive Homefront project on schedule, along with my useless but very real worries about teaching the class. And of course there was the work we still had to do at the Gables. And the lighthouse. Oh Lordy. And then there was the latest group of writers that Mac was having to deal with. Especially Lewis, who'd really gotten under my craw.

I blew out a breath. "You're right."

She fluttered her eyelashes. "You know I love to hear those words. Say them again."

"Shut up." I laughed. "Okay. Yes, I've been distracted. But not anymore."

"That's more like it." She smiled. "So what's the plan of attack? Want to double-team her?"

"It's always worked before."

She looked over my shoulder. "Wait. Here comes Eric."

"Perfect timing," I said. "And here's Travis and Linda."

All three of them slid into the booth, and Eric gave Chloe a quick kiss. "Hi."

"Hi, yourself," she said, but then turned her attention back to the interplay between Lewis and Whitney at the bar. "They're watching us," she murmured to me.

"Good," I said quietly. "Here's the plan."

Chapter Six

It wasn't much of a plan, and it grew even shakier when Eric leaned forward and gave me one of those raised-eyebrow frowns. "What are you up to?"

"Nothing," I said, way too quickly. It had been a while since I'd been grilled by the chief of police. "It's just . . . um, I was talking to Chloe, and we thought it would be nice if you and Chloe took Travis over and introduced him to Whitney. They've never actually met each other."

Chloe looked at me as though I'd thrown her to the lions. "Why me?"

"Well, I can't do it," I reasoned. "That would just make it worse."

"Make what worse?" Eric asked.

I took a deep breath, then exhaled slowly. "Were you aware that Whitney attacked Travis this morning?"

"What?" He said it through clenched teeth, and his gaze switched to Travis. "Is that true?"

Travis looked from Eric to me. "I don't know her

name, but yeah, some woman came up and started slapping at me for grabbing Linda."

"You didn't grab me," Linda insisted. "You were trying to protect me." She turned to Eric. "But that woman got the wrong idea. She walked right up and began to smack Travis on the back."

Eric looked to me for an explanation.

"You had to be there," I said.

Chloe leaned against Eric. "You know Whitney's a little whacko, right?"

Eric's lips tightened. He knew how Chloe and I felt about Whitney, but he couldn't really take sides since his closest ally in the department was Whitney's husband, Tommy, who was a good friend and a great guy. "Okay, let's do this. Travis, come with me."

I took a quick look around and saw that Tommy had joined Whitney and Jennifer. His presence would help, I thought.

"Do you want me to go, too?" Chloe asked.

"No, love." Eric stared at the bar. "I think I can handle it."

"My hero," Chloe said, and kissed him.

He slid out of the booth. "Come on, Travis. There's someone I want you to meet."

Travis reluctantly slid to the other side. "If you say so."

They walked over to the bar. I slid over so that I could finally get a good view of the action.

"I'm still going to talk to her," Linda said quietly. "She had no right to treat Travis that way."

"I agree with you," I said. "But I don't want you to get your hopes up that she'll change."

"She's basically an awful person," Chloe said cheerfully.

"I wish I could disagree," Mac murmured.

Mac's words reminded me that even he had been subjected to Whitney's cruelty awhile back. She had told him a particularly vicious lie about me, and he would never forgive the woman for that. Neither would I.

I turned to watch Eric and Travis at the bar. Whitney was obviously forcing herself to pay attention to Eric, but I could tell by her body language that she wasn't thrilled. Jennifer looked downright annoyed that their evil gossip session had been interrupted.

Lewis and Brian smiled congenially through the introductions. Finally, Eric finished the conversation and returned to our booth.

"Hey, Travis," Lewis called.

Travis turned to see Lewis and Brian approach and he stopped to talk for a brief minute. Then the two writers returned to their table, and Travis came back to our booth.

"That went pretty well," he said. "She was a lot nicer after Eric introduced us."

"That's great to hear," Mac said. "She won't give you any trouble now that she realizes you're friends with Eric."

I exchanged a quick glance with Chloe. I still wouldn't trust Whitney as far as I could throw her, but as long as she stayed away from Homefront, I would be happy.

"What did Lewis and Brian want?" I asked.

Travis took a sip of his beer. "They invited me to the retreat house to talk to them about storytelling."

We all needed a moment to absorb that odd information.

"If it were anyone else asking," Mac said finally, "I would say, go for it. But . . ."

"I'm right there with you, buddy," Travis said. "They asked real nice, but after their comments the other night, I'm a little gun-shy."

I nodded. "I don't blame you."

Travis chuckled sheepishly. "Call me overly sensitive, but I still remember every word they said. I don't think I could take another session like that."

"I would highly recommend that you don't," Mac said flatly.

"And I would agree," Eric said, then signaled the waitress to come over. "Let's get some food."

The six of us walked together to Linda's car. She had driven Travis to the pub and would drive him back to Homefront.

"It's been a weird day," Travis said, sounding tired. "A whole lot of good and a little bit of bad."

"I'd have to agree with that summary," I said.

"I assume the bad part had to do with all that breaking glass," Eric said.

"That was bad for everyone," I said. "Except there's a bright side. Eddie, the glass man isn't going to charge us to replace it."

"That's really nice," Linda said.

"Yeah." I smiled. "Eddie said that Homefront is the best and most inspiring gig he's had in a long time, so he's doing us that favor. He's a good guy."

Travis stifled a yawn. "Well, I'm ready to call it a day."

Eric gave him a pat on the back. "You and me both."

"See you when I see you." Travis shook Eric's hand. Then he glanced at Mac. "I just made a decision. I'm going to write about what happened today."

"It helps to write stuff down," Mac said easily. "Whether you want to read it out loud is up to you."

"I'll think about it."

As the men talked, Linda came over to me. "I'll be a little late tomorrow morning, but I promise I'll be working. That is, I'll be out collecting bits of things for the mosaics."

"Sounds like fun. What are you collecting?"

"I'm going to the beach to find some seashells."

I beamed at her. "I love that. It sounds awesome."

"I've done it before with my mosaics, and it really looks great. And I think it'll work for the tiny houses, too, because we live by the beach."

"Will you be gone all day?"

"Oh no. I'm just going up to the breakwater. I always find the best shells around there."

"The breakwater out by the lighthouse?"

"Yes. Something about the breakwater seems to attract a lot of seashells."

"Really? I never noticed. But now I will. So, maybe I'll see you in the afternoon?"

"Definitely." Linda gave a firm nod. "I should be back by noon or one o'clock at the latest."

"Come find me. I'll help you move your table wherever you want it."

"I'll do that."

A few minutes later, Mac and I said good night and walked home.

The next morning, I walked into the kitchen in time to see the sleek black cat skulk across the room as though he were stalking through the jungle in search of his next meal.

"You're so pretty," I said, and bent down to run my hand along the cat's soft, smooth back. Luke curled his neck into my hand, hoping for more strokes.

Mac stood at the counter, pouring a cup of coffee for me. "He's having delusions of grandeur. Thinks he's a jungle cat."

"There is a resemblance," I admitted, and stood. "But I think he's adapted to his new home nicely, don't you?"

Mac grinned and handed me the coffee cup. "I think I've adapted nicely as well."

"Very nicely." I moved close and kissed him. "Thanks for the coffee."

When we sat down to eat a quick breakfast of hard-boiled eggs, turkey bacon, and strawberries, I said, "Yesterday was just weird."

"The Whitney incident must've freaked you out."

"She's so bizarre. What was she even doing there?" I mentally shook that thought away. "Anyway, the broken glass slowed us down by a few hours, so I'm anxious to get an early start today."

"I'll track you down when I'm through with my meeting."

"What are you meeting for this time?" I asked.

He took a sip of coffee. "My team is meeting with the project manager to talk about fundraising and sponsorship."

"Sounds like a blast." I might've been smirking.

"Oh, it'll be a laugh riot." But I knew that Mac enjoyed the work he was doing for Homefront.

He and Eric and their friends who'd originally backed the Homefront project had lined up dozens of sponsors and organizations to obtain a million different things. We had been able to furnish all the houses, including lumber and building supplies, appliances and fixtures.

Since Lighthouse Cove was listed on the National Register of Historic Places, I had wanted to keep with the town's Victorian style, so a lot of the Victorian embellishments had been donated as well, such as scalloped shingles, mini turrets, and faux widows' walks.

All of the landscaping had come through the sponsorship program, too. The local nursery had donated the trees and flowers and sod for the lawns.

Inside the center, they had managed to obtain office furniture and computers. For the visiting nurse and dentist, there were medical supplies in case of emergencies. Even the barbershop's furniture and supplies had been donated by a local charitable organization.

"I'll probably be somewhere in the thirty-one to thirty-five block of houses," I said.

"I'll find you."

I smiled. "Good. Maybe we can have lunch in the café if you have time."

"Let's do it." He tore off a piece of bacon. "Oh, and don't forget, tonight we're doing that writing exercise thing at the beach with the writers."

"I won't forget," I said. Even though I wasn't looking forward to spending time with this particular group of writers, I always looked forward to spending time at the beach with Mac.

My crew made up for lost time on house number thirty-four. By noon, the guys and I were close to finishing the roof and had started on the siding.

I was just climbing down the ladder when Mac strolled up. "Hey Irish, is this good timing?"

I turned and saw him. "Perfect. I just finished stapling the underlayment."

"Wish I could've seen you in action," he said with a grin.

"You'll have plenty of opportunities."

"True. Although you've made good progress. Only twenty-five houses to go."

"That's right." I waved at Travis, who was slowly jogging our way. He was frowning and didn't see me at first.

"Travis," Mac called.

"Oh. Hey, Mac," he said. "Hey, Shannon."

"What's wrong?" I asked.

He waved away my concern. "I must've misplaced my tablet."

"No way," Mac said. "It's got all of your writing on it, right?"

"It's pretty much got my whole life on it," he said.

"Can we help you look?"

"Thanks, but that's okay." But he looked dismayed. "I think I must've left it at the café."

"You sure?"

He rubbed his neck. "No, I'm not. I'm always pretty careful with it, so I'm thinking it might've been stolen."

"Are you serious?" Mac asked.

"Well, yeah. I live a pretty spare life. It's not like I've got a lot of possessions, so it would be hard to lose it inside my house. I keep it on my desk unless I'm leaving the house to do some writing or take some pictures."

I gazed around at the property. "If you lost it anywhere around here, someone would find it and bring it back."

"Yeah. I'm not worried."

I frowned. "But your stories and your photos are irreplaceable."

"Not really." He grinned. "Everything's stored on the cloud. Thanks to Mac."

"Thanks to Mac?" I turned and looked at him.

"The entire property has internet access, and we've got a sophisticated data backup program built in."

"I didn't realize," I said, gazing up at him. "That was really smart."

"I'm a smart guy."

"Yeah, you are."

Travis sighed. "If the tablet doesn't show up in a day or so, I'll have to buy another one. They're pretty cheap these days, so once I get one, I'll be able to download my documents and photos from the cloud, and all will be good as new."

"That sounds pretty simple," I said. "But I still hope you find it."

"Thanks. Me, too."

"We're having lunch in the café," Mac said. "You want to join us?"

"Thanks, but no. I promised some of the crew I'd have lunch with them." He held up a bottle of water and a small brown paper bag that I assumed held his lunch. "We all meet in the picnic area."

"That's right," I said. "They love hearing your stories. One of these days, I'll join you all."

"Do that," he said.

He took off toward the small park that ran along the side of the property.

"You ready?" Mac asked.

I glanced up at the roof of the house next door. "Let me just tell Sean I'm going."

"I'll go with you and say hello."

Sean was holding his nail gun but stopped it when he saw us. "Hey, Mac. What's up?"

"Not too much. How're you doing?"

"Can't complain. Nobody listens."

I grinned at him. "I listen. I care."

"Yeah, right." He gave a short laugh. "What's going on?"

"We're going to the café for lunch."

"Fancy," he said, teasing.

"Linda should be back within the hour. If you see her, could you get some of the guys to help move her table wherever she wants to set up?"

At the end of the day yesterday, we had stowed the table inside house number thirty-three. Linda had draped a tablecloth over everything to keep the sawdust from settling on her tools.

"Sure," Sean said. "I'll keep an eye out for her."

"Thanks. We'll see you later."

"So tell me what to expect tonight," I said as we sat down with our sandwiches and soup bowls.

"I wish I knew," Mac said. "This is a strange group of writers. Talented, but strange. Usually I give the group a prompt or two and ask them to write a few paragraphs, and then if they want to, they read them aloud and talk about the exercise."

"What did you have in mind for tonight?"

"I was going to have them bring jackets and blankets and flashlights, and sit on the beach and write about a stranger that walks by."

I sipped a spoonful of the delicious tomato soup. "They just . . . walk by?"

"Yes. This is where their own creativity comes in. The stranger could be a boy skipping stones on the water. It could be a woman who claims to have amnesia. It could be an old man carrying a fishing pole. It could be some guy hiding from the police. He's got a gun."

"So it could be anyone. I get it. That's pretty neat."

He finished a bite of his grilled cheese sandwich. "And I kind of expect them to bring in the temperature, the darkness, the sea breeze, the smells, the sound of the waves, and all that good stuff. But I'm afraid this group might balk at doing the work. They're all a little too cynical and cool to be taking part in a simple writing exercise."

"If they don't want to do it, then we can come home, order a pizza, and have a nice evening."

He laughed and reached out to squeeze my hand. "There's that glass-half-full positivity I love."

I smiled. "I'm just a cockeyed optimist."

"Yeah, you are."

We ate in silence for a minute or so. Then I asked, "Are you going to talk to Lewis about his book?"

His lips twisted into a wry smile. "You mean, the book he hasn't written?"

"Yeah, that one."

"Since I heard about it thirdhand from Linda to you, I won't bring it up. He might be humiliated, or he might get angry. I really don't want to trigger him. He's too volatile."

"So mum's the word."

"Yeah," he said. "I'm sticking with that."

"Do you ever give advice to these writers' groups?"

"Sure. Most of them really want to connect and find out the big dark secrets of publishing. This is the first group that isn't interested in much of anything I have to say." He bit into his sandwich and chewed for a moment. "They do ask questions, but they've got their own answers built in. So they want to argue about it. Which is fine. I like a good healthy argument. But what they're doing is sort of . . ."

"Fake?" I said.

"Exactly. The question is fake. They don't really care what I have to say. They just want me to think they're smart or sophisticated or fascinated with a subject. It's tiresome."

It was my turn to squeeze his hand. "I'm sorry."

"Hey, I was naïve about this whole process. Now I know that it won't always be an uplifting experience." He shrugged. "Lesson learned."

"Well, tonight will be interesting either way."

"That's right." He held up his bottle of water in a toast. "As long as you're there to protect me, it'll be great."

"That's right." I laughed. "And if not, there's pizza."

Mac walked with me back to house number thirty-four. I stowed my bag inside the house and grabbed my tool belt. Sean walked up a minute later. "How was lunch?"

"Great. Grilled cheese sandwiches and tomato soup."

"Really? Like when we were kids?"

"Even better. They used sourdough bread for the sandwich, and the soup had chunks of tomato and fresh basil. It was delicious."

"I'll have to try the café one of these days."

"You won't be sorry," Mac said.

I glanced around. "Is Linda here?"

"I haven't seen her."

I checked my watch. It was one fifteen. "She said she'd be here between twelve and one, so she's not really late yet."

"Maybe she got hung up somewhere," Mac suggested.

"Probably. She'll be here." I gave Mac a kiss. "Thanks for lunch."

"My pleasure." He kissed me back. "I'll let you get back to work."

He turned and strolled away, and I watched him walk back to the parking lot. Even from this distance, he was so handsome, so dangerously masculine, I couldn't look away. Was there a better-looking man anywhere on the planet? I didn't think so. Not for me anyway. It helped that he was smart and funny and kind. And he loved me.

"He's a good guy," Sean said.

"The best," I whispered, then had to laugh at myself. "Let's get back to work. You ready?"

"Always."

Before I could get started on my job of installing vinyl siding, I was interrupted by Chloe, who strolled into view with her camera rolling and came in close on my stack of siding panels.

"Nothing more stimulating than vinyl siding," I said.

"It's a dream of mine to make it a regular feature of the show," she said, and continued to aim her camera as I grabbed the first panel.

"Your audience will love it," I said. I lined the panel along the bottom edge of the outer wall, then grabbed my hammer and one of the siding nails from a pocket of my tool belt. "Watch how brilliantly I hammer this nail."

She laughed. "Right."

"Do you want me to say anything?" I asked, as I hammered the first nail into the panel.

"I'll probably narrate over the video. Even though vinyl siding is a deathly boring topic, I think I can make it sound interesting if I highlight the fact that it's been around forever, and yet, it can be made to look vintage."

"That's exactly what we're aiming for," I said. "We want to give each house a bit of Victorian flair, and using different types and styles of siding is a good way to do it."

"I've seen a lot of it. Pretty clever stuff."

"Thanks."

"Okay," she said. "I'm going to get some wide shots of the property and maybe zoom in on a few guys working. I'll just keep on shooting, so ignore me."

I flashed her a big smile. "It'll be a pleasure."

"That sounded snarky."

I heard Sean chuckle.

"There," I said. "Someone thought I was funny."

"You force him to laugh at your jokes," she said.

"That's right," I said. "Laugh, or you'll be hanging drywall for the rest of your days."

"Wow." Chloe held up both hands. "That's harsh."

"Go away."

She laughed and walked away, pointing her camera every which way.

I went back to face my siding job. Here again, my crew and I had a good system and the work went quickly—or as quickly as it ever did when it came to nailing down siding.

It was repetitive work, and it involved hammering lots of nails into lots of slots in the panel. But as repetitive as it was, the work forced you to pay attention, because you couldn't just swing away with your hammer mindlessly. No, you had to be careful not to drive the nail all the way into the wall. If you did that, the siding panel would eventually bow and crack. It needed a few millimeters to breathe. It was tricky.

Still, I would be swinging a hammer for four hours straight. I tried to ignore the aches while assuring myself that my upper arms were awesome.

And even though I had to physically pay attention, I could sort of let my mind zone out. I mentally wandered from my construction class to my vegetable garden. I needed to plant more herbs and cut down the dill that had gone to seed. I wondered how my dad and his girlfriend, Belinda, were doing and made a mental note to call them soon. Chloe would want to have a get-together with the two of them and our Uncle Pete while she was here.

And before I knew it, I had installed half a wall's worth of siding. It looked good.

When we finally quit for the day, I stowed my tools and walked into the house to get my bag. And that was when I remembered Linda. I had completely forgotten about her! She hadn't shown up for work. Or had she? Maybe she had arrived and gone straight to her table and gotten some work done. But I couldn't imagine her not stopping to say hello.

I pulled the tablecloth away and looked at her boxes

of pottery and marble and glass. I stared at all of the mallets lined up along the end. They were a little out of line, probably because of the tablecloth. Other than that, it didn't look like she had done any work here today.

Maybe there was a family issue, I thought. Everyone had family issues once in a while. Or maybe, like me, she had simply zoned out somewhere. Maybe she'd stayed at the beach longer than she thought she would. Or met a friend and hung out all afternoon. It happened all the time.

I pulled out my phone and sent her a quick text. "Hope everything's all right. See you tomorrow."

She didn't text me back right away. Maybe she'd left her phone somewhere. I knew I would talk to her at some point and find out what had happened, but I let it go for now, said good night to my guys, and headed for my truck over in the parking lot.

Mac and I stopped for a quick dinner of cheeseburgers and fries at the Cozy Cove diner, then got a couple of caffe lattes to go. It was seven o'clock when we met the writers on the porch of the lighthouse mansion.

The town had always called this place "the mansion," although there were many Victorian homes in town that were much bigger. This one, however, had the distinction of standing next door to the lighthouse and had been the home of lighthouse keepers for over 150 years.

The sun had slipped below the horizon a few minutes ago, but there was still some light in the sky. All six of the writers were there, and they seemed excited to be doing the exercise with Mac. I was secretly thrilled that they were showing some enthusiasm because, why wouldn't they? This was MacKintyre Sullivan, after all.

We spent a few minutes hanging out on the porch as Mac introduced the exercise to them. I stood near the railing and watched as they all took seats on the beautiful wicker furniture.

"Okay," Mac said. "Everyone have their tablets or their notebooks?"

"Yes." They all waved theirs for him to see.

"Great. Rule number one, don't get sand on your notebook."

There was some light laughter from the women.

"You all have flashlights, right?"

"Yes."

"Good." Mac had informed them earlier that he kept a supply of flashlights in one of the drawers in the living room cabinet for this very occasion.

"You'll need a flashlight if you're writing in a notebook or journal, just to see the page. And you'll also want one for the walk down to the shoreline."

"Yeah," Annabelle said, frowning as the sky grew darker. "The sun is completely gone."

"That's right," Mac said. "So be careful, please. Bring snacks if you want any. And drinks are fine. I'm talking about soft drinks, water, coffee, tea. Personally, unless you're vying for the Hemingway prize, I'd avoid alcohol until you get back to the house. Also, please don't litter. Bring all your trash back here."

"I brought a shopping bag for any trash," Sheri said.

"Good thinking."

I was amused to see her preen over his mild praise.

"Shannon and I will be here on the porch. I figure

it's far enough away to give you all some privacy but close enough to hear if anyone needs help."

"That works for me," Hugh said.

"So here's the assignment," Mac began. "Write a short essay or story about yourself. You're sitting on the beach. And a stranger walks by."

There was silence for a moment.

"That's it?" Hugh said.

Brian raised his hand. "What else?"

"Who's the stranger?" Lewis asked.

Mac smiled. "It can be anyone you want it to be."

"Any examples?" Sheri asked hopefully.

"Nope." Mac chuckled, mostly to himself. "Except to remind you that you asked me to suggest a mood-setting exercise. So write in that context—if you want to. Set the mood. Again, it's your work. You're all talented writers. This is where your creativity comes in."

I remembered that Mac had used those exact words earlier that day when he was explaining it to me.

"Does the stranger have to be an adult?" Kingsley asked.

"No." Mac didn't elaborate.

Kingsley pursed his lips in thought. "Does it have to be a human?"

Everyone laughed at that.

"No," Mac said.

I found it interesting to see that they all craved some guidance from Mac, even though, as he'd just mentioned, they were all talented writers.

"So, it just has to be a stranger. Could be anyone," Lewis said.

Mac gave a quick nod. "That's right."

"Okay." Lewis said, a beach towel under his arm. "Let's go, you guys."

"You already know what you're going to write?" Annabelle asked, with a touch of annoyance.

"Maybe," Lewis said cryptically, and led the way down the steps. "Or maybe I'll wait for inspiration to strike."

Sheri picked up a folding beach chair and a tote bag, and followed the others.

"She's the smart one," I murmured. "Bringing a chair."

"Yeah," Mac said. When he saw that they had reached the edge of the sand, he yelled, "Hey, be careful out there."

There were some vague responses, then they were gone.

I crossed the porch and sat next to him on the wide sofa. "So now we wait."

"Yes." He pulled me a little closer.

We sipped our caffe lattes and snuggled on the wicker sofa.

"It's colder tonight than I thought it would be." I took another sip. "Or maybe I'm just feeling nervous for those guys sitting out there in the dark."

"They're fine," Mac said. "Here, I'll open up the blanket."

He set his drink on the side table, reached for the blanket we'd brought with us, and spread it across our laps.

"They didn't seem too cynical about the exercise," I said quietly.

"No. I have to say I was pleasantly surprised by

that." He chuckled. "Of course, they're probably out there right now, rolling their eyes, sitting on the cold sand, cursing me out as they try to come up with something creative."

"The way you explained it this afternoon, I think it's a really good exercise. You can go in so many directions with it."

"Yeah. I think they'll get something out of it."

Without warning, there was a horrific scream. Then another. Over the roar of the ocean waves breaking on the shore, the ear-shattering screams continued to fill the night air.

We both jumped up from the sofa.

"What in the world?" I threw the blanket down.

"Stay here," Mac commanded.

Had he gone crazy? "No way!"

"Then stay close," he said, and grabbed my hand. And we both ran to the beach.

Chapter Seven

Mac's flashlight picked out the group halfway across the wide stretch of sand. They were all standing and staring at something farther down toward the water.

"What is it?" Mac demanded.

"Over here!" Kingsley shouted.

Lewis sat in the sand with his head buried in his arms. I thought I heard him choking. Was he actually crying? I couldn't believe it.

I suddenly wondered if they were all bluffing. Then Annabelle simply shuddered, wrung her hands, and whispered, "Oh God. Oh God."

Unless she was an excellent actress, it didn't sound like a bluff.

"I didn't think it was real," Hugh whispered.

Sheri had her arms wrapped around herself. "We thought it was a joke," she whimpered.

"We were laughing," Brian confessed, and cringed at his words. "Laughing. I'm sorry."

Lewis sat up, and as Mac moved the flashlight beam

in different directions, I got a brief look at Lewis's face. I didn't see how he could fake that look of utter devastation. Shaking his head slowly, Lewis said, "We thought you were trying to trick us with a phony dead body."

Dead body?

Oh God. It was my turn to cringe.

"Where?" Mac asked.

They all pointed toward the water.

I followed Mac and his flashlight beam. The tide was rising, and the water lapped farther onto the shore with every wave. It hadn't reached the body yet.

She was facedown in the sand. It was clearly a woman. She wore a long skirt that feathered lightly in the breeze. As though she might've been dragged to this spot, her thin sweater was bunched up, revealing the pale, smooth skin of her back. Her tangled blond hair was matted with blood.

I recognized that pretty flowered skirt.

"Oh my God. It's Linda." The shock was causing my throat to close up. I'd only known her a few days, but already Linda was a friend. A good person. No, a *great* person. Who would hurt her? "How could this happen?"

Mac stepped closer and pressed his fingers to her neck to check for a pulse. He stood and walked back to me, shaking his head. He pulled me close and gave me one quick, hard hug. Then he said, "Call Eric."

I already had my phone out.

Eric had come alone and informed us that several of his officers would be here shortly. He moved all of us farther up the beach, away from the water, so as not to disturb the body. He needed to stay on the beach to keep an eye on the body and watch all of us while he was at it. He took a few dozen photos of Linda from various angles to document the scene. The water was still about ten feet from where she lay, and I prayed it wouldn't touch her before the other officers arrived and she could be moved.

I didn't realize I was crying until my vision went blurry.

The writers had slowly moved farther away from Mac and me and were now gathered a few yards away in their own circle. Eric assured them that as soon as the officers arrived on the scene they would escort them home and take their statements.

Lewis had taken the discovery of Linda's body the hardest. He'd still been sniffling when Eric arrived and now I noticed that Brian's eyes were wet, too. Sheri and Annabelle had shed some tears as well. The other two men were more stoic.

"She wasn't killed here," Mac said quietly, glancing back at Linda's body, which could be seen more easily now that Eric had pitched a battery-powered light tree nearby.

"You may be right," Eric said, "but I'm not willing to state categorically one way or the other. We'll wait for CSI to determine that."

In our little town, the crime scene investigation unit consisted of one man, Leo Stringer, and his occasional assistant, Officer Lilah O'Neil.

"Her sweater was pulled up from her waist and I'm wondering if that means she was dragged here." I felt my stomach dip as I said the words. My eyes were already raw from tears, and my head was beginning to ache, so I was determined not to cry again.

"You think she was?" Eric asked.

"I'm just guessing," I admitted. "As far as I know, she spent the day out here, collecting seashells for her artwork. So she could've been attacked right here, but . . ."

"There's no blood," Mac asserted, then glanced at Eric. "I checked for a pulse, but didn't move her. I used my flashlight to search the area before you got here. Someone hit her really hard in the head with a blunt object. But there's no sign of spatter anywhere."

I stared at Linda's body lying alone in the glaring light with the tide moving slowly up on the sand. "Maybe the water washed it away."

"High tide is just coming in," Eric said. "Still, Mac's right. There would be a lot more blood on the spot where she fell."

I took a long moment to dwell on the fact that the police chief was actually revealing details of the crime to me. It hadn't been that long ago when Eric would've told me to mind my own business and sent me home. Maybe he had mellowed because of my involvement with Mac, or maybe it was my connection to Chloe. I didn't really care. I just appreciated that he had grown to trust me. It shouldn't have mattered, though, because my friend was lying dead in the wet sand. Part of me wanted to lie down in a quiet room and cry for my poor friend. But I made an effort to follow their theories.

"Shannon may have a point about the sweater being pulled up," Mac said. "But that means that the killer had to have pulled her by her feet."

"Good point," Eric said. "So where did he pull her from?"

I stared at our surroundings. "The mansion? A car? The lighthouse?"

"All possibilities," Eric said. "We'll check out the house and any cars of its guests."

"Linda lives in town with her father," I said. "Maybe you already knew that."

He pulled out a notepad and began writing. "I know it now. Thanks."

"Julia Barton knows her really well. She'll have more personal information for you."

"Got it," he said.

The writers were clustered together a few yards away, and from where I stood now, I could hear their conversation. They were carrying on as though nothing else was going on around them.

Sheri said, "I'm so bummed. I got a couple of pages into my story, and it was going pretty well."

"I had a whole page finished," one of the guys said. "My stranger is an alien."

That was probably Kingsley, I thought.

"Mine is a cute little boy," Annabelle said, and giggled. "I think he's lost."

"Mine is a woman who turns out to be my real mother." Lewis grinned. "She gave me up for adoption, and she's been looking for me."

Sheri said, "Really? Is that true?"

His laugh was derisive. "No, dummy. It's fiction."

"Well, you never know," Sheri said defensively.

Incensed, I lowered my voice. "Can you hear them?"

Eric whispered, "What the hell are they talking about?"

"They're idiots," I said angrily. How could they stand there talking and joking when a beautiful woman lay dead on the beach only a few yards away? And less than ten minutes ago, Lewis was crying his eyes out. And now he was laughing? What a jerk!

"It was a writing exercise," Mac explained to Eric. Knowing I was upset, he gently ran his hand up and down my back. "I asked them to write a short essay about themselves sitting on the beach when a stranger passes by."

"That's a writing exercise?"

"Yeah. A creative writing prompt. Anyway, that's what they were doing out here."

Eric's eyes narrowed. "Sounds like they all wrote something while they were here."

Mac nodded. "They didn't get too far, but yeah."

"I don't care how far they got," Eric said. "I want their notes. I want everything."

Mac nodded. "I'll take care of it."

The chief thought for a moment. "No. Thanks, Mac, but I'll have Tommy handle it. I don't want to give any of those writers the slightest opportunity to turn on you."

"I don't want that, either," I said quickly. "Thanks, Eric."

And wasn't it interesting that even the chief of police recognized that these writers had no allegiance to anyone. Not to one another and not even to Mac.

A few seconds later, a beam of light flashed across the sand. I figured they had turned their flashlights on again and wondered if they were trying to get a better look at Linda's body.

In a flash, Eric stalked across to the group and grabbed something from one of them.

"Hey, that's mine!"

That was Lewis yelling, I realized.

Whatever he had taken from him, Eric slipped it into his pocket. "You can have it back at the end of the night."

"I was just recording the sights and sounds of the night," Lewis protested. "I use it in my writing."

"Sure you were, Lewis," Sheri taunted.

Kingsley snickered. "That's a big fat load of BS."

"Shut up," Lewis said, snarling.

Eric strolled over and said under his breath, "Jackass had his phone out, taking shots of the body."

"He's a piece of work," Mac murmured.

"Here comes my team," Eric said, as bright headlights lit up the night. "Now we can get to work."

Once the police officers and the CSI unit were on the scene, the three uniformed officers were told to take all of us civilians back to the lighthouse mansion. Eric and Tommy stayed on the beach with Leo Stringer and Lilah. I hoped they'd be able to move poor Linda's body before the tide got too high.

Once on the porch, each of the three officers took one writer into a separate room in the house to get their statements. Eric had told the cops to get copies of their writing exercises as well.

I recognized two of the officers, of course. Mindy Payton was a friend from high school, and Officer Garcia had worked on the last crime scene I'd been involved in. The third officer was a new face, and Mindy introduced us.

"Shannon Hammer and Mac Sullivan," she said. "This is Officer Rachel Timmons."

Rachel was tall, thin, and striking, with almond-shaped eyes and long, black hair worn in a thick pony-tail down her back. We all shook hands, and I said, "Welcome to Lighthouse Cove."

"Thanks," she said. "So far, it's a lot different from my last job."

"Where'd you come from?" Mac asked.

"I started out as an EMT in Oakland and made the move to the police academy after a few years," she said. "Stayed there for almost ten years."

"Oakland's a big city compared to our little town," Mac admitted.

"And parts of it are beautiful. It's right on the bay. And the food is fabulous. But this is a lot closer to home."

"Where's home?" I asked.

"I grew up in Eureka."

"Oh yeah," I said. "Just a thirty-minute drive up the highway."

She grinned. "I love it. And so does my dad."

"Well, it's great to meet you," I said. "Despite the circumstances."

Once all the statements had been taken, the officers left us to join the team on the beach.

Mac and I stayed for a few minutes to talk to the writers.

"I'm sorry you had to experience that," Mac said.

"Are you kidding?" Hugh grinned. "I mean, I'm sorry about Linda. But it's not too often that you get the opportunity to find a dead body right there in front of you."

I exchanged a quick look with Mac, and I was sure he caught my vibe of pure disgust.

Lewis seemed to have caught it, too, but he just

shrugged. "Hey, I was half in love with her, but what the hell? It's all grist for the mill."

I was about to turn apoplectic, so Mac grabbed my hand. "We've got to get going. But first, I know you all wrote a little something tonight and you handed copies over to the police. Nevertheless, if any of you want to talk about it or go over something else you're working on, let's find some time and get together."

"I'd love to talk about it with you," Annabelle said silkily. She was obviously flirting.

What was wrong with these people? Somebody had just been killed. They'd all seen the body. They'd been interviewed by the police. Did they understand they were suspects? Did they care? Clearly they did not. They would probably be thrilled if they knew that the police were looking at one of them as a possible killer. Once again, I wasn't sure they understood anything outside of themselves and their own little worlds.

"Uh, maybe," Mac said awkwardly.

I wasn't having any of it and just wanted to get away from them. "See you all later," I managed to say through my tightly pressed lips, reached for Mac's hand, and walked out the front door. I found our blanket and shoved it into the tote bag we'd brought.

We didn't speak until we got to Mac's car. He set down the tote bag and pulled me into his arms. "I'm so sorry."

I thought I had used up all my tears, but I was wrong. His words touched my heart, and I began to weep on his shoulder.

"I should've gone looking for her," I said, trying to talk through the tears. "I knew where she was going. Maybe I could've saved her."

"Where was she going?" Mac asked, rubbing my back.

I had to gulp in another breath before I could answer him. "She was coming up here. She wanted to collect some seashells for her mosaics, and she said the best ones are at the breakwater."

"She was out here?"

"Yeah." I was starting to get control of myself, and I could hear the deep suspicion in his voice. "Mac, I know these writers are strange and they're feckless and selfish. But they're not killers."

He unlocked the car door and I climbed inside. When he got into the driver's seat and turned on the engine, he sat for a moment, then turned to me. "I'm not sure I agree."

"What are you saying?"

He stared out at the beach, where several light stands had been set up near the shore. "It might be wrong of me to say it, but I wouldn't be surprised if one of them did kill Linda."

Homefront was in mourning. By early the next day, all of the vets and everyone on my crew had heard about Linda. Those who knew her were grieving at the news. Julia was inconsolable.

Some of my crew members had grown up in Lighthouse Cove and had known Linda from childhood. Others hadn't known her well but were nevertheless saddened by the news that someone from our town had died. I told Wade and Sean to leave it up to each individual, whether they wanted to keep working or take a few hours or a full day off.

Personally, when I was feeling down, I tended to

throw myself into the work. To each his own, as my father always said.

Mac, Eric, and Julia called a quick meeting of the entire Homefront village to let everyone know that a memorial service would be held at Linda's church next Monday.

Travis cried openly. "She was a beautiful soul. It's just not right."

"No, it's not," I said. And naturally, seeing Travis weeping brought my own tears out. We walked over to the small park and sat on a picnic bench.

"Can you tell me what happened?" he asked.

I was about to tell him when I noticed Julia hugging a few people. Then she caught sight of me, and Travis, and ran over to our table. She pulled me into a hug and held on tight.

"Oh my God, Shannon."

"I'm so sorry, Julia."

After a long moment, she turned to Travis and gave him a hug as more tears began to fall.

Finally, we all sat down on either side of the table. "You saw her, Shannon," Julia said. "Tell us what you know."

I kept it brief. "Mac and I were out at the lighthouse mansion, and we found her on the beach."

"Can you tell me how she died?" Julia asked.

"Are you sure you want to know?" I asked softly.

"I'm damned sure," she said.

I nodded. "Okay. Okay." I took a deep breath. "She was bludgeoned. Some kind of heavy object. I don't know much more than that."

"Oh my God." Julia put her arms on the table and lay her head down.

"You don't know what the object was?" Travis asked, wanting more basic information. "A two-by-four? Or maybe a pipe?"

I knew what he was getting at. The items he'd listed could be found on any construction site like this one. Did he think one of the construction workers did this? Or one of the vets?

I wasn't about to mention the writers, because if Travis thought one of those guys had anything to do with Linda's death, I was afraid he would hunt them down and take them out.

"I don't know, Travis," I said. "But I might be able to find out. If I do, I'll tell you."

"I appreciate it." He sniffed a few times and made a valiant effort to keep from crying again. Then he patted my hand. "We'll find this guy, Shannon. Linda was a good person, and she didn't deserve to die like that."

"No, she didn't."

We sat in silence for several minutes, wrapped up in our own thoughts.

"I'm going back to work," Travis said.

"Are you sure you want to do that?"

"I'm better off when I'm busy."

I nodded sympathetically. "I'm the same way. So how do you feel about vinyl siding?"

He flashed me a grateful smile. "I feel just fine about it."

"Then come with me and I'll set you up."

At house number thirty-four, Travis and I carried a stack of siding panels out to the exterior wall, where I'd left off the day before. Then I handed him a box of siding nails, and he was good to go.

"That should keep me busy for a while," he said, strapping on his tool belt.

"Thanks, Travis," I said. "By the way, have you found your tablet yet?"

He scowled. "No. And I'm about to order a new one. Just wanted to wait a few days in case someone found it."

"I'm sorry."

"We have bigger worries to deal with than my tablet."

"Yeah, we do," I said, and knew he was thinking of Linda. I patted his shoulder. "I'll be around if you need anything." Then I walked into the house to leave my bag and grab my tool belt.

I came to a stop when I saw Linda's mosaic table in the kitchen area. I wanted to cry all over again, remembering how we'd spent so much time talking about her collection of mallets and all the interesting stones and glass she had collected.

I wondered if she had actually made it to the beach yesterday to find her seashells. Had she put them in a bag or a pocket? I would have to ask Eric if he had found any of them.

It would be a nice tribute if we could create something special from all of her seashells and stones and glass. I made a mental note to talk to Niall about it. As a stonemason, he tended to work with bigger stones than these, but I knew he could do something great with mosaics if I asked him.

I pulled away the tablecloth and gazed at all the boxes of stones, pottery shards, and glass chunks. The hammer and hardie were exactly where she'd left them. And all the mallets were lined up in order—

No. I stared at the table. No, they were not in order.

"Something's wrong," I muttered, checking the antique mallets on one side and the more modern ones on the other. Where was her big, heavy wooden mallet? The one that her grandfather had created out of white ash and black walnut and weighted down with molten lead?

On a hunch, I counted the mallets. I remembered counting twelve before, but now there were only ten. One of the other mallets was missing as well, and I couldn't figure out which one it was. I looked under the table and all around the empty, unfinished room. The mallets were gone.

"Shannon," Eric said, talking on his speaker phone. "You know I'm not going to tell you anything about the investigation."

"But I might have some important information for you. I just need to know the shape of the murder weapon."

"Tell me what you know," he said reasonably, "and I'll tell you if you're right."

I scowled. "Eric, don't make me have to tell Chloe how exasperating you are."

He laughed. "You don't think she knows?"

I sighed. Of course she knew. It was hardly a viable threat, darn it. "Okay, fine. Linda has a set of mallets that are really unusual."

"Did you say mallets? Like, croquet mallets?"

"No, like mallets. Like hammers but different. Linda used a bunch of different mallets in her mosaic work. She used them to break up stone or marble or glass. Niall has a bunch of them. Have you seen them?"

"Yeah, I've seen some of his."

"Right. So one of Linda's mallets was handmade by her grandfather. It's heavy, made of wood and reinforced with lead inside, so it packs a wallop. The face of the head—you know, where you strike the stone—is a big four-inch square block."

He didn't respond right away and my stomach sank.

A tingling feeling traveled across my shoulders and down my spine. "That's it. That's what killed her. Am I right?"

"Where did you last see this mallet?" he asked.

"It was on her mosaic table. You know, where she did her work. We keep her table stowed inside house number thirty-four. But I'm looking at the table right now, and that mallet is missing."

"Of course it is," he muttered angrily.

"Oh, wait." I brightened. "I have a picture of it. Not that it'll help that much, but you'll be able to see what it looks like."

"I'll meet you at thirty-four."

Eric gazed at Linda's mosaic table. "She's got quite a collection of weapons here."

"They're not weapons," I insisted. "They're tools for her artwork."

"Look like weapons to me."

I gazed at him steadily. "Have you ever looked inside Chloe's tool chest?"

"Don't remind me. The woman could wipe out a small battalion with the weapons—I mean, *tools*—she's got."

I wasn't about to remind him that he and I had met for the first time when someone had stolen some of my tools and used them as deadly weapons. I still got chills when I recalled being interrogated by Eric for hours and wondering if I'd wind up inside a jail cell before the night was over.

I pulled out my phone. Clicking into my photo collection, I handed it to Eric. "Here's a photo of the big mallet I was talking about."

He stared at the photo, swiped the screen, and stared at a few more shots. "It's a beauty all right."

"Yeah, it is. Did I tell you her grandfather made it?"

"Yes." He swiped again. "Okay, good. I can see your hand in this one, so I can figure out the scale." He enlarged the picture and stared some more. Then he took hold of my hand and held it up. Squinting, he looked at my hand and then back at the photo and nodded.

"Can you send me those photos?"

"Sure. So you think that's the murder weapon?"

"Pretty darn sure. Now we've got to find it."

I winced. "So it's missing."

"Yeah." He clenched his jaw. "When we find it, we'll find Linda's killer."

I blew out a breath. "I've got more good news for you."

He glared at me. "I'm not going to like it, am I?"

"Nope." *Don't draw it out,* I thought. *Just say it fast.* "There's another mallet missing."

"What?" He sort of shouted the word.

I winced. "I counted them the other day. I should've taken a picture of the whole collection, but I didn't. So I'm not sure which one is missing, and I have no idea what it looks like."

"But you're sure there's a second mallet missing."

"Absolutely. There were twelve here, and now there are ten."

I was leaving Homefront for the day when Vince, the project manager, came walking quickly toward me.

"Shannon, glad I caught you."

"What's up, Vince?"

"I have a little project for you to consider."

"You're scaring me," I said with a laugh. "There are no little projects around here."

He grinned. "Well, let me show you and you'll decide."

"Okay."

He led the way into the community center, turned left, and walked to the end of the hall of offices. He opened the last door. The room was large and still un-finished, with the subfloor exposed and no baseboards yet. There were a couple of big windows along the one wall that looked out to the village, but otherwise, the room was a blank slate.

"It's a nice space," I said. "But wasn't this supposed to be your office?"

"I don't need anything this big. And remember, it was originally going to function as a second conference room, but it turns out to be superfluous."

"You sure?" I asked. "You are the big boss, after all."

"Tell the other guys, will ya?" He laughed. "The truth is, I like having my office closer to the front door. It's big enough for me, and I can keep an eye on every-thing that's going on."

"Makes sense." I stepped into the room and gazed around. "So what do you have in mind for this space?"

"Any chance we could turn it into two smaller offices?"

I walked the length of the room and then checked out the width, counting my steps to gauge the size. I counted electrical outlets, lighting fixtures, and windows. I didn't have my stud finder with me, so I began to knock on the surface of the wall at short intervals, listening for the change in tone from hollow to solid that indicated the presence of an upright support beam, better known as a stud. I quickly found them.

"Of course," I finally said.

"I'm bringing in two more counselors and I need the space."

"So, you won't need to add any extra windows or electrical outlets? Just a partition wall."

"Just the wall," Vince said.

"Okay," I said after another moment studying the space. "We could build a partition wall right here." I held out my arms to indicate. "I can't go too much farther because of this window. So one office would be, oh, approximately sixteen by twenty feet, and the second office would be about sixteen by sixteen feet. Is that okay?"

"Those are reasonable sizes for an office, right?"

"Sure." I was still mentally measuring. "And we really lucked out by putting in a second door off the hall, so we won't need to build one into the partition."

"That was dumb luck." He seemed to be mentally measuring the space as well. "So even in the smaller room, you can still fit a desk in there with a couple of chairs and a filing cabinet or two. Maybe an extra table at one end for a printer. I think that'll work."

"Sure it will. We can do it easily."

Vince smiled, knowing I was already hooked on the project. And why wouldn't I be? It wasn't exactly a challenge. And it would be fun to work inside the center for a while. There was always a lot going on.

I thought about the timing, tried to picture my schedules and my crew assignments. "I don't want to pull any of my guys off the tiny house project right away. We've got a well-oiled machine out there, and I would hate to interrupt the momentum."

"Agreed. I've never seen a crew work with such single-minded determination."

I beamed at the compliment. "Thanks." I walked around the room again. "Don't mind me, I'm just thinking out loud here. I'll ask my sister to help with the framing and the drywall." I didn't think Chloe would mind contributing some of her time to a good cause. But I frowned, considering everything that would have to be done. Glancing around, I said, "I'd rather not deal with electrical, and it looks like you've got plenty of outlets on these longer walls."

"Yeah, we won't need more outlets."

"It'll keep the cost down," I muttered.

"I like that."

"We'll finish off the rooms when we're done with the partition." I paced as I made notes. "Lay down tile over this subfloor. Paint, of course. Baseboards, light fixtures, outlet covers, window shades, hardware."

Vince was beaming, and I realized he was letting me blather on because he was so happy I'd agreed to do the job.

"Sorry," I said. "Just thinking out loud."

"Think away," Vince said. "If you'll give me a ballpark budget, I'm happy to have you start whenever you can."

"I'll work it out tonight and get back to you to-morrow."

"Sounds good." We shook hands. "Thanks, Shannon."

Mac and I spent a quiet evening watching an old movie surrounded by our sweet little critters. We made a big healthy salad for dinner with veggies from the garden, which I'd been cultivating ever since I was seventeen and needed a hobby. Mac did his part by grilling chicken breasts and cutting one of them up for the salad.

I had come home earlier and gone straight to my office to work out a budget for Vince. I'd made a list of supplies and equipment we'd need. After that, I'd given Wade and Carla a call to let them know about the additional job we'd be doing for the center. Once that phone call was finished, I shut down my work brain and settled in with Mac and the little ones.

My heart still ached when I thought about last night's discovery of Linda's body on the beach. Every time I saw that image in my mind, I wanted to cry. And yet I'd been able to come home and work on numbers and dates and talk to my foremen as though nothing had changed in my world. I had been compartmental-izing my thoughts all day. Work had helped keep the pain at bay. The new project in the community center helped. But now, faced with the reality of Linda's death, I just wanted to curl up and rock myself to sleep.

Mac patted my back, then walked into the kitchen as a local commercial came on, touting a hardware super-store's huge sale. "Our huge selection of tile work! Backsplashes! Kitchen and bathroom floors! Peel and stick! Accents and trims! Prices slashed through Sunday!"

"Oh no," I whispered, and burst into tears. I couldn't stop. Why did it have to be a commercial for tile work? For backsplashes? Of all things! As inane as the subject matter was, it reminded me of Linda and I continued to sob quietly.

Robbie seemed to feel my pain and cuddled up on my lap. Both cats moved to either side of me on the couch and gave me little headbutts to show they cared.

The unconditional love of animals was a true miracle, I thought.

Mac returned with a bottle of beer and noticed that I had lost it. "Hey, hey. Come here." He picked up Luke and sat down next to me with the cat in his lap. "I'm sorry, sweetheart." He pulled me close to him and simply rocked me as if I were a baby, and he whispered sweet, loving words that made me cry even harder.

After a few minutes, I took a few long, slow breaths in and out. I felt waterlogged. "I'm sorry. It just hit me hard."

"Don't be sorry. She was a good friend and a good person."

"Honestly, I barely knew her, but I felt like we connected. You know?"

"I do, love. Once in a great while, a person touches your life, and you're irrevocably changed for the better."

I sniffled. "I hate that someone hurt her."

"I do, too."

We held on to each other through the next inning. I was glad to have the baseball game on because we both needed the background noise and activity.

During the next commercial break, Mac picked up his cell phone. "Sorry, love, but I just want to check and see if I got an email from one of the corporate board members I met with. They were supposed to vote on how much . . . holy cow."

"What?"

"Check this out."

"What? An email?"

"Not exactly." He scratched his neck as he read his phone screen. "It's the daily listing of new publication deals. And under the list of so-called 'hot new properties,' there was a blurb about a new manuscript written by Lewis Bondurant."

"Lewis Bondurant?" I frowned. "Is that Lewis from the writers' retreat?"

"Yeah, that's him. The blurb said that he'd just submitted his latest book yesterday, and both his agent and his publishers are lauding this modern adventure story as the next huge blockbuster hit."

"But . . . that's just weird," I said. "Linda told me he couldn't even figure out how to start his next book."

"Yeah, I remember." Mac reasoned. "That's why this jumped out at me."

I thought back to my conversation with her. "Linda felt bad because his writer friends were so jealous of him. He'd hit it big on the first book, so now they wouldn't even try to help him plot out a second one."

Mac gave a cynical snort. "It's not because they're jealous. It's because he's an obnoxious jerk."

"There's that. Linda was so worried about him because he was freaking out."

"Sounds like he was laying it on thick for Linda.

That's his style, after all. Always thirsty for any kind of attention."

Mac sipped his beer and thought about it for a long beat.

I watched him. "What are you thinking?"

"Just trying to thread a few facts together."

"Okay." I waited.

He sat forward, his elbows resting on his knees. "The other night at the pub, Lewis approached Travis with an offer to come talk to the group."

"Right, and Travis wasn't buying it."

"Smart man. But soon after that, Travis's tablet was stolen."

"That's right." I gazed at him, knew what he was thinking. "Lewis had to have stolen it."

"Oh, yeah."

"And you really believe he would send his agent someone else's story?"

"Actually, I do think that," Mac said evenly.

"But Travis writes adventure stories about wrestling bears and stuff."

"You know, I actually think he really did wrestle a bear or two in real life."

"Okay, that's pretty amazing, but you know what I mean. Travis writes about the wild frontier. The mountain man. The rugged individualist. Living off the land. All that stuff. Lewis isn't anything like that. How could he get away with it?"

"Because his first book was a huge hit," Mac said. "His agent and editor think he's a genius, so they're going to believe he wrote anything he sends them. Even if it's a story about a mountain man wrestling a bear."

"I guess that's why they call it fiction."

Mac laughed. "Exactly. But I'm concerned that Lewis might try to pass off some of Travis's other stories as his own, too."

"I thought he mainly wrote short stories."

"He does, but according to Eric, he's also got three really good book-length novels on his tablet. One of them is a romance, and it's supposed to be amazing."

"You're kidding. A romance?"

"Well, it's a romance about a guy who meets a woman in Alaska, and halfway through the story, he has to rescue her from a raging river. It's sort of a modern Alaskan version of *The African Queen*."

"Oh, I loved that movie. Very romantic."

Mac chuckled. "Travis is a wonderful storyteller. If Lewis stole the tablet and downloaded one of Travis's novels, then sent it to his agent under his own name, I can understand why his agent would be popping champagne right now. His stories are just that good."

"But it's so wrong. And it's got to be illegal."

"Do you think Lewis cares?"

"It'll be easy enough to prove that he stole the story," I insisted. "If he did."

"Lewis wouldn't consider any of that. He won't expect anyone to put the pieces together for a long time."

"You don't think so?"

Mac shrugged. "It'll be close to a year by the time the book comes out."

"Well, he should pay for stealing someone else's idea," I groused.

"He doesn't care," Mac said. "He doesn't consider anyone's feelings outside of his own little universe."

"And he doesn't believe anyone is as smart as he is."

"The guy's a real prize." Mac shook his head in annoyance. "And I hate that we're spending more time dwelling on him."

"We really have to do something about it." I gazed at him, then took a few seconds to give Robbie a quick scratch behind his ears while I thought through everything we'd talked about. Finally I looked back at Mac. "So, how do we set a trap for him?"

Chapter Eight

Before Mac went to work the next morning, I reminded him of our big dinner date that night. We had been invited by my best friend Jane Hennessey to attend her first dinner party in the beautifully renovated dining room of her Gables Hotel.

"I didn't forget," Mac assured me. "I'm looking forward to seeing all the work you've done on the place."

"It looks spectacular, if I do say so myself."

After he went to his office, I called Chloe.

"What?" she said, her voice raspy from sleep.

"It's Shannon."

"It's seven o'clock in the morning," she whined. "What can be so important?"

"I've got a little construction job I'm hoping you'll help me with. Starting today."

She groaned. "I'm on vacation."

"You work in television," I said. "You're on vacation every day."

"How dare you?"

I just laughed.

She huffed. "Listen, missy. I happen to be a very important person. I don't have to take this abuse from you."

I was still chuckling. "So you'll help me?"

I could hear her grumbling and grunting and breathing heavily, and I imagined she was throwing the covers back and sitting up in bed. Finally she said, "What's it for?"

I smiled. "Homefront's project manager wants one of the big offices turned into two smaller spaces, so we'll be building a partition wall."

"Fun," she said, and yawned. "When do we start?"

I gave her all the details, and she assured me that she would be there.

"How are you holding up?" she asked, her tone turning serious. I knew she was talking about Linda.

"I'm okay. I had a little breakdown last night, but I'm better this morning. It hits me at the weirdest times."

"If you need to talk, I'm here."

I almost burst into tears hearing her say that, but I managed to maintain. "Thanks, sweetie."

"Just remember," she said resolutely. "Eric will catch whoever did it, and they will pay."

I spent the early part of the morning gathering materials, equipment, and supplies for the job inside the center. Once our prep work was done, I estimated that the framing itself would take about an hour. Then we'd start hanging drywall. That would take another day or two. Once the drywall mud was applied, it would be another day before it would be completely dry. Then we'd start sanding the surfaces, applying more mud, and so on.

I doubted Chloe would be able to stay for the whole job. Once she left town, I would have to steal a couple of guys from the tiny house project to finish things up.

Chloe met me at the community center at noon, and I showed her what we had planned for the big office.

"That shouldn't be too hard," she said. "The framing will go quickly, but the drywall will take a few days."

"That's what I figure."

"Okay, we've both done this a thousand times," she said. "It won't be a load-bearing wall so we'll just need a bottom plate and single top plate."

"Right. We'll build the entire frame on the floor, and then we'll raise it and brace it."

"Perfect." She splayed her hands. "Piece of cake."

"You shouldn't say that."

"Sorry." She batted her eyelashes. "Did I jinx the whole project?"

"Luckily, we have this wood here so you can knock on it."

"Ha ha," she said, but I noticed her rapping her knuckles on the stack of two-by-fours.

The lumber was piled on top of a thick piece of plywood on one of our utility carts. On the bottom shelf of the cart were my toolbox and power drill. And next to the utility cart was my circular saw table, an eight-foot ladder, and four folding sawhorses.

"How'd you get all this stuff over here?" she asked.

"Hmm. I might've had some help."

"I'll bet you did."

I ignored her. "We're going to move all of this lumber into the room. We'll lay it all on the floor along the far wall for easier access. Basically, I don't want to leave anything out in the hall."

"Good point."

"Then you can help me carry this piece of plywood into the room, and we'll lay it across two of the sawhorses. It's going to function as our utility table."

"That works."

I could feel the worry lines sprouting on my forehead. "I'm sure I've forgotten something, but we'll muddle through it together."

She turned and looked at me. "You haven't done anything like this in a while, have you?"

I was taken aback. "What do you mean? I do this stuff every day."

"I mean, on your own." Her smile was shrewd. "You've got Wade and Carla and Sean and Johnny and all the other guys running around doing this setup and prep work for you. Am I right?"

"Fine." I had to sigh. "You're right. I've turned into a spoiled little princess."

"I should talk." Chloe laughed. "If you're a princess, then I'm a queen."

"Now that is the truth."

Somehow we managed to haul all of the two-by-fours into the office and onto the floor in an orderly pile. We set up the sawhorses and placed the heavy plywood on top to make a utility table. I brought in my toolbox and set it up on the floor, and finally, I wheeled in my circular saw table and plugged it in.

I was pulling out my stud finder when a shrill beeping filled the air.

Chloe held her hands over her ears. "What in the world is that?"

I shook my head in disgust. "It's my lighthouse alarm." I grabbed my phone and stopped the alarm.

"Why do you have a lighthouse alarm?"

"Because," I explained, "we've caught kids sneaking in there, and with the repairs we're doing, it could be dangerous."

"So now what do we do?"

I stared at my phone. "First, I check out the video, and depending on what I see, I call the police."

"Ooh, I want to see." She leaned over my shoulder to get a look. "It's kind of dark."

"It looks like there's a bug on the lens." I grimaced, then turned up the audio. "Never mind. We can still hear them."

There was a lot of female giggling and manly guffawing as the intruders climbed the circular stairway inside the lighthouse.

"Who is that?" Chloe said. "They sound like a bunch of knuckleheads."

"That's exactly what they are." And I was furious! "It's the writers. I can tell from their voices."

"What voices? All I hear is a bunch of laughing."

"Yeah, but it's them. Without a doubt. I can tell."

"So, wait. You're telling me that the writers staying at Mac's house just broke into the lighthouse?"

"Yes, and it's not the first time they've done it, either." I stared at the screen for another minute, but I never did get a look at their faces. Then the voices began to dwindle as they moved farther up the stairway toward the lens room.

"So what do you do now?"

I smiled determinedly. "I call the police."

"You won't reach Eric. He's meeting with the town council."

"Shoot." So instead of calling Eric directly, I called dispatch and spoke to Ginny Malone.

"You got kids sneaking into the lighthouse?" she said when I told her what my problem was.

"It can be dangerous in there," I explained. "They could get hurt. Could you send a car out to check on them?"

"You bet, Shannon."

"Thanks, Ginny." I ended the call and glanced up at Chloe. "We'll see what happens."

We took some time to measure the space precisely, then I had to determine where we would place the partition wall. With my stud finder, it was easy to locate the ceiling and floor joists that would be used to hold the wall in place.

The room was precisely sixteen feet wide, and I had brought sixteen-foot lengths of two-by-four lumber. So that was kind of perfect, I thought. It hadn't happened by chance, of course. I had helped build this place, so I already knew most of these measurements by heart. But it never hurt to double-check.

We ran a chalk line across the floor to indicate where the floor joist was located. This would be where we placed the bottom plate of the frame once we lifted it off the ground.

Chloe took charge of marking the top and bottom plates at sixteen-inch intervals using her speed square— or "Speedy," as she called it—and a thick pencil, and those marks showed where we would nail each two-by-four to the plates.

Now it was time to saw off the ends of our ten pieces of vertical lumber—our studs—to fit the height of the room. I was using ten-foot lengths of two-by-fours, and since this ceiling was ten feet high, we subtracted the width of the top and bottom plates—one and a half inches times two—and cut down each piece of wood to precisely nine feet, eight and three-quarter inches.

I couldn't build the frame ten feet high because I wouldn't be able to tilt it into place. I needed some wiggle room. Once it was in place, I would use a shim to snug the fit.

We built the frame on the floor and braced the bottom plate against the far wall so nothing would slide as we nailed the studs into the top plate.

Since we had taken all that time earlier to prep and measure and mark everything so precisely, the actual building of the frame took almost no time at all. It certainly helped to have my nail gun with me. Although, with a relatively simple job like this, it wasn't an absolute requirement.

"Good job," Chloe said. "High five."

We tried to slap each other's hand but missed.

"We are pitiful," she said.

"Yeah, but we do good work." I gave her a hearty pat on the back. "Thanks."

"And thanks to Dad," she said, and we both grinned. Our father had taught us everything we knew about construction.

"Measure twice, cut once," I said. "Words to live by."

We took a five-minute break to use the bathroom and check in with our respective boyfriends. I'd brought apples and string cheese, and we munched and chatted for another five minutes.

"So, is tonight casual?" Chloe asked.

To say I was shocked didn't begin to describe my reaction. "Are you actually asking my advice on what you should wear tonight?"

She looked as if she wanted to bite off her tongue. "I didn't want to call Jane and bother her. Just answer the question."

"Okay." I smiled. "I think Jane wants this to be a festive occasion, so I would go with something dressier."

"Great. I can do that."

I tore off a piece of cheese. "I can't wait for you to see the place."

"I can't, either. It's been months since I went through it the first time. It was so incredibly creepy."

"The Gables isn't creepy anymore. It's clean and beautiful and really awesome."

The Gables was formerly known as the Northern California Asylum for the Insane. When the developers decided to refurbish the place, Jane immediately put in a bid on the north wing, hoping she could turn the space into a small hotel, much like her Hennessey Inn near the town square. She and I had had to overcome mold, mildew, and dry rot, along with a ghost or two and a really vicious murderer in order to turn those creepy halls into a sparkling new Hennessey Hotel.

I tossed my apple core into the wastebasket. "You ready to get back to work?"

"Let's go."

Back in the room, I tested the weight of the frame by lifting the top a few inches off the floor. "Heavier than it looks," I murmured. "Ready to raise this thing?"

"Do you have something to brace it with?" she asked.

"Yeah, that's what those two extra sawhorses are for." I walked to the far wall and brought one of the folded sawhorses over, then opened it up so that it stood on its own.

Chloe did the same with the second one. "Okay, these will hold up. Are you ready?"

"Yeah. Count of three." I counted to three, and we both lifted the top plate up a few feet. "Hold it." I grabbed the sawhorse and wedged it under the frame. We lifted it a few feet higher, and Chloe wedged her sawhorse farther under to take the weight off of us. We went back and forth two more times, lifting the frame and wedging the sawhorse, until the frame was standing exactly where we wanted it to be. Then we used two-by-fours wedged diagonally against the walls to brace the frame until we could attach the top plate to the ceiling joist.

I tested the braces and found them tight and firm, but I didn't like taking chances. "Instead of leaving these braces overnight, I'm just going to go ahead and screw the whole thing to the ceiling joist."

"That's a much better plan," Chloe said.

"Can you check me as I go?"

"Sure."

I grabbed a handful of four-inch wood screws and tossed them into the front pocket of my tool belt. I needed the screws to be long enough to go through the top plate, the drywall, and ultimately into the ceiling joist.

I installed a T-25 star driver on my power drill and climbed the ladder up far enough to comfortably do the job. As I screwed each section of the top plate to the joist, Chloe would check that the frame was still plumb. She used the four-foot level and held it firmly against the vertical stud to make sure that the frame was straight up and down.

"It's good," she said.

When the top plate was done, I climbed down off the ladder and proceeded to do the same thing to the bottom plate, attaching it to the floor joist every few inches. I worked on my hands and knees and asked Chloe to give me the thumbs-up one last time before I scurried across the floor to secure the base plate.

When I was finished, I stood up and stretched my back and neck. I set the power drill down on the plywood table and bent over to touch my toes. And groaned.

"I'm getting too old for this," I said.

"Shut up," Chloe said, laughing at me. "You're not even old enough to run for president."

I would get no sympathy from her, not that I expected any. I stretched a little more and then looked around at what we'd accomplished. "Hey, we rock."

"Totally rock."

"Ready to drywall?"

"Good God," she said, horrified. "I'm a human being, not a machine."

With a laugh, I pulled my phone out of its pocket and checked the time. "Oh shoot, it's already five o'clock. We'd better pack it up for today. We still have to go home and get ready for tonight."

She unbuckled her tool belt. "Good. So we're back here on Monday?"

"Yes. Monday morning I want to hang the drywall and start on the mud."

"Count me in," Chloe said, as we packed up tools and folded up the ladder and sawhorses.

"Great," I said. "We'll start at eight o'clock."

"In the morning?" She glared at me. "You're a heathen."

I followed her out of the room, laughing as I locked the door behind me.

The dining room at the Gables Hotel had once served as the indoor recreation room of the old asylum. On rainy days, the patients would sit in this room playing cards, quilting, drawing, or simply sitting in one of the many chairs that lined the walls and staring out at the rain-soaked lawn. When the sun was out, the staff would bring their patients outdoors to take in the fresh air. There, they would dance or exercise or work in the garden or simply sit on the grass and ponder the world.

Jane's mother had been a patient here off and on for many years. It hadn't been a fun time for Jane. Because of it, she had been driven to bid on the property in an attempt to bring some beauty and light into this dark place where her mother had spent so much time.

And Jane had succeeded. The wide hallways had been painted a very pale shade of sage that brightened the rooms. Newly installed ceiling fixtures and cleverly shaped wall sconces further lightened the spaces. The wood bannisters and newel posts of the massive stairway had been polished to a shine so bright, I could almost see myself in the wood.

We walked into the expansive dining room, and I heard Mac utter, "Wow."

It was even more beautiful than I remembered from a few weeks ago, when my crew and I had put the finishing touches on the reconstructed coffered ceiling and applied the final coat of sealer on the beautiful

blond wood wall paneling. The lighting was softly re-
cessed under the layers of crown molding within the
coffers. The western-facing wall was covered in floor-
to-ceiling windows that showed off the stunning view
of the ocean and coastline.

I could proudly take credit for the sleek wood fin-
ishes and the intricate ceiling design, but the rest of the
room was pure Jane. Her natural elegance and grace
shined in every corner. There was white linen, glitter-
ing crystal stemware, and shiny silver place settings on
each table. Delicate flowers graced every surface, and
leafy trees in large pots were used to create intimate
dining spaces here and there around the room.

The long table in front of the center window was set
for a party of twelve. I knew for a fact that my friends
and I would be the only diners in the room tonight. I
might've felt odd about that, but since I knew that this
was Jane's first test run of the kitchen and waitstaff, I
felt pride and excitement instead.

Jane greeted Mac and me with hugs. Then she
spread her arms out wide and turned around. "Well,
what do you think?"

"It's even more eye-popping than it was just a while
ago." I held on to her hands and squeezed. "You're going to have a waiting list a mile long within a week."

"I'm blown away, Jane," Mac said. "It's just gorgeous."

"Thanks, Mac," she said. "You were a major part of
making it happen. I'm so happy you're here."

Mac had been an investor in the development project and had been forced into a confrontation with a
former resident who wasn't happy about it. While there
were some intense moments, Mac and I had come out

of the experience even closer than ever. He had moved in with me shortly after that.

Niall Rose, Jane's fiancé, handed each of us a glass of champagne, and I gave him a hug, too. He was a good-looking barrel-chested Scotsman who wore a kilt on special occasions like this one.

Mac walked over to the window. "That view doesn't hurt."

Jane turned and watched him. "It's breathtaking, isn't it?"

"It's a great view and all"—I shrugged—"but the food better be good."

With a laugh, she gave me a light swat on my arm. "Trust me, it's drool-worthy."

"I absolutely trust you," I said, grabbing her for another quick hug. "It's going to be wonderful."

"It's out of this world," Niall said, rubbing his stomach. "We've been taste-testing all week."

I pulled him aside for a moment to ask him if he would mind completing three of Linda's mosaic backsplashes. "She was barely able to get started on the project, but I would love to have some of her touches included in the last few houses. I know the mosaic work isn't what you're used to doing, but I would so appreciate it if you would step in to finish what she started."

"Ah, Shannon." His big arms wrapped me in a hug, and I almost lost it right then and there. That had been happening a lot lately. "Of course I'll do it for you. I met Linda on a few occasions and found her to be a lovely woman and a true artist."

I had to take a few seconds to control my tear ducts. "Thanks, Niall."

Within minutes, Marigold and Rafe arrived, followed quickly by Emily and Gus. Gus Peratti had been everyone's favorite auto mechanic for years. He and Emily lived in a beautiful old Victorian home that was haunted by the woman who had fallen in love with Gus's grandfather. It was a long story, but as long as Gus was living in the house, it seemed that the ghost was happy.

Lizzie and Hal walked in a few minutes later, apologizing for being late. "Marisa was trying on prom dresses."

"You're not late," Jane said, and gave them both a hug.

"My heart." I pressed my hands against my chest. "It hurts to realize she's old enough to go to the prom."

"It's given me a few tough moments, too," Hal confessed.

Lizzie patted his shoulder. "Daddy can't deal with our little girl turning seventeen."

"I don't think I can, either," I said.

"How's Taz handling it?" Gus asked.

"In typical brotherly fashion," Lizzie said. "By mocking and ridiculing her as often as possible."

"That's my boy," Hal said with a grin.

I had known their two children since they were born, and it really did tweak my heart to know that Marisa would be going off to college within months. Her brother Taz—short for Tasmanian Devil, of course—would be sticking around for a few more years, thank goodness. He enjoyed working part-time at Paper Moon, their book and paper shop on the town square, and I knew Hal and Lizzie loved having him there.

"Oh, here's Chloe and Eric," Jane said, and we all turned to greet them.

Chloe stared up at the ceiling with her mouth open in awe. She gave Jane a big hug. "I'm going to need a minute."

"Take all the time you want," Jane said.

Chloe pressed her hands to her heart. "It's just . . . it's sensational. So much more sophisticated and elegant than I ever dreamed possible." She grabbed Jane's hand and reached for mine. "I'm so proud of you both."

"Thank you, Chloe," Jane whispered.

"And by the way," Chloe added, "you are perfect in this room. You look wonderful."

"Aw." Jane, who had the most romantic heart of all my friends, had dressed in a gracefully flowing long skirt and filmy, rose-colored top. It suited her personality and spirit. She gave Chloe another hug. "Thank you."

Chloe continued looking up. "Seriously, Jane, you did an amazing job."

"It's all because of Shannon," she said. "I mean, she and her guys made it happen."

"It helps that the ceilings are twenty feet tall," I said. "Really adds to the drama."

"I would love to film this room for the show," Chloe said. "In fact, I'd love to film the whole place."

"That would be fabulous," Jane said. "Anytime."

"God, this space," Chloe said, still looking in every direction. "I'm so glad I took some video of it when you first started because I'll really be able to highlight the work you've done. You've turned it into a showcase."

"Wait'll you see the hotel rooms," Niall said. "They are extraordinary."

"I'd love to see them," Marigold said.

Jane nodded. "We'll give you all a tour after dinner."

Marigold clapped her hands. "I can't wait."

Even though the hotel was completely clean and refurbished, the place still gave me the occasional chill. After all, some of us had almost died confronting that former resident of the asylum. Jane had made the difficult decision to keep the basement baths just as they had been in the past, as a stark reminder of what had taken place in the old asylum days.

Mac and I had run into some serious trouble in the "Baths," as they called that area. Jane had asked us both whether to keep them as is or demolish them. It was not an easy decision, but it seemed important to have a historical record of what happened here.

For contrast, Jane had designated one room off the main hall as "Grace's Room." Grace Hennessey was Jane's mother, and it was she who had inspired Jane to buy the property and replace those old memories with newer, lighter ones. The room had a serene elegance, with its comfortable couches and chairs, its view of the ocean, and its display of vintage photographs and artwork created by the patients. Jane's hope was that other relatives of patients would find some peace here.

I managed to let those complicated thoughts drift away as a waiter offered me a glass of champagne and a delectable selection of hors d'oeuvres on a small plate. I had a sip of the bubbly, then took a bite of one of the appetizers—and realized that Jane was staring at me.

"Well?" she asked.

"I can't talk right now." I closed my eyes. "I'm having a private moment with this wrapped pesto-burrata, sweet-corn thingy."

"Isn't that amazing?"

"Mmmm-erm," I mumbled.

She laughed and left to mingle with the others. A little while later, we all took our seats at the table.

"We're serving lots of small dishes tonight," Jane said. "That way you can get a good idea of what's on the regular menu."

"Sounds wonderful," Emily said.

Chloe leaned over and whispered, "My goodness, we're all so well behaved tonight. I know that's not the way you girls usually act when you get together."

I had to laugh. "True, we're a pretty raucous bunch. But this room is so fancy, it makes you want to talk in hushed tones, doesn't it?"

She glanced around. "Totally."

"And this is Jane's first dinner here," I added, "so it's special for all of us."

"I'm so glad she invited me."

"You've become part of the group," I said.

"That's so nice." Chloe sniffled. "I have to admit I've tried not to be jealous that you have so many good friends."

"But you have lots of friends," I protested.

She shook her head. "They're mostly work friends. If I ever leave the show, I'll never see them again."

Her words made me sad, but I didn't want to dwell on it. Instead I said, "Well, look around, because these people are your friends now, too."

"Including me." Eric had been listening, and now he took Chloe's hand and brought it to his lips. "I love you."

I sighed, turned to Mac, and smiled.

"Pretty nice evening," he said, kissing me.

"It's the best."

The staff was quietly attentive as they served dishes and filled wineglasses. Every small plate was accompanied by a new and different wine. As dusk turned to dark, the world outside the windows turned magical with the moon rising in the sky and reflecting on the water.

We chatted and laughed and talked about everything that had been going on lately. I told them all the latest happenings at Homefront and the progress we'd made on the tiny houses.

"Shannon," Lizzie said quietly. "I heard that you found Linda."

I gasped. "Where did you hear that?"

She raised her eyebrows. "Seriously? Are you familiar with the term *small town*?"

"Yeah," I muttered. "Just didn't expect to talk about it tonight." And in my defense, I wasn't actually the one who had found Linda. That dubious honor went to those six writers. But I wasn't about to bring up that point just then.

"I wasn't sure whether to mention it," Lizzie said. "But everyone in town has heard about poor Linda. It must've been such a shock for you."

"It was."

"Linda was such a sweetheart," Marigold said. "It broke my heart when I heard the news."

"Is there anything we can do to help?" Jane asked.

Emily spoke up. "Yes, Shannon. Whatever you need. We can help."

Lizzie nodded in sympathy. "Just tell us what we can do."

"Please, Shannon," Jane said. "Linda was a good friend. We would all be glad to help you find the person who killed her."

I didn't dare look at Eric. "I'd rather we didn't talk about this while the, ahem, chief of police is sitting at the table."

"Oh, don't mind me," Eric drawled. "Go right ahead."

It was true. My girlfriends and I had actually been helpful in the past when it came to digging up information and hunting down suspects. Among the five of us—now six, with Chloe—we knew just about everyone in town. So it had never been a problem to approach our friends, neighbors, and fellow shopkeepers and grill them—er, *question* them—about certain suspicious characters they might've been aware of.

Still, Eric was sitting *right there*.

Mac caught my horrified expression and squeezed my hand. "You have nothing to be ashamed of. You all could give the Baker Street Irregulars a run for their money."

Emily smiled. "We're not quite as scruffy, but we get the job done."

"And Eric is much better looking than Sherlock Holmes," Chloe said. "Although not quite as quirky."

I took another bracing sip of wine. "I'm afraid you guys can't help with this one." I glanced at Eric. "I have no idea what direction Eric's investigation is taking, but as far as I'm concerned, the most suspicious characters are those six writers who are staying at Mac's mansion. And nobody in town knows them well enough to have an opinion."

"I know them," Lizzie said. "They've all come in a few times to ask about book signings. And they do like to spend money."

I exchanged a look with Mac. "Are they doing a book signing?"

Mac's jaw tightened. "No."

"I was a little confused at first," Lizzie explained, "because you usually set up a book signing for each writers' group."

Mac winced. "Sorry. I was just getting started on a new book and got distracted. But once they were here for a few days, I decided to blow off the book signing."

Maybe it was harsh, but I was glad Mac had forgotten to set up the book signing. He had done enough for them.

"Lewis Bondurant's first book has been a big seller for us," Lizzie said. "And I heard his next book is going to be even bigger."

Mac and I exchanged a quick look. As a bookseller, Lizzie would be up on all the latest publishing news.

"What have you heard about the new book?" Mac asked.

Lizzie sipped her wine. "There's a lot of buzz, but not much substance. I guess that's to be expected."

"Right," Mac said. "They want to tease you a little."

Lizzie nodded. "Exactly. Anyway, I've heard this book is a real departure from the first book. More of a romantic adventure, believe it or not."

"That's different," I said.

"I'll say," she said. "And I have to admit, I'm intrigued."

I trusted my friends without qualification, but I wasn't ready to bring up the possibility that Lewis had stolen the story idea. Not until Mac and I could prove it.

"The two women came into the tea shop the other day," Emily said.

"Two women?" I asked, distracted by the thought of Lewis.

"The writers," she explained. "They bought a dozen scones and a large bag of biscuits."

"What did you think of them?" Mac asked.

"A bit pretentious," Emily said, "but pleasant enough. Except they did try to bargain down the price."

"Why?" I asked, annoyed on Emily's behalf.

"They said that one of the scones was broken"— Emily frowned—"but it wasn't broken when I put it in the box. I'm very careful with my baked goods."

"Yes, you are," I said, in her defense.

"Nevertheless, I subtracted the price of the one scone," Emily admitted.

"*Pretentious* is the right word," Lizzie agreed. "But to be fair, we get that from a lot of people who visit from big cities. They can't help themselves. It's like, they're shocked—I tell you, shocked!—that we read books here."

Mac laughed. "Yeah, I hear that a lot."

"I met one of them," Marigold said. "A blond fellow. He came into Crafts and Quilts just this morning and took pictures of all the quilts. I was fine with that, but then he started a conversation with me, and he kept the video going."

"What did you do?" I asked.

"I told him to stop." Marigold shook her head. "What's wrong with people?"

"Do you know this guy?" Rafe asked, on the defensive after Marigold's statement.

"Yeah, I know him," Mac said, his jaw set in a hard line. "Don't worry. It won't happen again."

Thankfully, Lizzie changed the topic, moving on to the subject of the newest cool papers and pens and other good stuff she and Hal were selling in their store.

Marigold and Rafe told us about their ice cream venture. A year ago, Rafe had cashed in his partnership in a high-tech start-up and bought a five-hundred-acre farm outside of town. It had a barn, and he figured, why not fill the barn with milking cows? So what else could they do with all that milk but start making ice cream?

"By the way," Jane said. "We're serving Rafe's ice cream for dessert, among other yummy goodies."

With that announcement, there were more toasts and cheers.

"Jane, everything is fantastic," Hal said.

"Thanks, sweetie."

I thought the time was just about right, so I stood, held up my wineglass, and gazed at my best friend since first grade. "Jane, you amaze us all. Thank you for this wonderful evening. You've brought a new level of excellence and beauty to the Gables and to Lighthouse Cove. Your mother would be so proud of you."

She looked at me and shook her head. "You're determined to make me cry, aren't you?"

I smiled. "Is it working?"

"Yes, damn you." She dabbed at her eyes with her napkin, and everyone laughed. Then we all toasted her by clinking our wineglasses and drinking heartily.

"I see that it's come to that time of the evening when we do our best to make Jane cry," Emily said in her soft Scottish brogue. Gus helped push her chair back, and they both stood up. Emily took a deep breath. "So I would like to take this opportunity to announce my engagement to this darling man, Gus Peratti."

"About damn time," her brother, Niall, shouted and raised his glass.

"How does Mrs. Rawley feel about this?" Lizzie asked. Mrs. Rawley was the ghost that haunted their home.

"She's blissfully happy," Emily said.

Everyone cheered again and laughed as Gus grabbed her in a classic swoony kiss.

And as predicted, my romantic friend, Jane, burst into more happy tears. But she wasn't alone this time as my girlfriends and I dabbed our own eyes at the joyous news.

Chapter Nine

The next day was Sunday. Mac, Chloe, and I piled into Eric's SUV and drove inland through the forest, winding around dangerous curves for an hour until we reached the edge of the Anderson Valley wine country.

We were still a few miles from the town of Navarro when I remembered to ask Eric about the lighthouse. My mind was really slipping, I thought. I had too much going on.

"Did your patrol find anything when they went by the lighthouse yesterday?"

"I've been meaning to tell you what happened," Eric said. "I apologize, because the short answer is no. By the time they got there, everyone had already left the scene."

I scowled. "Rats."

"I will disclose that Ginny got the message to me right away," he said. "I wanted to make sure you knew."

"Ginny's great," I said.

"Yeah, she is. But the rest of us were held up by a little fracas at the high school."

"A fracas?" I smiled at the old-fashioned word. "I like it."

"Well, I didn't like what I saw at the school. It wasn't our kids, but the visiting team had a couple of hooligans who were here to make trouble."

Hooligans, I thought. Another excellent word.

"What happened?" Mac asked.

"They were actually fighting among themselves," Eric said. "Our team just sat back and shook their heads. But then the visitors started to turn on our guys, and we hurried in to break it up. We called the parents of the fighters to come get them. I wasn't going to let them get back on the team bus and drive off into the sunset. First of all, because they would've kept fighting. And second, I wanted some accountability from the parents. So we ended up staying for several hours."

"Doesn't that sound like fun?" I said.

"Bet those parents weren't too happy to make that drive," Chloe said.

"No, they weren't. We made it clear that the other team would not be invited here again, and Coach Wilkins is calling the county organization to complain about them."

"Good," Mac said.

"Those kids aren't the only visiting hooligans," I grumbled.

"What do you mean?"

"I mean those freaking writers. They're nothing but trouble. They invaded the lighthouse again, and I really can't wait for them to get out of town."

"It won't be long now," Mac said, squeezing my knee in sympathy.

True, I thought. Unless one of them had killed Linda. Then they'd be sticking around for a while, in a jail cell.

I hated to complain about them again, especially because I knew that Mac was starting to take it personally. He blamed himself for bringing them to town, but it wasn't his fault that they were behaving like grown-up hooligans.

"I've got to get over to the lighthouse tomorrow. I'll take Wade with me. We'll do another walk-through and make sure they haven't damaged anything inside the building."

"Just what are you expecting to find?" Eric asked in his best police-chief tone.

"With these people, I wouldn't be surprised to find graffiti all over the place."

"Really?" Chloe asked.

I scowled. "No. But I still want to make sure."

I forced myself to relax and take in the beauty around us. It only took some deep breaths and a few minutes of gazing at the rolling green hills covered in grapevines to chill me out.

A few minutes later, Eric turned into a long driveway and parked near a beautiful glass-walled building. It was Bella Rosso, Uncle Pete's vineyard and winery. It never failed to bring a happy smile to my face. The views from the tasting room were spectacular, and today the weather contributed, with breezy blue skies covering the valley and the dark green mountains in the distance.

My father and his beloved Belinda greeted us at the

door leading into the rustically elegant tasting room. They had first met right here, soon after Uncle Pete hired her as his new winemaker. She had worked in some of the greatest winehouses in Bordeaux before coming back to California and settling in the Anderson Valley.

"Dad," I whispered. "You look great."

"I'm feeling pretty great these days." A while ago he had been living in an RV parked in my driveway. Then he bought a boat and lived on it until he met Belinda. Recently he had moved out to Uncle Pete's ranch house to help with the ongoing construction of the winery and to see Belinda more often. "We're in the middle of building a small room off the main barrel room to house the concrete casks."

These concrete barrels were the latest thing in wine fermentation and aging. Shaped like big eggs, they were about seven feet tall and six feet in diameter at their widest point. On our last visit, Belinda had explained that concrete was ideal because it was a neutral material as well as being semiporous. This allowed for micro-oxygenation similar to a wood barrel, but without the added oaky flavor.

That made sense, even to a science-free brain like mine.

Belinda gave each of us a big squeezing hug. "It's so good to see you. I love it when you visit. It makes your dad so happy."

Uncle Pete came in a minute later, and there were more hugs.

After a few minutes of catching up on all the goings-on in our lives, Belinda said, "We thought we'd take a walk around the vineyards to show you our latest plantings, then we'll have a little lunch."

"Sounds wonderful," I said.

While we walked, we talked about Homefront and the progress we had made over the last month. "Dad, you won't believe how many houses we've been able to build in such a short time. It's heartening to see things coming together to make it happen so quickly."

I was determined not to mention Linda's murder. I knew it would upset Dad, and I wanted this visit to be carefree and enjoyable for him and for all of us.

I told them about my construction class, and Chloe talked about the latest excitement on her TV show. She made Dad shed a tear when she announced that she would finally be able to move to Lighthouse Cove next month. She would still commute to Hollywood about ten days a month or so, but she would live most of the time with Eric.

I took a quick glance at Eric. He looked awfully pleased as well.

Belinda gave Chloe a big hug. "I'm so glad it's happening at last."

"Me, too. My schedule has been completely whacko for months, but it's starting to calm down, and I'm going to make it happen."

"Yay!" I said.

"With that good news," Belinda said, "Let's have a celebratory barrel tasting and then lunch."

I loved barrel tastings. Every time I visited Uncle Pete, I gave thanks to the wine gods for allowing my uncle to grow grapes and make wine. And for allowing me to indulge in the rich, fruity deliciousness of Pete's award-winning Pinot Noirs and Cabernets. And straight from the barrel with the help of a little tool they called a "wine thief," which made it so easy.

Lunch was lovely and relaxed. Belinda and her crew filled the table with platters of caprese salad with creamy Burrata and fresh basil; a pasta salad with a Greek twist that had tomatoes, cucumbers, bell pepper, Kalamata olives, and chunks of feta; and a charcuterie board with every kind of sliced meat you could imagine, along with ramekins of fig jam, peach preserves, and honeycomb. There were tangy cornichons, dried fruits, and whole salted pecans, as well as six different kinds of cheeses, from hard Manchego to warm Brie.

Another platter held everything to make our own tacos, along with a stack of homemade tamales and mini quesadillas filled with champagne grapes and Camembert.

"Uncle Pete, you've outdone yourself," Chloe said. "Everything is wonderful."

"Huh?" he said. "Did you think I fixed all this food?"

"Then who did?" Chloe asked.

Belinda laughed. "Don't look at me. I can barely cook cold cereal."

"Don't let her fool you," Dad said fondly. "She cooks great cold cereal."

We all laughed, then I asked, "So who puts all this together for you?"

"This spread was put together by one of Belinda's assistants. He usually works his magic in the barrel room, but I think he was born to be a chef."

I wouldn't disagree. The food was amazing. And then there was dessert. Hot fudge sundaes with homemade ice cream.

"Is this Rafe's ice cream?" I asked.

"You bet," Belinda said. "Isn't it the greatest?"

"I would have to agree," Eric said.

It came as no surprise when Chloe and I both asked for second helpings. This had always been our favorite dessert, so we were in heaven. I was getting full and sleepy, and I wondered briefly how my stomach would fare on that winding, curvy ride home. But this dessert, along with the company, was totally worth it.

A while later, Dad, Belinda, and Uncle Pete walked with us to the car.

"I hope you can get into town sometime soon," I said. "I really want you to see how much the village has grown. I feel so good about this project."

"Me, too," Chloe said. "Of course, Mac and Eric are the miracle workers who made all the pieces come together."

"We had a lot of help," Mac said.

"It's a remarkable achievement all around," Pete said. He nudged Eric, and the two men walked across the parking lot, talking about something.

Dad glanced at Belinda. "We can probably get away sometime next week. I'm anxious to see how much it's changed since the last time we were there."

"You saw it in the beginning when the first few houses were going up," I said. "Now it's becoming a thriving village."

"We'll put our heads together," Belinda said, "pick a date, and give you a call."

"Good."

There were more hugs all around. Then we climbed back into Eric's SUV and hit the road.

As we started to head west, I asked, "What did Uncle Pete want to talk about?"

"He was in town last week for a meeting at the wine bar."

"He came into town?" I glanced at Chloe. "Did you know that?"

"He was only here for the meeting with his staff," Eric said. "But while he was here, he heard about Linda Rutledge. He wanted to ask me what happened and whether or not Shannon was involved."

"Why me?" I asked, hating to sound so defensive.

"Shannon, you know why," Chloe said.

"I guess I do, but it's not fair."

Mac slipped his arm around my shoulder.

Eric met my gaze in the rearview mirror. "I don't like it any more than you do. I wish I could do something to prevent it. I know it can be really painful."

I thought of Linda again and had to suck in a breath. "This time it really hurts."

Chloe turned around in her seat and patted my knee. "Maybe you could look at it the way Marigold sees it. As a gift."

"How can that be a gift?" I wondered, trying to keep from whining.

"Because you not only find dead bodies," Mac pointed out. "You also try to find justice for them."

I blinked.

"Good point," Eric said. "I'll be happy if it never happens again. But if it does, I want you to know ahead of time that I admire your persistence in tracking down the people responsible for the crime."

I stared at his eyes in the mirror. "I really appreciate you saying that, Eric."

"But," he added, scowling at me in the rearview mirror, "I'd appreciate it even more if you didn't always try to face down some crazy whacked-out killer all by yourself."

"I'd go along with that," Mac said mildly, giving me a light squeeze.

I laid my head on his shoulder. "I'm right there with you."

I showed up at the lighthouse at six thirty the next morning. I had called Wade the night before and asked him to meet me, and naturally, he was already there waiting for me. I joined him at the lighthouse door. "Sorry to get you up so early, but I really need to check on things."

"No problem," he said genially. "I'm usually up and out around this time anyway." We both had keys to the door, so he opened it, and I stepped inside.

The cavernous structure looked the same as usual at first glance. It was an impressive sight to stare up at that circular iron staircase that ascended well over 120 feet to the lantern room.

"Looks okay so far," Wade said. "You want to go all the way up?"

"Yeah. Sorry. I just don't trust the people who've been breaking in here lately."

We both knew who I was referring to.

"Didn't think we'd be getting this much exercise this morning," he said, and swept his arm upward. "After you."

I took the first step. "Here goes."

We climbed twenty steps up to the chained-off landing where the circular iron steps began. We both slipped under the chain.

"It's not like we put up any great barriers to get in here," he murmured.

"Just a dozen warning signs and a locked door," I said cynically. "Who would pay attention to those?"

"Apparently, not these people."

The iron staircase was steep and narrow, and as I moved up, I used my flashlight to make some quick checks of the spots where I knew there was some weakness. Despite that, the staircase was still remarkably strong after so many years.

There were several landings with space enough to accommodate two or three visitors who wanted to take a quick break from the staircase and look at the view from the window. Beneath each window was an old wooden bench for anyone who needed to rest. I checked to make sure that the wood hadn't been damaged or destroyed, then continued up to the next landing.

At the top, the wooden door that led out to the catwalk was damaged. Someone had jammed the lock and jabbed at the old splintered wood until it gave way.

I shook my head, almost speechless. "This makes me so angry. What gives them the right to destroy things?"

"They feel entitled," Wade said. "Probably think that because they paid money to attend the retreat, it gives them the right to do whatever they want."

"Yeah. That's kind of sick."

"It sure is." He swung the door open to check the damage. "We were going to have to replace this door anyway."

"I know, but that's no excuse," I said. "Let's check the lens room. If they damaged the lantern room or the Fresnel lens in any way, I'll have them arrested."

I arrived at the community center thirty minutes later and quickly began to set up everything for us to start hanging drywall. I had changed our start time to nine o'clock, and since the memorial service for Linda would take place at eleven o'clock, I was determined to get at least a good hour of work done before we had to leave.

Wade and I hadn't found any damage to the lens or lantern room. In fact, it didn't look like anyone had been in there since he and I did our last walk-through.

We decided that the writers must've stopped at the catwalk and simply hung out there, enjoying the view. If so, it was a good decision on their part, because I'd been deadly serious about trying to have them thrown in jail if they'd gone any farther.

Just thinking about it made my muscles tighten, and I had to force myself to shake it off and get back to the work of finishing this partition wall.

The first thing I did was nail a three-foot-long two-by-four to the middle of the frame. I made sure it was perfectly level, because I planned to use it to steady and level the large sheets of drywall before sliding them up to the ceiling and screwing them down. Later, I would remove the two-by-four from this side of the wall and nail it to the other side.

As with so many handy tricks, I had learned this one from my father. It was especially helpful when I was the only one hanging drywall. But even with another helper around, it still made the work easier.

I laid out all of the tools we would need for the job. I checked my power drill to make sure I had the right drill bit.

A lot of people nailed their drywall sheets, but I had always used screws. I'd seen too many nails pop up after a while and it wasn't pretty. Basically, it ruined the look of the finished wall. Screws tended to stay put.

At a little before nine o'clock, Chloe walked into the room carrying a cardboard tray with two caffe lattes. When she saw me, she frowned. "Darn. I thought I'd beat you here."

"I got here early to set everything up."

She handed me one of the lattes.

"Thanks." I took a sip. "Delish."

She set her purse down in the corner. "You're all ready to go with the drywall panels. Did elves deliver them in the night?"

"Yes. They're good little workers."

She smirked. "I love elves."

I took a long drink of my latte. "We've only got an hour or so before we have to leave for Linda's memorial."

"We should be able to get one side of the wall covered in that time."

"I think so, too."

"I brought my power drill," she said. "But it's still in the car. I thought it was more important to get the lattes in here than bother with power tools."

"I love your attitude. So regal."

She laughed. "I'll go get the drill."

Once again we lucked out with our measurements—although it wasn't really luck at all. I already knew the wall was sixteen feet wide and the drywall panels were four by eight feet. That meant that we only needed two panels to cover the top part of the wall. As far as I was concerned, the fewer panels, the better. It meant less drywall tape, less mud, and less hassle.

We slid the first panel all the way up to the ceiling and then starting drilling the screws into the studs.

As we worked, Chloe and I carried on a meandering conversation in low tones. We talked about our trip to the winery and chatted about Dad and Belinda and Uncle Pete.

Chloe asked me how I was feeling about Linda, and I told her what it was like to find her lying in the sand the other night. Then I told her about the writers and how they'd behaved.

"They're not very pleasant people," she said.

"And so immature," I added. "I feel bad for Mac because every other writers' group has been great. We thought it would always be that way, but I guess it was just a matter of time before we got a dud."

"Hey, you might never get another dud group again."

"That would be wonderful."

We continued drilling screws into the drywall, then hung another piece.

"I wish I knew who hurt her," I said.

"Do you know how she died?" Chloe asked.

I glanced around, then felt foolish for doing so. It wasn't like anyone was listening to us. "Yeah, but don't tell Eric I told you."

She smiled. "I won't."

I took a deep breath. "She was hit in the head, bludgeoned with one of her own mallets."

"Oh, that's awful." She stopped drilling for a minute and looked pensive.

"What's up?"

"There's something I forgot to tell you. I'm not even sure it's important, but it might mean something."

"Tell me."

Chloe laid her power drill down on the plywood table. "Just last night, I was looking at all the videos I took this last week. I was right outside in the parking lot, getting a wide shot of the property, and I saw someone running at the far end, carrying some tools. At least, I thought they were tools. I thought it was one of your guys, carrying a couple of small pickaxes or some hammers. But now I'm wondering if they might've been mallets. I just couldn't see well enough."

"It could've been any of our guys," I said.

"Yeah, except that he was running between houses and clutching the tools." She wrapped her hands around her chest. "Like this. Holding them close to his body. None of us carries tools that way."

"Not usually."

"The immediate impression I got was that he was hiding. He moved quickly from house to house as if he was trying not to be seen."

"Are you sure about this?" I asked. "It sounds weird."

"I'm pretty sure," she said. "Oh, and he wasn't dressed like any of our guys."

"How was he dressed?"

"From where I was standing, I thought he might be wearing khakis or Dockers and a big brown jacket."

I chuckled. "You're right. It doesn't sound like one of our guys."

"The guys on your crew wouldn't be caught dead in Dockers. I mean, not while they're working anyway."

"Agreed. It's definitely a blue jeans crowd." I stared out the window and saw all the activity going on. It was a good thing to see. *Inspiring,* I thought. "You know, it could've been one of the vets."

She blew out a breath. "I never thought of that. You're right." She pursed her lips in thought. "But even the vets

I've seen don't usually run around with tools." She waved her hand away. "Look, it's probably nothing."

"Can you zoom in on the image?"

"I tried that and it just got blurry." She gave me a considering look. "But look, you're around here all the time. You might be able to take one look at the video and know who it was."

"Yes," I said eagerly. "I want to see it."

There was a scuffling sound out in the hall, and I suddenly wondered if someone was listening to our conversation. Not that it mattered, but I was in a jumpy mood lately. I reminded myself that we were in a hurry. "We need to get this done and go to the memorial."

"Yeah, sorry." She picked up her power drill. "I'm probably blowing this way out of proportion. But why don't you and Mac come over for dinner tonight, and you can take a look at the video?"

"Great idea. I'll let Mac know."

She smiled wryly. "And I'll let Eric know that we're having company."

"Has he seen the video?"

"Nope." She smiled. "We'll all look at it together."

The memorial service for Linda was lovely, although I spent most of the time observing the people. Was Linda's killer here among the crowd? How would I recognize him? Or her? I didn't know what to look for. Suspicious moves? Clutching tools? A mallet in their pocket?

I suddenly remembered Eric's words in the car yesterday. Was I trying to face down a whacked-out killer? I didn't think so. I was just trying to figure out the truth.

There were photographs of Linda everywhere. Her

entire life was memorialized in pictures, from the time she was born, all the way through school and into the army. Examples of her mosaic artwork were hung on the walls, and I still marveled at how talented she was. And beautiful, too, as all those photographs proved.

Julia spoke of Linda and the courage she showed in the military and what her friendship had meant to her. I was glad I'd brought a handful of tissues because I was not able to keep from sobbing through some of it.

I was so glad that Mac was here with me. When he put his arm around my shoulder and held me close, I was pitifully grateful for his quiet strength and his love and support.

A friend of Linda's played guitar and sang some of her favorite songs, then played quietly while people gathered in small groups and shared memories of their friend.

Travis approached and simply wrapped his arms around me in a warm hug. "God, I miss her."

"I do, too."

"I lost some buddies during the war, and there were times when I didn't know if I could make it through another day without them."

"I'm so sorry."

"Thanks." He let me go, then sniffled, trying to get a grip on his emotions. "But the thing is, believe it or not, this is worse. You know, Linda and I were just friends. I'd only known her a short while, but she was so good, so honest, so fresh and real. God, losing her feels like I've lost a limb. It's like a part of myself is gone. She was so . . . vital."

"I didn't know her very well," I said, "but I liked her from the first moment. It makes me sad to know I won't see her and talk to her again."

He was quiet for a long time, then he said, "I can see her in my mind. I know she's here with us."

I stared at him, then nodded. "I'm glad."

A while later, I spotted Annabelle, Sheri, Hugh, and Kingsley. I wondered where the other two writers were. At a side table filled with tiny pastries and cookies and a huge coffee urn, I managed to corner Sheri to ask her about Lewis.

"I didn't see him here," I said casually. "I guess he must be really bummed about Linda."

Sheri narrowed her eyes. "I'm not a fool. I know you and the cops are trying to frame Lewis for Linda's death."

"What?" I was truly taken aback. She was wrong, and the only thing I could do was deny it rigorously. "No, I'm not. I would never do something like that. Why would you even say it?"

"Because I'm not stupid," she said indignantly. "I'm warning you. Leave Lewis alone."

She stomped off, leaving me a little breathless. I hadn't thought Sheri was stupid at all. However, since she was so passionate about standing up for the odious Lewis, I might have to reconsider.

I wasn't sure why she was so angry, but then I thought about it. The way she'd been defending Lewis so ardently, I suddenly had to wonder if maybe she was jealous of Linda. And if she had been jealous of Linda, then Sheri just might have a motive for murder.

Chapter Ten

After the two-hour service, I wanted nothing more than to throw myself into work. I had always found it the best remedy for whatever was getting me down. Chloe felt the same way, so as soon as we returned to the community center, we quickly jumped right back into the job of hanging drywall.

She once again strapped on her tool belt. "You ready?"

"Yeah." I took a deep breath and blew it out. "Sorry. But that was rough."

"I know. But wasn't it nice to see how many people were there?"

"It felt like the whole town came out." I buckled my tool belt, checked the pockets. "So many people talked about how lovely and gentle she was."

"I only met her that one night in your construction class, but she seemed like a real sweetheart."

"She was."

Chloe checked her power drill, revving it once to make sure everything was ready to go. "What the—?"

"What's wrong?"

She stared at the tool. "My drill is set in reverse."

"Oh. You must've accidentally nudged the reverse button before we left."

"I didn't," she muttered. "Why would I do that?" She went ahead and pushed the toggle button back to its normal position.

With drywall hanging on the top of the partition wall, I had to bend down and look through the frame to see the other room. I saw the sawhorses folded up on the far wall. Standing upright, I said, "Well, heck. Now that the drywall is up, I've got to go all the way around to the other door to get those sawhorses."

Chloe laughed. "You can handle that long walk."

I made an impatient sound, somewhere between a grunt and *humph*.

Chloe pulled out her claw hammer and pointed to the partition frame. "We won't need this temporary two-by-four here anymore, so I'm going to take it off and attach it to the other side of the wall."

"Good thinking. I'll be right back."

I walked out the door and turned down the hall. On the other side of the wall, I pulled the sawhorses closer to the frame and opened them up. As I'd done before, I would use the sawhorses to cut the panels down to size.

Cutting drywall was the easiest part of the whole process. I always used a long steel T square to mark the cutting line, then run my X-Acto knife down the line. I usually cut through it twice because the drywall we used was five-eighths of an inch thick, and the first cut didn't always get through it. Then I would turn the panel around and easily cut through the thin paper backing.

I studied the unfinished partition wall from this side. "We built a pretty great wall," I said loud enough for Chloe to hear.

"Oh yeah, we did," she said from the other side. "We totally rock."

I glanced up at the top plate of the wall and frowned. "What the heck?"

"What?" Chloe asked.

I stared at the sight and wondered if I was hallucinating. I knew for a fact that I had screwed the frame to the ceiling joist before we hung the first drywall panel. I moved closer, squinted harder. "This is bizarre."

All the screws were gone. They were just *gone*.

"I think I'm having an out-of-body experience," I said.

Chloe wasn't listening. "Darn. There's always one nail that won't budge." I could hear her straining.

And suddenly the heavy partition wall was moving, leaning, then falling toward me.

"Chloe!" I shouted.

She screamed. "Shannon! I can't stop it!"

I dropped to the floor between the two sawhorses and curled up under them, then wrapped my arms around my head.

I could still hear Chloe's screams, but I couldn't respond. All I could do was whimper in panic as the wall came crashing down on top of me. I couldn't feel it, though, and for one sickening moment, I thought I might be paralyzed.

It felt like minutes, but it was probably only a few seconds. I heard Chloe scrambling and stumbling and swearing, then suddenly she came rushing down the hall and over to my side of the wall. She was followed quickly by two men I recognized as veterans.

"She's buried under there!" Chloe shouted.

"I think I'm okay," I whispered. Except I wasn't sure.

The air around me shifted, and I realized that the frame was being lifted up. I wasn't paralyzed at all. And I was still breathing. I was alive.

"Shannon! Where are you hurt?"

"I'm not sure." I managed to croak out the words, my body still curled around the sawhorse.

"Oh my God," she cried. "I'm so sorry! It's all my fault."

"No, it's not." I couldn't say much else for another minute, until one of the vets pulled the sawhorse away, and I slowly rolled over onto my back and stared up at Chloe.

"What happened?" I asked.

She was breathing hard and talking fast. "I was pulling out the nails in the two-by-four, and I had to push really hard against the wall as a lever to force one of them loose. I must've pushed so hard that I loosened the partition wall and caused it to fall over on top of you."

"No." I was still lying flat on the floor, catching my breath. "No, you didn't." I pointed up at the ceiling. "Look. Top plate. Screws are missing."

After I was finally able to push myself up off the floor, I had to test my legs and flex every muscle in my body to determine if I was injured anywhere. I was fine, just a little freaked out and achy from throwing myself onto the floor. We thanked the vets, then Chloe and I decided to walk away from the ugliness of the fallen wall for a few minutes. We locked the doors and walked down the hall to the café, where we ordered tea and cookies. Cookies made everything better.

I happened to know that the cookies here were amazing. That was because they were baked daily by my friend Emily Rose at her tea shop on the town square. She supplied the café with dozens of cookies and pastries every day, and the café promptly sold out of them. The vets who lived here were smart people who knew their cookies.

Happily the café had restocked the cookie supply after the lunch rush. We bought a few for the two guys who had helped us, and they were perfectly happy to take cookies for payment. Everyone loved Emily's cookies. They were comfort food of the highest order.

And comfort was what Chloe and I needed at that moment. We sipped our tea and slowly pieced together what must've happened.

"I told you my drill was set in reverse mode. Someone must've used it to remove all the screws."

I nodded. "I thought you had accidentally changed the rotation."

"Would you have done that?" she asked pointedly.

"No, of course not."

"Right? And neither would I."

"I know that." I squeezed her hand. "I just never imagined someone else would do it, so I brushed it off as a mistake."

She blew out a breath, and I could tell she was

drained of energy. "I'm just glad those sawhorses were sitting there," she said. "They broke the fall."

"I barely managed to drop down in time to avoid the wall itself."

"You managed to do that while the wall was falling?"

"Yeah. Then I covered my head and got as close as I could to the sawhorse."

"That was fast, smart thinking."

I grimaced. "I should've brought hardhats for both of us. I just didn't think we would need them for this job." I stared at the cookie in my hand, hesitant to accept what I knew was true. "Someone unscrewed all of the top and bottom plate screws. Someone walked in and did that while we were at the memorial service."

"I still can't believe it," Chloe whispered, shaking her head. "It's, like, diabolical."

"Maybe. But it's idiotic, too. First of all, anyone could've seen them do it. We'll have to ask around, see if anyone saw someone enter our room. And second, that wall wasn't going to kill us, right? It's basically just the frame, so it's not heavy enough yet. But yeah, it battered me a little."

Chloe rubbed her head. "Me, too."

And that's when I noticed the lump on her forehead. "Wait a minute. Are you hurt?"

She held up a hand. "Just a bit. I'm more concerned about you."

"I've got some aches and bumps, and my wrist is a little twisted. But the sawhorse took the brunt of the wall's weight. But what happened to you? How did you get hurt?"

She tightened her lips. "I sort of . . . fell forward . . . with the wall. When it hit the sawhorse, the wall stopped abruptly, but my head . . . kept going. My forehead slammed into one of the studs."

I stared at her. "Oh, ouch. You were hurt way worse than I was."

She rubbed both hands over her face, then she sniffled a little. "I thought I squished you."

I reached for her arm. "I'm okay."

"Me, too." She wiped her eyes. "These are just a few post-wall-falling tears."

I had to laugh but slowly sobered. "Chloe, someone deliberately sabotaged our work."

She gazed at me for a long moment, then pulled out her phone. "I'm calling Eric."

Eric made it to the center in fifteen minutes. He checked out Chloe and me, then went around and questioned all of the vets and employees in the community center, then backtracked and checked inside every office in the building for anybody he hadn't talked to. He stopped at the café and questioned the two fellows who shared the jobs of cook, busboy, and dishwasher. Nobody had seen anything odd or suspicious.

Chloe and I showed Eric the room where we'd been working. The partition wall lay at an awkward angle over the sawhorse.

"What happened when you returned from the memorial service?" He pulled out a notepad and pen. "Give me every detail."

"Before we get ahead of ourselves," I said, "I want to mention that prior to leaving for the memorial, I distinctly heard a shuffling sound out in the hall. I didn't think anything of it, but now I wonder if someone was listening in on our conversation."

"The door was open?" he asked.

"Yes. It was getting a little stuffy in here so I opened both doors."

He nodded. "What were you talking about?"

Oh, shoot. I'd put my foot in it this time, I thought, but proceeded to answer him. "I was just telling Chloe about Linda's mallets and wondering if one of them could be the murder weapon."

His eyes narrowed in on me, and I speculated that despite his kind words on the way home from the winery yesterday, he might be ready to cart me off to jail for spilling the beans about the mallets.

Luckily, Chloe spoke up, distracting him. "I told Shannon about something I'd seen on one of my videos." She described the person she'd seen, his clothing, the fact that he might've been carrying a couple of mallets, and how he was skulking around.

"Oh, and I invited Mac and Shannon over for dinner," Chloe added. "So we can watch the video together. One of you might recognize the guy."

Eric tried to maintain his cool. "So what happened when you returned from the service?" He looked at Chloe. "You said you checked your power drill?"

"Yes, and I noticed that it had been switched to reverse."

"Did you touch it?"

"Well, yes, because I didn't notice it until I pulled the trigger to test it, as I always do. That's when I saw it rotating the wrong way, and I pushed the toggle button to fix it."

"So you touched it in all the usual places."

She smiled. "Yes."

He nodded patiently, although I figured he must be

frustrated at the fact that he wouldn't find any finger-prints on the power drill.

He looked at me. "Shannon, you notice anything?"

"Not until I walked into the other room and saw that all the screws were missing."

"Did you find any screws scattered around?"

"You mean the spent screws? No. He must've taken them with him." I frowned. "Or she."

"You have any reason to believe a woman might've done this?"

I stared at him for a moment and wondered if he was implying that women couldn't handle power tools. Then I realized who I was talking to. And who his girl-friend was. Chloe would kick his butt if he ever even thought it.

I leaned forward. "I had a conversation with Sheri at the memorial service. She's the dark-haired writer in Mac's retreat group."

"Yes, I know who you're talking about."

"I mentioned that I hadn't seen Lewis at the service and wondered if he might be upset because he seemed to really like Linda. It really set her off. She accused me of trying to maneuver Lewis into taking the blame for Linda's murder."

"Meow," Chloe murmured.

"Right?" I nodded. "She's very protective of him, and she's also very jealous. I was thinking while I spoke to her that if Sheri thought Linda was trying to steal Lewis away from the group—and especially from *Sheri*—it might be enough motivation to kill."

"She sounds kind of obsessed," Chloe added.

Eric was jotting it all down. "So you didn't see Lewis at the memorial service?"

My eyes widened as I realized the implication. Lewis might've been in here, sabotaging our work. "I didn't even think about that. I was thinking about Sheri. But no, I didn't see him at the memorial. Pretty sure he wasn't there."

"If he wasn't at the service, he could've been here," Chloe said. "Screwing around with our screws."

"Well put," I said, and every muscle in my body tightened another notch. "That creep."

"Don't point the finger at him just yet," Eric said mildly. "Other than Lewis, were the rest of the writers at the service?"

His words forced me to take a virtual step back and think for a minute. "I didn't see his friend Brian there, either. But maybe I just missed them. I did see the other four. But any one of them could've made it over here and unscrewed everything. They'd have plenty of time to do it since we had to stop at home and change clothes." I held up my hands in apology. "I don't know why I'm so eager to accuse the writers of doing this. Why in the world would they come here and try to hurt us? I'm obviously dwelling on them too much, but they bug me. Sorry."

"Don't be sorry. They bug me, too." He did a quick read through his notes, then asked, "Did you lock the doors when you left for the service?"

I had to think. "I remember locking this door, but I realize now that I never checked the other door, the one down the hall. When I went around to get the saw-horses, it was unlocked." I winced. "It might've been unlocked the whole time."

Eric studied the framing of the partition wall. "And that's the side of the wall where the screws are exposed."

"Exactly," I said, and pointed. "If he came in through this door, he wouldn't have seen the screws in the top plate because the drywall was already in place. Not true of the other side." I stared at the frame for a long moment. "So follow along with me for a minute."

"Okay."

I acted out my words. "He used the power drill to take out the screws on both the top and bottom plates. The ladder was folded up and lying against the far wall. He would need to use it to get to the top. And for both the top and bottom plates, he probably put his hands on the wood surface while he was doing all that unscrewing."

"That's good, Shannon," Eric said. "That's a really good point. His prints might be all over your equipment."

I felt gratified. "Thanks."

"I'm going to call Leo and have him check out this room. I'll let him know about the ladder and the plates. Not sure what he'll pick up on the wood, but if anyone can find a print, Leo can."

"Oh, hey," I said. "The intruder might've left fingerprints on that unlocked door."

"Possibly."

"Oh wait. I opened the door after that, so I probably wiped them away." I cringed. "Sorry."

"I'll still have Leo check it." He brushed his hands together to get rid of the bits of sawdust that were still flittering around the room. "I'll be here a while longer waiting for Leo."

"Okay," Chloe said. "I'm going to go home and prep for our dinner guests."

"Does that mean you'll call and order pizza?" Eric asked.

"And a salad," she added with a smile.

I grinned. "We're not worthy, but thanks. It's our favorite meal."

"Ours, too," Eric said, and pulled Chloe close for a hug.

"Chief Jensen? You in here?" Vince the project manager stuck his head into the room. "There you are, thank God."

"Hey Vince, what's up?"

"Somebody attacked Parks," he said frantically. "He's badly injured."

"Did you call an ambulance?" Eric asked, already striding toward the door.

"No. I didn't think. I knew you were here, so I just ran."

"I'll do it," I said. "Chloe, you go with Eric."

I had offered to make the call because I'd had way too much experience calling for an ambulance over the last few years. I knew exactly who to call and what to say. As soon as I gave Eric's message to Ginny, the dispatch operator for both the police and the ambulance services, I ran like the wind to catch up with Chloe and Eric.

When I reached Parks's house, I could see his inert form sprawled on the sidewalk nearby. Blood was seeping out from beneath his head.

Several veterans and a few of my crew stood close by. I was aware that some of the veterans had been medical technicians or nurses while in the military, so they knew enough not to move Parks until the police arrived.

I spied Heather, the blond medical technician from my construction class, crouched on the ground next to

Parks, monitoring a little machine attached to his index finger.

"Is he alive?" I asked. But how could he be? I wondered. With all that blood?

"He's alive," Heather said. "He's still unconscious, though. His oxygen level is decent, but his heart rate is low. That's to be expected." She sighed. "I'm hopeful that he pulls through without too much damage to his brain functions."

"Thanks, Heather." It was good to know the med-techs were on the scene, I thought.

I found Chloe standing a few feet away and moved to slip my arm through hers. "Are you okay?"

She leaned her head on my shoulder. "Oh God, Shannon. This has been a horrible day."

"Yeah, not one of our best."

We had just attended Linda's memorial service, and now someone else from Homefront had been attacked.

"They said Parks isn't dead," I whispered. "Just unconscious."

"Oh, thank goodness."

The wail of a siren could be heard in the distance, growing louder as it approached.

I glanced across the Parkway and saw Travis run out of his house and head straight for Chloe and me.

"What happened?"

I explained as well as I could.

"Does anybody know how it happened?"

Heather heard his question and turned. "He was hit in the head with some kind of heavy object."

"Oh man," Travis said. "Damn it. Who would do this to Parks? He wouldn't hurt a living soul."

"I don't know." I pulled him close for a hug. Travis and Parks were good friends. "I'm sorry."

As I tried to comfort him, my mind was brimming with fear. *A heavy object?* Had Linda's missing mallet thief found another victim?

Travis's question reverberated. Who would do this to Parks?

Parker Bellingham Jones the fourth, I thought warmly. He was such a character. Staring at his familiar face and scraggly beard, I prayed that he would survive.

I had to hope that I'd counted correctly, and only *two* mallets had been stolen from Linda's mosaic table. Because it appeared that someone was getting a real taste for murder with mallets.

Because of Linda's memorial service earlier in the day and the attack on Parks later that afternoon, Mac had canceled his writing workshop that night. I was still debating whether to go ahead with my construction class tomorrow night. My heart wasn't in it, but maybe it would be a beneficial way to work through the pain, bring the women together, and give them space to talk about their feelings. Afterward, we could take out our frustration and anger with a hammer and nails. I could confirm that it was almost as gratifying as ice cream.

Mac and I decided to walk the six blocks to Eric's home, so I grabbed a jacket to wear over my sage green tunic, black skinny jeans, and short black boots. I had seen Mac earlier at the memorial service, but I hadn't had a chance to catch him up on everything that had happened since then. I described in detail the disaster of the falling wall and then shared the pain of seeing

Parks lying unconscious on the sidewalk with his head bleeding.

Mac stopped and stared at me. He pressed his hands against my cheeks, then leaned forward and kissed me. "I'm so sorry."

"Yeah. It was pretty horrible."

He wrapped his arm around my shoulders and we continued walking. "I'm sorry I wasn't there with you."

"Me, too."

"Do you know how Parks is doing?"

"I was going to ask Eric when we get there." I leaned into him. "I just hope Chloe's video reveals who stole the mallets. We might be able to put all of this to rest very soon."

We walked a full block in silence, each of us thinking our own thoughts. Finally I looked up at him. "Linda told me that it was impossible to go to war and not come home without a touch of PTSD. She admitted that she'd had a mild case of it herself. Mostly consisting of the occasional nightmare."

"She had been luckier than some on that front, I guess."

I hesitated, then said, "We've never talked about it, but did you ever have PTSD?"

He was silent for a long moment. "Yeah, I did, but for me, thankfully, it was never debilitating. I guess I'd have to go along with what Linda said. It's a cliché, but war can be hell. If it doesn't affect you in some way, you might want to check your pulse."

We crossed the street holding hands.

"Even if it's something minor," he continued, "like nightmares or the occasional flashback, it can be pretty rough while it's happening."

"It sounds frightening. Seeing how Travis reacted to the shattering glass the other day? It just about broke my heart."

"Yeah, it's hard to stand by and watch when it's a friend or a loved one. That's why I started writing," Mac said. "I didn't plan to write a book, but it turned out that way. To this day, I put all my fears and anger and worries onto the pages."

"That's why you told Travis to write stuff down."

"Yeah. It helps. That's been my experience anyway."

We reached Eric's house and knocked on the front door. Within seconds, Chloe swung the door open. She wore a peach-colored sweater over black skinny jeans with black flats.

"Hi! Come in!"

Once inside, she gave each of us a hug. "Hey, we're twins." She pressed her skinny jeans–clad leg against mine.

"Aren't we groovy?" I said.

She laughed. "The grooviest." Then she sobered. "How are you doing?"

"I think I'm doing better than you." I brushed her bangs aside. "You still have a bump."

"It was bugging me, so I took some ibuprofen a little while ago."

"I'm so sorry." I gave her a light kiss on the cheek.

"Someday we'll laugh about it, right?"

"I hope so."

"Okay, we have wine, beer, sodas, water, coffee. What would you like to drink?"

"Do I smell pizza?" Mac asked, glancing around the wide-open living room.

Chloe grinned. "Yes, you sure do."

"Then I'll start with a beer and switch to wine with dinner."

"I'll have a glass of red," I said, knowing Chloe would be pouring from a bottle of one of Uncle Pete's best Pinots or Cabernets.

"Come into the kitchen," she said. "That's where it all happens."

As with every other house in Lighthouse Cove, the outer shell of Eric's home was Victorian in style. But his kitchen was big and sleek and very contemporary. It somehow suited his bigger-than-life frame with its wide white quartz island and gleaming, oversized stainless steel appliances. On the opposite side of the room, a kitchen table and chairs were placed next to a picture window that overlooked a charming garden filled with flowering plants and fruit trees. A cobblestone pathway meandered around the trees and led to a rustic wrought iron table and chairs under a grapevine-covered pergola.

It was lovely and whimsical and completely antithetical to Eric's no-nonsense style, which made the view even more delightful to me.

He stood at the sink, rinsing off a few plates from an earlier meal and putting them in the dishwasher. The sleeves of his denim work shirt were rolled up, and he wore a chef's apron over faded blue jeans with leather sandals. I watched my sister beam at him as he finished with the dishwasher and turned to start pouring wine into glasses. When Eric smiled and leaned over to kiss her, I experienced a moment of pure joy that they had found each other. Chloe had spent so many years living away from us because of someone else's malicious acts, but now, finally, she was blissfully happy, and I couldn't be more pleased.

Eric pulled two bottles of beer from the refrigerator and handed one to Mac while Chloe brought me a glass of wine.

"It's Pinot Noir," she said.

"My favorite."

"Mine, too."

"Cheers," Eric said, and we all clicked our glasses and bottles together.

And at that moment, his phone began to buzz.

"Are you kidding me," he muttered and pulled it from his pocket. His eyes went flat, and he walked out of the room, but not before he answered sharply, "Jensen."

The three of us stared at one another and tried to hear something that would give us a clue to the identity of the caller. But Eric said nothing, just listened to whoever was speaking. Finally he said, "I'm leaving now. Be there in ten."

"Can you tell us what's going on?" Chloe asked when Eric came into the kitchen.

He looked at each of us. "That was Tommy. He got an anonymous call from someone who claims they saw Travis carrying a couple of mallets into his house."

"Sounds fishy to me," Mac said instantly. "The caller I mean, not Travis."

"That's what I thought," Eric said, untying his apron and hanging it inside the pantry closet.

I frowned. "Nobody knows that a mallet is the possible murder weapon except the killer."

Chloe held her wineglass and pointed at me. "Along with whoever might've overheard us talking about it when you heard those footsteps outside the offices."

"It might be one and the same person," I said.

"I'd rather not speculate right now," Eric said, closing off the conversation. He gave Chloe a quick kiss. "You guys stick around. I've got to go, but I still want to look at that video."

"We're not leaving without our pizza," I said, and made Eric laugh.

And then he was gone.

Chapter Eleven

Mac stared out the kitchen window, deep in thought. "Someone is trying to set Travis up."

"Oh, absolutely," I said, tearing off a piece of the crust. "I'm betting on Lewis."

Chloe nibbled on salad. "Tommy might be able to identify the voice of the caller."

"They could've disguised their voice," Mac said.

"Coward," Chloe said with a sneer.

We were all silent for a long moment, sitting around the table with our own thoughts. And pizza. I bit into the crust, then took a sip of wine, and mentally thumbed through the possibilities. I was still set on Lewis being the one who'd made the anonymous call about Travis hiding the mallets. I could envision a full scenario that included Lewis as the bad guy and Travis as the good guy. From day one, Lewis had been jealous of Travis because he was friends with Linda. Lewis had stolen Travis's tablet and stolen his story idea, too. Lewis had snuck into Travis's house to hide the mallets to set him up as Linda's killer.

The only thing that didn't fit was the idea that Lewis killed Linda. What was his motive? He liked her! And she had been nice to him. So that one fact made all the rest of it seem unlikely.

And yet I still suspected him. Maybe it wasn't fair, but I was okay with it. I had developed such a strong dislike for the man. I hadn't liked him from the first minute he looked up at me and took my picture. It had been weirdly insulting! Even worse, I didn't like the way he had treated Mac.

And still, I couldn't see any reason why Lewis would kill Linda. So I'd have to backtrack and look elsewhere.

But who else would've accused Travis of hiding the mallets in his own house—which was the same as accusing him of killing Linda?

One of the other writers? Why? What if it was one of the veterans? Maybe Travis had been feuding with a neighbor. But I couldn't believe something like that could happen without the rest of the village knowing about it.

What about Julia? She had been Linda's closest friend, but she had admitted from the beginning that there was some jealousy when it came to the two women competing for men. I brushed the thought away. It was obvious that they had been joking about it. I didn't believe for one minute that Julia had anything to do with Linda's murder.

Could it be one of the Homefront workers? But again, what would their motive be? It didn't make sense.

Chloe set down her wine. "Eric will never believe that Travis could hurt someone. Especially not Linda.

Travis and she were dear friends. You saw them together."

"They seemed like they really cared about each other."

"And same goes for him and Parks," she said. "They were great friends. Travis wouldn't do anything to hurt either of them."

"It's not Travis," I said emphatically. "I don't care if they found the mallets in his house."

"What about that woman?" Chloe asked. "That friend of Linda's. Maybe she's not such a good friend?"

I frowned at her. "Are you talking about Julia Barton?"

"Yeah, that's the one. How well do you know her?"

I had just gone through the same thought process concerning Julia so I couldn't exactly dismiss the question. I glanced at Mac, and he looked back at me with eyebrows raised. The fact that we were once again discussing murderous intentions should've been repugnant to both of us. But from the first time we met, we'd been faced with murders in Lighthouse Cove so Mac had turned it into a guessing game. Suspects, motives, opportunities. He called it the Scooby-Doo game, after the cartoon characters who were always getting involved in mysteries and then spending their time hashing out the possibilities.

"Julia is a lovely woman and a very good friend of Linda's," I said, and took a quick bite of my pizza.

Chloe gave a shrug. "Oh well, it was just a shot in the dark."

"However," I continued, "Julia did admit to me that they weren't always friends. You know they grew up here, right?"

"Yeah," Chloe said.

"She said that they ran into the same prejudices and obstacles that we did. You know, the rich kids versus the townies."

"So who's the rich kid and who's the townie in their relationship?"

"Julia's father was a carpenter," I said. "He used to work with Dad."

"That's right. Mr. Barton," she said cheerfully. "We talked about this. I remember him."

I smiled. "He's a good guy."

"So, what about Linda's father?" Mac asked.

"Linda's father is a wealthy lawyer. And guess what? He's a friend of Whitney's father."

"Whitney rears her ugly head again," Chloe muttered, then rolled her eyes. "That whole townie discussion makes me tired. It's the one thing I never missed about Lighthouse Cove."

"Yeah, I'm over it, too." I gave her hand a quick squeeze, knowing what she'd gone through all those years ago.

"So how did Julia and Linda become friends?" Mac asked.

"They wound up in the army together and became best buds."

Chloe smiled. "That's kind of a nice twist."

"It is," I said. "Linda told me that she could always count on Julia."

"Oh wow." She blinked her eyes. "That almost makes me want to cry."

"But wait," Mac said. "What if Julia's townie feelings festered for years? What if their friendship was a total charade? What if, when Julia met up with Linda in the army, she plotted it all out?"

Chloe and I just stared at him.

He threw up his hands. "I don't buy it, either. We'll strike Julia off the suspect list."

"Good," Chloe said.

He held up his finger. "Except, just one more possibility for the sake of argument. Maybe Julia was jealous of Linda."

"Jealous, why?" I asked.

Mac picked up his beer. "Well, Linda completely captured the attention of Lewis."

I stared at him in disbelief. "So you think Julia was secretly crazy about Lewis?"

He laughed. "Good God, no. I was trying to keep the scenario going, but I just can't go there."

"Thank you," I said. "But just in case you harbor doubts, let me put your worries to rest once and for all. Julia couldn't stand Lewis. She didn't trust him around Linda because Linda was too nice and friendly and open around him. Julia was worried about Linda spending any time with him. And now I'm thinking she was right to worry."

Chloe's phone rang and she ran to answer it. "Oh, Eric. Are you okay?"

She listened for a minute and then said, "Okay, keep me posted. If you think it's going to be more than an hour, call me."

She ended the call and looked at Mac and me. "He'll be home in an hour and asked if we would save him a piece of pizza."

"Oh, that's sad," I said.

"I know," Chloe said. "I feel sorry for him having to work so late."

"No, I mean it's sad that we have to save a piece of pizza for him."

Chloe slapped my arm. "Pizza hog."

"Couldn't we save him some salad instead?"

She slapped me again. "Meanie."

I laughed. "Okay, fine. We'll save him a piece of the pizza he bought for all of us."

"That's good of you." She got up, brought the wine bottle to the table, and poured more into our glasses.

"Did he tell you what's going on?" Mac asked.

"A little bit. He said that Travis was taken to the police station, where Tommy is now interrogating him."

I frowned. "Why Tommy?"

"Because Eric is recusing himself," Chloe said. "He's too good a friend of Travis's to be impartial."

"Eric must hate that," I murmured.

"You know he does," Chloe agreed.

"Is Tommy in charge of both murder cases?"

"As long as Travis is a suspect, I guess Tommy's in charge."

"Well then." I exchanged a look with Mac, then glanced at Chloe. "We've got to figure out who the real killer is."

"Did Eric say anything about Parks?" Mac asked.

"No." Chloe looked ready to cry again. "I'm really worried about him."

"No news is good news," I said immediately. "Let's wait until we hear something."

Mac and I stayed with Chloe and ate pizza and salad, and discussed suspects and motives. We wanted to wait until Eric got home so we could all look at the video together.

An hour later, Eric walked in the door. Chloe jumped up and ran to greet him.

"Come have some pizza," she said, and walked with him into the kitchen.

"We saved you a piece," I said quickly.

Chloe gave me a dry look. "We saved you *three* pieces and some salad. You want a beer?"

He ran a hand up and down her back. "I think I'll have a glass of wine."

He poured himself a glass of the Pinot Noir while Chloe warmed up a piece of pizza. Then he sat down at the table, looking beat.

"Do you want to talk about it?" I asked.

"Two bloody mallets were stuffed inside a plastic bag and shoved into Travis's closet."

Mac snorted. "Because every killer keeps his bloody weapons in a plastic bag in their closet."

Eric gave him a cynical look. "Right? Some people can be so dumb."

"Worse," I said. "They think *you're* dumb."

"That's a big mistake," Chloe said, and set a plate down in front of Eric with a big slice of pizza and some salad.

"Yeah. Big mistake." He picked up the pizza, folded it, and took a bite. "Oh man. That's good."

"The best," Mac agreed.

"It really is the perfect food," I said.

"So what's this about Tommy?" Mac asked.

Eric shrugged. "I recused myself, so he took over."

I gazed at him. "Not for long, I hope."

"I'll still run the case, but Tommy will take charge

of everything connected specifically to Travis. Any questioning, searching of premises, that sort of thing."

"Sounds complicated," I said.

"It's a little tricky. We'll work it out."

Chloe brought him another piece of pizza, and he gazed up at her adoringly. "Thanks, babe."

I'd probably react the same way if she brought me a piece of pizza. It was really good.

Eric's phone rang and he grabbed it, then looked around the table at us. "Sorry. This won't take long."

He said hello, listened for a minute, and then said, "Good. Okay. Thanks, Tommy. See you tomorrow."

He set the phone on the table, screen side down. Then he took a long sip of wine. Finally he said, "Travis has been interrogated and released with a warning not to leave town."

"That's . . . good, right?" I asked.

"As good as we can get for the moment," he said. "For now, it's all circumstantial. Nobody saw him do anything. Except we've got some anonymous jackass insisting that he saw Travis run into his house carrying two bloody mallets."

"That's just ridiculous," I said.

"Yeah," Eric said, and took a healthy bite of that second piece of pizza. "We know that, but not everybody seems to agree."

"What's that supposed to mean?" Was someone bad-mouthing Travis, I wondered.

"Now that Tommy's in charge, he's determined to stay impartial. But it's almost like he's bending in the opposite direction. He said a few things about Homefront not being safe."

"Eric, he got that from Whitney," I said. "We all know she's an idiot."

Chloe huffed out a breath. "Then he's an idiot if he's paying attention to her."

"They're married," Eric said. "What else can he do?"

"Tommy's great," I said, "but he's way too easygoing when it comes to placating Whitney."

For a minute, we were silent, drinking wine, thinking about the murder.

"I want you to know I'm honing in on Lewis," Mac said. "I don't trust him and I don't like him. He was flirting with Linda the whole time, meeting her at the pub, so he must've liked her. But he's squirrelly. Maybe she told him to buzz off, and he took it badly."

"I honestly can't see her saying something like that," I said. "But more importantly, Lewis told Linda about the problems he was having with writing a new book."

"He did?" Eric said.

Mac and I stared at each other, suddenly realizing that we'd never told him about Lewis's issues with starting his second book. So we told him the whole story now.

"The reason this is important is that once Travis's tablet disappeared, Lewis suddenly sent his agent a full manuscript."

"You think Lewis stole an idea from Travis?"

"I think he stole the entire book," Mac said.

"And the only person outside of the writers' group who knew he didn't have a story idea was Linda."

"And then Linda was killed," Eric murmured. "So he steals Travis's tablet, finds one of his great stories on there, sends it to his agent, then remembers that he told Linda his sob story."

Mac nodded. "You've got the gist of it."

"But Lewis really liked Linda," I said, playing devil's advocate.

"True," Eric said.

"But then, Lewis is squirrelly," Mac countered with a crooked smile.

I looked at Chloe. "Remember in the pub, when Travis was sitting with Linda? Remember the look on Lewis's face?"

"If looks could kill," she said.

Eric shook his head. "There's too much psycho stuff here. So he kills Linda and then tries to frame Travis, who he considered his main competition for Linda."

"That's really sick," I said.

Mac reached over and squeezed my hand.

"And don't forget," I said. "There's that conversation I had with Sheri at the memorial."

"Oh yeah," Chloe said. "The woman scorned. Or whatever."

"She was jealous of Linda," I said.

We took a few seconds to think about all that. Eric finished his pizza, then asked, "How does Parks fit into all this?"

I shrugged. "Maybe he saw the real killer go into Travis's house."

Eric stared at me. "You're good at this."

"I've had some practice," I said, with a smile for Mac.

Mac just grinned. "That's my girl."

I reached for my wineglass. "You know, we haven't even touched on the other writers in the group. They're all squirrelly, if you ask me."

"They're an odd group, for sure," Chloe said.

"Let me think about all this," Eric said. "Damn, I

really need to talk to Travis myself. I didn't get a chance tonight."

Mac leaned his elbows on the table. "Can you talk to him as a friend and not jeopardize the investigation?"

Eric scowled. "I've got to think about it. Maybe I'll talk to Tommy tomorrow."

Chloe leaned over and asked, "Do you want a third piece of pizza?"

"No thanks, babe." He stood and took his plate to the sink. "I want to watch that video."

His phone rang again, and his shoulders sagged in defeat. "I've got to take this." He connected the call. "Hey, Tom." He listened for a few seconds. "Hold on for just a quick minute."

I stifled a yawn.

"Sorry, guys," Eric said

"It's okay, Chief," Mac said. "It's getting late anyway. Why don't you two go ahead and look at it tonight, and Shannon and I will check it out tomorrow night?"

I winced. "I have my construction class. Unless I cancel it."

"You can come over anytime and look at it," Chloe said. "Morning or afternoon."

"I want to get back to our partition wall tomorrow morning, so how about later in the afternoon."

"Works for me," Chloe said.

"I can do it then, too," Mac said.

"Thanks, guys." Eric walked out of the kitchen to resume his talk with Tommy.

"If you do watch the video tonight," I said to Chloe. "Let me know what Eric thinks."

"I will." She gave me a hug. "Sleep tight."

"Don't let the bedbugs bite," I said, finishing the little poem our mother always recited. Then I hugged her back. "Will you be able to help me with the wall tomorrow?"

"Of course. I'll be there by eight."

I sighed with relief. "Thanks, kiddo."

Chloe gave Mac a big hug, and then we left and walked home. As soon as we stepped into the house, Robbie went wild with joy, and both cats wove themselves like ribbons around and between our ankles.

Mac had fed them earlier, so I changed their water, and he gave them all a treat. Then we turned off the lights and went upstairs to bed, where I fell a sleep as soon as my head hit the pillow.

"Good morning," Chloe said when she walked into our workroom the next morning. "I brought coffee for you."

"Wow, thanks. You're, like, a goddess." I lifted up one of the cardboard cups and took a life-affirming sip.

"That's even better than being queen." She set her things down and grabbed her own cup. "So how are you feeling?"

"A little achy, but I'm fine. What about you?"

"Well, I truly gave myself one good knock on the head." She brushed aside her bangs, and I got another look at the bump on her forehead.

"Oh, honey." I came in closer. "It's still red. I'm so sorry. You really got the worst of it."

"I'm popping ibuprofen every so often, so it doesn't hurt as much as it might. I think our fears amplified the pain."

"You're right. I was scared to death for a few minutes there."

"Me, too." She buckled her tool belt and straightened her shoulders.

I knelt down to check out the condition of the base plate. "The fact that someone purposely tried to sabotage us fills me with a white-hot rage."

"I feel the same." She scowled. "What can we do to find them?"

"I've been thinking about it. We know it's connected to Linda's murder and the attack on Parks. The killer must've been listening to our conversation, don't you think?"

"Without a doubt," she said.

"So when we find the killer, we'll find the person who screwed around with our wall."

"How do we find the killer?"

"We've got to watch that video."

"We'll do it this afternoon." She took a few deep breaths, bent over and stretched to get her muscles going, then stood and gave me two thumbs-up. "Now let's get that wall back into place."

"Let's go." But first I closed both doors. "I'm not going to lock them in case anyone needs to get in here. But at least if they're closed, nobody can eavesdrop."

"Good thinking."

We removed the piece of damaged drywall that had been broken when the wall fell, then lifted the frame back into place, using the sawhorses to bear the weight as we went. "Hey, thanks again for last night. It's just too bad that Eric had to leave."

"I know. That was a bummer. And he's really worried about Travis."

"So am I. In fact, if we take a little break later, I'd

like to track him down, just to let him know we're on his side."

"That would be nice," Chloe said.

I reached for a handful of four-inch screws and put them in the front pocket of my tool belt. Then I carried the ladder down the hall to the other side of the partition.

"Apparently," Chloe continued, "he wasn't allowed to stay in his house last night. It's a crime scene for another day or two."

"Where did he stay?"

"He bunked with one of his buddies who lives a few houses away."

"That's good. But it still sucks." Climbing the ladder, I went through the process, once again, of screwing the top plate into the ceiling joist and waiting for Chloe to check for plumb. She gave me a thumbs-up to reposition my ladder for the next screw.

"It really does." Chloe opened up the sawhorses and laid out the new drywall panels. "By the way, Eric actually enjoyed himself last night, especially when we were trying to help him figure out suspects and motives."

"I'm glad he considered it helping and not interfering."

"Why would he think that?"

I chuckled. "Well, it took him a long time to trust me. After all, I think I was his first murder suspect in Lighthouse Cove."

"What are you talking about?"

I had to think for a minute. "I guess I never told you the whole story of how I met him."

"Tell me now. We have nothing but time."

"Okay." I got another screw in, then moved the ladder over. "It was a few months after Eric moved here and took the police chief job. People around town were talking about him. My girlfriends were googly-eyed about him. But I hadn't met him." I screwed in another screw. "Then one day, I went to check on a house I was refurbishing. A neighbor had reported hearing water running in the basement, so I went down and found the sump pump clogged up. And that's when I stumbled over a dead body."

"Ew!"

"Yeah, it was creepy for sure," I said. "But here's the kicker. I had gone out on a date with the dead guy the night before. He had tried to make a move, and I wasn't happy about it. So I kicked him and ran away, but not before I told him that if he ever tried that again, I would kill him."

"Oh, great."

"Yeah. We were on the beach, and I had an audience of dozens of people lined up on the pier right above us."

"Oh God, Shannon."

"So anyway, I found the body and raced back upstairs to call the cops. Eric shows up looking like some kind of Viking god, and I have to walk him through this funky old house to find the basement door. I left him there and waited out on the front porch. And a while later, he comes up and shows me a plastic evidence bag with my pink pipe wrench inside, all smeared with blood."

"Oh, jeez."

"Yeah." I could laugh about it now, I realized, and ran another screw into the top plate. "Tommy was there, and he vouched for me, but Eric didn't know me from Adam, and he'd heard about me threatening to kill the guy. So I wound up being his prime suspect, and he interrogated me for a few hours. I thought I'd end up in a cell, but he let me go home." I shared all the sordid details of finding more bodies and trying to figure it all out. "And then someone coshed me in the head with my own pink hammer, and Eric figured maybe I wasn't the killer after all."

"Wow. I knew you had some stuff happening around that time, but I guess I never got the full story."

"Those were good times."

She shook her head. "Sounds like they were frightening times."

"That, too. But just around that same time, I met Mac."

"Ah." She smiled. "A happy ending."

"And the killer kidnapped Whitney, and I ended up saving her life."

"Now that sucks."

I laughed. "I love you."

"Back at you."

I continued working with my power drill until all the screws were inserted right where they'd been a few days before. Then I got down on my hands and knees, and repeated it for the base plate.

"Hey, I completely forgot to ask if you and Eric had a chance to watch the video last night."

"No. He was on the phone for an hour with Tommy, so I cleaned up the kitchen and finally went to bed."

"Well, maybe we can all watch it this afternoon, like you suggested."

"I'll see if Eric can be here."

"I hope he can. I don't like the idea of watching it without him."

"Neither do I. We could do it later, but you have your class tonight."

"Actually, I'm still debating whether to cancel it or not. What do you think?"

She thought about it as she marked another piece of drywall. "You should go ahead with it. It can be another way to memorialize Linda."

"Good point."

"I'll come if you want me there."

"I would love you to be there, but I'll understand if you'd rather not."

"Let me think about it."

"Okay." I remembered something else I'd forgotten to ask about. "Have we heard anything about Parks yet?"

"Eric talked to the doctor in charge early this morning. He said that Parks hasn't regained consciousness, but they're confident that he will very soon. His vital signs are good. They were going to take him for a brain scan later this morning."

"That's really scary."

"I know."

"I hope he comes out of it soon. He could tell us who hurt him and killed Linda."

"Whoever did it is going to pay."

"Damn straight," Chloe said fiercely, and ran her X-Acto knife down the line she had marked. "I know you think it's one of the writers, but why? Why would they kill Linda?"

"Because . . . they're squirrelly?"

She chuckled but then said, "So far, all the incidents

have happened here at Homefront. The writers have nothing to do with this place."

"But they do," I insisted. "They came to Mac's workshop that first night, and Lewis met Linda here at the same time. And he kept coming back to see her." I pulled the leftover screws from my pocket and put them back in the box. "In fact, I had to ask him to leave the other day."

"Really?"

"Yeah. It was the day Linda started working on the mosaic backsplashes. He just walked right over and wanted to talk to her. I knew she wouldn't brush him off, even though she was officially on the job. So I did it for her."

"It does seem like it's all connected to Homefront."

"Right? Lewis met Linda here and Parks was attacked here. And our partition wall was sabotaged here."

"But Linda was found on the beach," Chloe said.

"But she might've been killed somewhere else and taken to the beach." I told her about the drag marks and the way her sweater was rolled up her back.

"You keep her mosaic stuff inside one of the houses, right? Maybe she was killed right there and then taken to the beach."

"Why would someone do that?" I wondered.

Chloe frowned. "Maybe the killer is trying to implicate the writers."

That actually made sense in a twisted kind of way. But then whoever had done this was twisted anyway.

"I'm ready for a break."

"Me, too."

We locked the doors and walked down the hall to

the café. I stopped when I saw Julia coming out of Vince's office.

"Julia."

"Oh, Shannon."

I gave her a big hug. "How are you doing?"

"Not well," she admitted. "I cry a lot and I'm angry and I don't know what to do. She was my best friend." She absently twisted the ends of her belt. "And the part that really gets to me is that we knew each other for years but didn't become friends until much later. I feel like I lost all that time when we could've been best buds and having fun and going on adventures and . . . oh, you know."

"I'm so sorry. She was a sweet person and a good friend."

"Yeah, she was."

I took a deep breath. "I was wondering whether to cancel tonight's construction class. What do you think?"

"Personally, I don't think I can handle it."

"I understand."

"All of the women in the class were friends of Linda's, and you know, we lady vets have to stick together." She smiled.

"That's a good rule to follow."

"I suppose it would make sense to get together for the class, but I just can't do it. I'd like to cancel the class for this week and then come back next week feeling a little more prepared and ready to go."

"Then consider it canceled," I said. "I'll ask the office to make the announcement."

"I can make the announcement," Julia offered. "It'll give me a chance to commiserate with everyone."

"Okay. Thanks." I thought of something else. "About her mosaics and equipment. The only person I know who does anything close to what she does is my stone-mason, Niall, so I have asked him to step in and finish what she started."

"I know Niall," Julia said. "He's a fabulous artist and a really good guy."

"He sure is."

"And I guess I should ask her father if he'd like to keep her things when Niall is finished."

I winced. "Maybe Linda told you that he was always against her learning the craft from her grandfather. He might get a little testy about it."

She thought about that. "You know, I think I'll save that conversation for another day. After all, Linda might have written out a last will, making the entire conversation moot."

I patted her shoulder. "That's possible. Let me know what the verdict is when you find out." I gave her another hug. "Call me if you want to talk."

"I just want to find out who hurt her."

"I want that, too," I said. And I was determined to get some answers.

"I've been craving these cookies all night," Chloe said as we entered the café, and she quickly bought a package of three.

"After stuffing myself with cookies and pizza yesterday, I'm sticking with something healthy." I picked up an apple.

"An apple. That's not boring at all."

I laughed as I took my apple to the cash register and paid for all of our snacks.

"It's such a nice day," she said. "Let's walk outside for a few minutes."

The sky was blue with puffy white clouds, and I could smell the sea breeze. "I love it here."

"I can't wait to move back permanently," she said as she nibbled on a cookie.

"I can't wait, either." I took a bite of my apple and savored the sweet, tart taste. "I'm so excited for you. And for me."

"I know. It's going to be fun."

"Hey, Chloe."

We both turned and saw Travis walking our way. Chloe and I exchanged a quick glance. This was perfect. He was just the person we wanted to see.

"Hey, Travis," we said in unison.

He grinned. "You two are a sight for these old eyes."

"You're not that old," Chloe said with a laugh. She hugged him. "How are you doing?"

He hesitated, then said, "I've been better."

"I'm sorry," I said.

"Yeah." He folded his arms across his chest. "I'm just stumped. I can't believe anyone would suspect me of hurting Linda or Parks. I haven't known either of them very long, but I already considered them two of my best friends."

"I know," Chloe said.

Then he shook himself out of his down mood. "I'll be okay. I'm going to lay low, do my work, and write. It really helps me think. Mac was right about that."

I gave him a hug. "Sounds like the best thing you could do for now."

"Yeah. But just now I want to get some lunch."

"We'll walk with you," I said.

As we walked, Chloe said, "Travis, we know you didn't hurt Linda or Parks."

"Somebody's trying to set you up," I said.

"But who would do that?" he wondered. "I'm sure I've pissed off plenty of people in my life, but not to this extent. I thought for a little while that it was a random thing."

"You mean, they just happened to pick your house?" I said.

"Stranger things have happened."

"It's not random," Chloe insisted.

"No, not after what happened to Linda," I said. "And then Parks. And then our wall being sabotaged."

He stared at me. "What's that about a wall?"

Chloe told him what happened to the partition wall.

"Oh man, that's a whole different kind of dirty trick." He ran his hand across the back of his neck. "So, definitely not random."

"And don't forget," I said. "Someone stole your tablet."

"Oh hey." He grinned. "I found it."

I exchanged a look with Chloe. "You found it?"

"Well, it sort of just reappeared yesterday. When the cops came to check out my closet, I happened to look at my desk, and it was just sitting there."

"Just sitting there," I repeated slowly.

Chloe looked at me. "Another mystery?"

"Hmm," I whispered. "Actually, things are getting clearer."

"How can you even say that?" she said. "I'm more confused than ever."

"Yeah," Travis said. "What're you thinking, Shannon?"

"Just that whoever hid those mallets is the same person who stole your tablet. And that person is also Linda's killer."

His mouth twisted into a frown. "The tablet did reappear at the same time the mallets showed up."

I knew Mac was convinced that Lewis had not only taken the tablet but stolen one of Travis's story ideas. If the tablet appeared at the same time as the bloody mallets, it was one more reason to suspect that Lewis had killed Linda.

I pulled out my phone. "I'm going to call Eric. He needs to check Travis's tablet for fingerprints."

The phone call took less than two minutes. Eric thanked me and we ended the call. I looked at Travis. "He'll probably call you later to get a look at the tablet."

"I won't touch it until I hear from him."

"Good thinking," Chloe said, patting his back. "Let's go inside and get you some lunch."

"Sounds good. I'm starving."

He got a bowl of soup and a ham sandwich, and the three of us sat inside at one of the tables.

We talked about construction work and the progress we were making on the tiny homes. Travis said he was looking forward to having more neighbors to talk to. "I love it here," he said. "I just hope people don't think I had anything to do with this craziness."

"You'll be cleared of suspicion in no time. I know it."

"You're a good friend. I've been really lucky with my friends."

"Travis," I said carefully. "Is there anyone around Homefront that you've had a run-in with? An argument?"

He took a spoonful of soup. "I know what you're

asking. But honestly, I'm clueless. Although . . ." He considered, then said, "When I moved in here a few months ago, there was another guy, Stewart, who wanted my house. He put up a pretty big stink over them picking me first. Accused Eric of putting his finger on the scale."

"Eric would never do that," Chloe insisted.

"I know. And that's not how they operate here. Unless there's a sudden critical need, they work on a first come, first served basis. And when enough people express interest, they start a lottery. Right now, there's a whole list of people waiting to move in, and they'll all get a place eventually, but they might not get the first place that comes available."

"That makes sense," I said. "So what about this guy Stewart?"

He shook his head. "He wanted the house and couldn't understand why I got it before him. But it's no big deal, because now he's got his own place, and he's pretty happy. He even made a point of telling me how much better his location is than mine."

"So he's not mad at you," Chloe said.

"No." He chuckled. "I think he was feeling a little embarrassed that he made such a big deal about it. But we're pals now. No biggie."

"What about the writers? Didn't you have any run-ins with Lewis or any of them?"

"Not really. He gave me the stink eye a few times when he saw me talking to Linda at the pub, but that's hardly a reason to kill someone. Or frame someone."

I wondered.

"Besides," he continued, "he really liked Linda. Why would he kill her?"

Because she knew that Lewis didn't have another book in him, I thought. And then Lewis stole Travis's tablet and voilà! Lewis suddenly had a manuscript. It still made me so angry! But I didn't say any of that to Travis because I didn't want to upset him until we could prove it beyond a shadow of a doubt.

I tossed my apple into the trash can. "Guess we'd better get moving."

"I should head out, too," he said, and carried his tray to the cart where others were stacked.

"Hang in there, Travis," Chloe said, and gave him another hug.

"You, too, Chloe." Then he gave me a quick hug. "Thanks, Shannon."

We watched him walk away. Then I turned to Chloe. "You ready to work?"

"I am if you are."

I didn't answer right away. "What I'd really like to do is look at that video."

Her eyes widened, then she smiled. "Awesome idea. Let's go."

As we crossed the parking lot, I heard little tapping noises coming up behind us. I turned around and saw Whitney prancing as fast as she could in her idiot stilettos.

"Wait just a damn minute, you two," she said. "I saw you talking to that man."

"What man is that?" Chloe asked.

"That horrible man." She looked past me to catch a glimpse of "that man" and pointed at Travis. "There he is. I warned you that he was a dangerous troublemaker. Now Linda Rutledge is dead, and that other poor fellow is in the hospital."

Chloe groaned. "You leave Travis alone. He didn't do anything."

"On the contrary, I witnessed him attacking Linda. She was my friend and now she's dead."

She wasn't your friend, I thought. "As usual, you have no idea what you're talking about."

"He didn't attack Linda," Chloe persisted. "He was protecting her. They were good friends."

She snorted. "Protecting her. Get real. I don't even know why I talk to either of you."

"I don't, either," I said. "Why don't you shut up and go away?"

She stomped her foot. "You think you know everything, but you're wrong. And believe me, my committee will be addressing the town council on this issue very soon."

I narrowed in on her. "What committee is this?"

"If you must know, it's the Committee to Protect the Reputation of Lighthouse Cove."

"Wow, you just made that up on the spot, didn't you."

"I did not. It's real. And we're coming after you."

"And just who is on your committee?" I asked.

She lifted her nose even higher in the air. "It's none of your business."

I ignored that. "I'll bet your committee consists of two people. You and Jennifer Bailey. Two pillars of society."

"If pillars were shrews," Chloe muttered, making me laugh. But then Chloe stepped right up to Whitney and shook her finger in the woman's face. "Let me remind you who my fiancé is. He's Police Chief Eric Jensen. And Travis is one of his best friends. Both of them served our country with honor, dedication, and distinction. So you might think long and hard about that before you attack him again."

Whitney stomped her foot again, which had almost no effect except to weaken the flimsy heel of her shoe.

"Stomp some more," I said, "and you'll stick that heel so far into the grass, you'll fall flat on your face."

She gasped, then lifted her feet tentatively.

Chloe giggled.

"Townies," Whitney snarled, and took mincing steps over to her black Mercedes-Benz sedan.

What was she doing here? Had she just been passing by and jumped at the chance to harass us? Chloe was right. She was a shrew.

"You never should've warned her about getting her heels stuck," Chloe said.

I sighed. "Tactical error on my part."

We watched her slam the car door and gun the engine. Her tires screeched as she fishtailed out of the parking lot.

"I really liked what you said about Travis and Eric."

"It's true," she said.

"I know. I liked it."

Chloe stared at Whitney's car and shook her head slowly. "What a disaster she is."

"Every time I'm forced to talk to her, I feel dumber afterward." I slipped my arm through Chloe's. "Let's go watch that video."

Chapter Twelve

On the drive to Eric's house, I called Mac. "I'm in the car with Chloe, and we're going to watch the video."

"You going to Eric's?"

"Yeah."

"I'll meet you there," he said, and ended the call.

I turned to Chloe. "Mac's coming over."

"Cool."

"Do you want to call Eric?"

She checked her watch. "He's in a meeting with his team. I'll text him when we get home."

Mac drove up in his SUV just as Chloe was parking her BMW.

"Perfect timing," I said, and walked over to kiss him.

Chloe unlocked the door and walked in as a low-key beeping sound was emitted. "Just have to turn off the alarm."

She stopped in front of a key pad and pushed a series of buttons. "Okay, we're good."

"Glad to hear it," I said, and followed her through the kitchen to a comfortable family room with a massive wide-screen television on the wall. "So you haven't watched the video on this screen yet?"

"Not yet. I watched it on my camera, but its screen is too small for me to see what's going on."

"That shouldn't be a problem with this screen," Mac said.

She smiled. "Yeah." She pulled her camera out of her tote bag and turned it on, then clicked a few buttons. Then she turned on the television, pushed another few buttons, and a shot of Sean flexing his muscles appeared on the screen.

"Oh, he'd love that shot," I said.

"I can isolate it and give it to him."

"His birthday's in a few weeks."

Mac coughed theatrically. "Can we move along?"

I smiled. "Sorry. I'm easily distracted."

"I'm going to let it roll from here," Chloe said, and sat down in one of the wide chocolate brown leather chairs. "It's about two minutes in from this point."

I took a seat on the comfy matching leather sofa, and Mac leaned against the paneled wall.

"Hey, this looks really good," I said, watching Chloe's video. "I think you've got some interesting stuff for your show."

"Yeah, it'll go with what I'm planning for next season." She pointed to the screen. "So here I'm walking toward the community center, and I'm about to turn and do a panorama shot. Here we go."

"What are we looking for?" I asked.

"The guy I'm talking about is way in the background

near the last row of houses. Can you see him?" Chloe got up and stood near the screen and pointed. "This guy right here."

The person was so far away that it was hard to see facial features. He was wearing a brown jacket and a ski cap that covered his hair.

"That jacket," I said quietly.

"I see it," Mac said. "Is that fringe?"

"Maybe. I wish I could see his hair."

"I can try to zoom in," Chloe said. "Give me a second." She froze the frame, then went in reverse for several frames. Then she pushed something that suddenly enlarged the picture. It went blurry at first but then cleared up.

"That's as close to perfect as it gets," Mac said. "And yeah, that's a brown suede jacket, heavy on the fringe."

"Just like the one Lewis wears."

"In case I didn't mention it before," Chloe said, "That's a very expensive jacket."

"You called it cowboy rock star," I said.

"That's about right."

"And it still doesn't suit him."

"I can't make out his face from this distance," Mac said, "but I'm pretty sure it's him."

"Who else would it be?" Chloe asked.

"Just wish I could see his hair." I grimaced. "The body language is a little off."

"That's because he's skulking around," Mac suggested, "carrying something."

"Mallets?"

"It could be. Hard to tell, but it does look like tools." I demonstrated. "He's carrying them like this, so the heavier tops are here, above his arms, and the handles are down below."

"Yeah," Chloe said. "I get that. And Eric said they were in a plastic bag, right?"

"Yeah," Mac said.

"Wish I could see his hair color," I lamented for the third time. "Sorry to whine. But his beachboy hair is unusual enough that it would nail him for sure."

"It's him," Mac said decisively.

"Okay," I said, willing to go along. "The jacket is clearly his."

We watched as Lewis ran behind one of the houses, then hurried across the open space and went straight to Travis's house.

"Oh man." Mac whistled. "Eric should see this right away."

But Chloe already had her phone in her hand. "I'm on it."

While we waited for Eric to arrive with Tommy, I had time to ponder the mystery. "I want to watch it again when Eric gets here. I know he's carrying something, but there's still something off about him. I wonder if someone is impersonating him. Maybe Sheri stole the jacket and wore that ski cap to disguise herself. Or Brian." I frowned. "I don't even know Brian. I probably wouldn't recognize him on the street."

"I'm not sure anyone knows Brian," Mac said. "He's always in the background."

"Yeah. Very passive," I said.

"He's really loyal to Lewis," Mac said. "Maybe he was jealous of Lewis spending so much time with Linda."

I had to think about that. "You know, that first night in your writing workshop, I was watching the two of them and Brian was the one who saw Linda first. She and Julia were standing by the door, and Brian elbowed Lewis and said, 'Wow, she's pretty.' Then Lewis turned and looked at the women and said something like, 'Forget it, dude, she's out of your league. Or above your pay grade.' Something like that."

"Well, that was rude," Chloe said.

"Yeah, I thought so, too. But I think that's their dynamic. Brian saw her first, but Lewis got the girl."

"That could get old," Mac agreed.

"Maybe it was Kingsley." I sank down in the chair. "I'm grasping at straws again."

"What if the two of them did it together?" Chloe said, her eyes gleaming with humor. "What if that's their thing?"

Mac grinned. He really loved playing the what-if game. "So Lewis kills, and Brian hides the murder weapons."

"That's just sick," I said. "But we've seen some strange things happen around here."

"Maybe the whole group gets involved," Mac said, chuckling. "Sheri's a librarian. She could easily research a few hundred different ways to kill."

"Now that you mention it," I said, "Sheri is definitely protective of Lewis. She might be willing to do anything he asked her to do."

"You think that's their dynamic?" Mac asked.

"Oh, who knows?" I shook my head. "They're all a bit odd."

Chloe came to attention. "Eric is home."

"You've got bat ears," I said. "I didn't hear anything."

"I can tell the sound of his car."

Eric walked in ten seconds later, followed by Tommy.

"Hey, Chloe," Tommy said.

"Hi, Tommy."

He grinned when he saw me. "Shannon! How you doing?"

"I'm great, Tommy. How're you?"

"Couldn't be better."

He greeted Mac the same way, and I was reminded once again that Tommy was the most mild-mannered, friendly guy I'd ever known. The fact that he was still married to Whitney was a question for the ages.

"Let's roll this video," Eric said, all business.

Chloe sat down and rolled it.

Eric and Tommy both stood and watched it.

"I'm going to freeze it here and zoom in."

Eric nodded. "Good."

She froze the shot, then played the scene again two more times.

Finally Eric looked at me. "Is that Lewis?"

"Probably. But after watching the video a few more times, I can't say one hundred percent that it's him. The ski cap is the problem for me. Lewis has that really distinctive blond hair, so it throws me off when I can't see it."

"He's vain," Chloe said. "He knows his hair is distinctive, so he would've known he had to wear a ski cap or something to cover it up if he didn't want to draw attention to himself."

"Good point," I said. "But also, I thought the jacket looked a little too big on that person. But that might be due to the awkward way he's carrying those tools."

"I can't imagine one of the other writers would try

to frame Travis," Mac said. "Unless they're all enablers."

"Good point," I said. "Frankly, if the person in that video is actually one of the others, I'll still bet that Lewis is pulling the strings."

"So let me ask you this," Eric said. "Do you both agree that it's one of the writers?"

"Oh, without a doubt," Mac said.

I nodded. "Absolutely."

Eric looked at Tommy. "Let's go talk to the writers."

"Right on," Tommy said.

But before they could walk out, Eric's phone rang. He grabbed it. "Jensen."

Because Tommy was with him, Eric put it on speaker. "Chief, it's Ginny. I'm transferring a call to you from someone named Sheri. She just overheard two men arguing about Linda Rutledge. She's afraid one of them killed that poor woman."

"Go ahead and transfer, Ginny."

A second later, incomprehensible screaming burst from the speaker.

"Sheri!" Eric shouted. "Are you in trouble?"

"Help me!" she cried. "They dragged me out of the house, but I escaped! But they're coming after me. They'll kill me!"

"Where are you?"

"The beach! Please help me!"

"Where, Sheri?" Eric demanded.

"I-I'm at the retreat," she whimpered. "Help."

"She's at the mansion," I said.

A look passed between Tommy and Eric, then both men raced out of the house.

Mac looked at me. "Let's go."

We got as far as the front door before I heard Chloe yell, "Wait for me!"

"Come on!"

We jumped into the SUV as Mac was starting the engine.

One mile up the highway, my phone alarm began to shriek. "It's the lighthouse alarm."

"Check the video," Mac said. "Tell me what you see and hear."

"Okay." I pressed the app and turned off the alarm, then stared at the video. The picture was dark as usual, but I could still see Lewis and Brian struggling on the narrow stairs with Sheri in tow. They were trying to drag her up to the top of the lighthouse. She was screaming.

"They've got Sheri," I said. "They're in the lighthouse, not the mansion."

"I'm calling Eric," Chloe said.

The chief picked up on the first ring.

"Shannon's alarm went off," Chloe said loudly into the phone. "Those two guys are inside the lighthouse, not the mansion. They're dragging Sheri up to the top."

"Thanks babe. We're on our way."

I was still watching the screen and listening to the audio. "I can't see Sheri anymore, but I can still hear her screaming. They must be getting pretty far up inside the tower."

"Poor thing," Chloe said. "She told Eric that she escaped, but they must've gone after her and dragged her back."

I put the phone up to my ear so I could hear better over the highway noise. "Now the guys are shouting, 'Get her!' 'Get back here, you bitch!'"

It sent chills across my shoulders. "They're just awful."

"So much for all of them being good friends," Chloe said.

All of a sudden, I saw Sheri racing past the camera, going down toward the door. Her hair was streaming wildly, and she was screaming. "I think she escaped again!"

"Yay!" Chloe cheered.

"The guys are after her," I reported. "Their shouts are getting closer."

"My nerves are shot," Chloe declared. "I don't know how you can be so calm."

I had to laugh because I was literally sitting on the edge of my seat. "Trust me, I'm not that calm."

Mac turned off the highway and onto Old Lighthouse Road. He usually drove slowly over the potholes and ruts, but not today. His SUV bumped and bucked over craters and cracks that he'd deliberately never bothered to fix, assuring me that this pitted old road helped keep out the riffraff. Given that we were now in pursuit of at least one creepy killer, that philosophy wasn't working for me.

"Hold on," Mac shouted.

I grabbed the chicken strap over the door to keep myself upright. "You okay back there?"

Chloe was being tossed left and right as Mac's tires hit another hole in the road. "I'm okay. Not sure my stomach will make it, though."

Mac came to a sharp stop in front of the lighthouse, right behind Eric's SUV.

From here, I could see the writers' cars parked in a neat row behind the mansion. Lewis's black Audi was there and a small white SUV was parked next to it. It looked familiar and I wondered whose it was. Was it the same SUV that was parked at Homefront the night Lewis showed up for his "date" with Linda? Had one of the writers been following Lewis?

We all jumped out of the car and Chloe pointed up. "Look! They're out on that catwalk. I think they're fighting."

"And that flimsy wrought iron is on the list to be replaced," I said. "It won't hold up to their weight and all that movement."

"They're insane," Chloe said.

"I can see it shaking from here," Mac said. "They're both going to die up there."

Eric aimed his SUV's side spotlight up toward the top of the lighthouse, illuminating Lewis and Brian as they fought.

"Will that help?" Chloe asked, since it was the middle of the afternoon and still sunny.

"If they didn't already hear the siren and see the flashing lights on our car, they'll see this one. It's so bright it's blinding."

"You want them to know we're here," she said.

"Yeah." Eric grabbed Mac's arm. "Two things." He pointed to his back seat, where Sheri was huddled in a blanket. "First, watch her. Don't let her out of the car. I'm taking her in for questioning."

"Got it."

"Second," Eric continued, "we've called for backup. Should be here any minute. Send one of them up to the top. The others should keep order down here. Tell them not to let any of the writers leave."

"Roger that," Mac said.

Then Eric and Tommy went racing into the lighthouse.

"Be careful," Chloe cried, then rolled her eyes. "Like they'll take that advice."

I patted her back. "It's the thought that counts."

I noticed the other writers had come out of the mansion and were standing on the pitted pavement staring at the top of the lighthouse where their buddies appeared to be yelling and pushing at each other. The four of them could've been watching a tennis tournament for all the emotion they showed. I shook my head. Lewis was a total creep, but the rest of them weren't much better.

I returned my gaze to the catwalk. Those two up there weren't fighters. Most of their attacks were with words, although they did get a few slaps and pushes in.

I was growing more frantic, watching and wondering when the catwalk rail would crumble into the ocean. And then I suddenly had to blink to clear my vision. "Am I seeing things, or is Lewis actually holding up his phone?"

"You're seeing just fine," Mac confirmed. "That numbskull is recording their fight."

"He's obsessed with that phone," Chloe said.

Two black-and-white patrol cars came barreling down the Old Lighthouse Road and skidded to a stop a few yards back from Mac's car. As soon as Mindy got out of the car, Mac stopped her. "Message from the chief. He's up at the top of the lighthouse, and he needs one more officer up there, stat."

"Did he say why he only wants one of us?"

I leaned forward. "There's already four men up there in a small space. You won't be able to fit too many more."

"Makes sense," she said.

"Who's that?" Rachel Timmons asked, pointing at Sheri in the back seat of the chief's SUV.

"A witness," Mac explained. "Eric's going to want to question her. I can keep an eye on her unless one of you wants to take over."

"We'll take over. Thanks, Mac."

"No problem."

Mindy adjusted her equipment-heavy belt. "Rachel, you mind watching the witness?"

"Not at all," Rachel Timmons said.

"Garcia, you want to go up, or shall I?"

He took a good, long look at the height of the light-house tower and saw the two guys squabbling outside on the catwalk. "You go ahead. Timmons and I can watch this crowd."

"Works for me," Mindy said jovially. "I can use the exercise." And she went running into the lighthouse.

Brian and Lewis continued screaming at each other, but it was impossible to hear what they were saying over the roar of the ocean and the cries of the seabirds. According to Sheri, they'd been arguing over Linda Rutledge. Was one of them accusing the other of killing her?

Without warning, Brian yanked the phone away from Lewis and hurled it into the ocean.

The crowd gasped in unison.

"Can't really blame him for doing that," Mac said.

Annabelle cried out, "Brian, that was mean!"

One of the guys, Kingsley or Hugh, I couldn't tell which, shouted, "Watch his left hook, Brian."

"Watch his left hook?" Mac said under his breath. "That's all the advice he can give this guy?"

"They're all crazy," I whispered.

Lewis screamed his outrage and reached for Brian's throat. He began to throttle him, and Brian was helpless for a moment as he tried to pry away Lewis's fingers. Then Brian stomped on Lewis's instep—a classic defense move for someone with no upper-body strength—and caused him to howl in pain. Lewis bent over and raised his tender foot. Again, we couldn't hear the words, but while Lewis was down, he wasn't out. He reached out with his fist and punched Brian in the stomach. Then he managed to pull himself up to his full height and punch Brian in the face. He clearly wasn't a trained fighter, but his punches appeared to be landing.

"This is brutal," Mac said. "Neither of them know what they're doing, but they're managing to hurt each other."

"Ouch," I said, although I had no sympathy for either of these two morons.

"That'll teach him not to take Lewis's phone," Chloe murmured.

Brian held up his arms to protect his face. Lewis kept swinging, and I wondered how long they could last. But in a surprise move, Brian managed to grab hold of both of Lewis's arms and slowly began to push him toward the railing.

"Oh no!" I shouted, along with everyone else.

"Where's Eric?" Chloe demanded.

"He might not want to go out on the catwalk," I said. "We haven't reinforced it yet, so it's a little weak."

"Do you think he's made it all the way to the top?"

"He and Tommy were moving pretty quickly."

It could take a while to get all the way up there, I thought. The steps were high and narrow and curved.

And being so close to the ocean, they could also be slippery from the moist salt air. It was a treacherous climb in the best of circumstances.

"I wish I had binoculars," she said, then jogged over to where the writers were standing and turned to stare up at the top. After a minute, she came back to report. "I can see Eric inside the glass room."

"Good," I said with some relief. "So he made it up there."

"Why doesn't he grab those guys and get them down here?"

"They might've locked the door to the catwalk," Mac suggested.

"No, they broke the lock," I said, remembering the state of the old weathered door.

Chloe frowned. "So Eric could step out and grab one of them."

"He might be hesitant to distract them."

Chloe made a sound of disgust. "At this point, they're both going to fall to their deaths anyway. He might as well go for it."

I exchanged a look with Mac. She made a good point.

Our gazes were suddenly drawn back to the catwalk as Brian pushed Lewis right up to the edge of the railing. Without warning, Brian gave him one strong shove and Lewis fell over the railing.

"Oh my God!" I screamed.

Everyone joined me, screaming and gasping in horror.

"Holy crap," Chloe cried.

"Noooo!" Sheri shrieked.

I hadn't noticed that she had left the SUV and was

now standing next to the car, staring up at the catwalk. I guessed we'd all been a little distracted.

Rachel Timmons rushed over and opened the back door. "Get back in there."

Sheri looked ready to argue, but Rachel straightened up and stuck her thumbs inside her equipment belt in an aggressive, no-nonsense pose. Sheri climbed back into the car like a docile little lamb.

She had managed to take our attention away for a minute, but now we all looked up and saw that miraculously, Lewis had managed to snag the bottom rail with one hand. Now he was dangling precariously in the air 120-some feet above the jagged rocks and the ocean spray.

"This is insane," Chloe said.

The door to the interior swung open, and Eric stepped out, grabbed Brian's arm, and twisted it behind his back. Within seconds, he had the writer off the catwalk and inside the lighthouse.

There was applause from the crowd for Eric and catcalls for Brian as they both disappeared from sight.

His so-called friends really didn't like him, I thought.

"Are they just going to leave Lewis hanging?" Chloe wondered aloud.

As if on cue, Tommy stepped out onto the flimsy catwalk. With two halting steps he made it to the railing where he crouched down, braced himself, and reached through the rail to grab hold of Lewis's hand.

Lewis's scream of fear could be heard by all of us. I couldn't blame him.

Then Tommy reached down with his other hand and Lewis managed to clutch it. In an amazing show of strength, Tommy pulled the guy up through the bottom spokes of the railing and dragged him onto the grating.

Lewis lay there for a couple of minutes while we all held our breath. Finally, Tommy helped him to his feet, and they both wobbled to the door and disappeared inside.

"Okay, that was pretty heroic," Chloe admitted.

"Sure was," Mac said.

The writers began to applaud and shout out praise for Tommy.

It had been quite a show.

"Now what?" Chloe wondered.

"It's a long way down," I said.

She nodded. "Too bad we didn't bring refreshments."

"Look at this," Mac said, and nudged his chin toward the writers.

We turned and watched Annabelle approach Rachel Timmons. They were close enough for us to hear the conversation as Annabelle asked if she could talk to Sheri.

"Sorry," Officer Timmons said. "You'll have to wait till later."

"Are you kidding me?" Annabelle cried.

"Nope. She's a witness and, frankly, so are you. We don't want you talking to each other until we interview you."

"That's so stupid!"

"What's stupid is you giving me a hard time," Timmons said. "Now you can either wait out here quietly, or you can wait in the black-and-white."

Insulted, Annabelle tossed her hair back. "Not in this lifetime!"

"Then do yourself a favor and go stand over there with your little friends," Timmons said.

"What. Ever." Annabelle stomped her foot—a movement that, after dealing with Whitney, looked distressingly familiar to me—and flounced away.

"They continue to be awful people," I said to Mac.

He shook his head. "Even the halfway normal ones make me want to throw them all out."

"You probably should," I said.

He held up two fingers. "I'm this close to doing it."

All of a sudden, the lighthouse door was flung open, and Brian came flying out, his hands cuffed securely behind his back. He stopped, looked around, and was clearly taken aback by all of us staring at him. He looked relieved to see his writer friends and ran over to them. "He tried to kill me! Did you see it? He's out of his mind! I was so scared."

Eric walked out the door of the lighthouse, seemingly unbothered that the man was running around loose. After all, Brian was handcuffed. Still though, Officer Garcia intercepted him, grabbed his arm, and led him back toward the chief's SUV.

"I want to talk to my friends!" he protested.

"You don't always get what you want," Officer Garcia said mildly. "You pushed that guy over the rail. You could've killed him."

"No! He tried to kill me!" Brian cried.

Eric met Officer Garcia halfway. "Thanks, Carlos. Can you hold him for another minute or two?"

"Sure, Chief. He's not going anywhere."

Eric walked over to his SUV and opened the back door. He leaned in and said something to Sheri, who nodded and smiled flirtatiously.

"Did you see that?" Chloe asked.

I snorted. "The batting eyelashes? Yeah. It just gets better and better."

Eric slammed the door shut and turned toward the lighthouse. And waited.

Another minute or so later, Lewis walked out into the sun. He looked around, and when he saw Brian, he shook his fist at him. "You bastard! You tried to kill me!"

"He's a liar!" Brian shouted to the crowd, then faced Lewis. "You're a fraud and a cheater!"

"Well, you're a thief and killer!"

"They really seem to know each other well," Mac said.

"I've rarely heard Brian's voice," I said. "It's deeper than I thought it would be."

"He doesn't talk much," Mac agreed. "But he's talking now."

All of a sudden, I couldn't help myself. I had just been thinking about Linda and how unfair it was that she'd been killed. She had been a good woman, warm, kind and compassionate. And now, seeing these two spoiled men shouting and spewing at each other like grammar school bullies, it made me sick to think of Linda sparing them one minute of her time.

I took a few steps forward and shouted, "Which one of you removed the screws in my wall?"

For some reason, that shut everyone up. Brian and Lewis both stared in my direction. The other writers stared at me. And having stared down more than a few killers in my life, I knew in that instant who had done it.

But before I could accuse anyone, Lewis began to sway. "I'm going to be sick," he mumbled, and weaved back and forth. He tried to take one more step toward Brian, then dropped to the ground in a dead faint.

Annabelle screamed, "Lewis!"

Sheri threw the car door open and rushed out to grab him.

I looked at Chloe. "I don't get it."

"Me either. It's like they're in a cult."

The cult of Lewis, I thought. Maybe it was his thick blond hair that appealed to them. Or his depraved sense of entitlement. It couldn't have been his personality.

"Get away from him," Brian said in a growl.

Sheri stroked Lewis's cheek, then looked up at Brian with tear-filled eyes. "Why are you always so mean to Lewis?"

Brian glared at her with bared teeth. "Because he stole my life."

Chapter Thirteen

Lewis wasn't moving.

Eric and Tommy rushed over and knelt down next to him. Eric checked Lewis's pulse while Tommy unbuttoned and loosened his collar.

"Don't move him," Eric said, then stood up and yelled, "Garcia, Timmons."

Rachel Timmons came right over. "Did he really pass out?"

"Looks like it. Tom, what happened in there?"

"I watched him take a hard fall down the lighthouse steps," Tommy said. "It happened at the base, just inside the door. He hit his head on the concrete, but he got right up and insisted he was fine."

Carlos Garcia frowned. "So this is, what? A delayed reaction?"

"I guess." Eric gritted his teeth. "He might need a brain scan, and I don't want to wait for an ambulance. Carlos, get the trauma bag out of Tommy's SUV."

"On it, Chief."

"Timmons, we need your EMT expertise. Keep this guy alive, will you?"

"You got it, Chief," she said.

Rachel crouched down, pulled a small black monitor from her fanny pack, and checked Lewis's vital signs. Garcia raced to the car and pulled a large duffel bag from the back. He returned to Lewis, knelt down, and wrapped his neck in a brace. Then he began to piece together a sturdy portable stretcher that they called an immobilization board. I'd seen them use this once before. At one end of the stretcher, Rachel arranged a contraption that looked like two boxes strapped together. They called it a "head bed" and it would help keep Lewis's head and neck stabilized while they transported him to the emergency room.

"We've got to be careful with him," Eric said. "We don't know what sort of injury he might've sustained."

Carlos finished putting the stretcher together and the four of them—Eric, Carlos, Rachel, and Tommy—carefully lifted Lewis onto its surface, strapped him on, and adjusted the head bed. Then they each grabbed a corner of the stretcher, lifted it, and slowly carried it over to the cargo section of Tommy's SUV.

Tommy quickly lowered the two back seats to make room, then Rachel climbed into the back to keep Lewis stable while Carlos took the driver's seat.

"Don't let him out of your sight," Eric warned them.

"Yes, sir." Carlos started the engine and took off for the highway with sirens blaring.

Eric escorted a teary-eyed Sheri back to his SUV and opened the back door for her. She sighed and climbed inside again.

"Do you think Lewis is faking it?" I asked Mac in a low voice.

"Tommy did say he hit his head, but you never know. The guy's proven to be a pretty decent liar."

Eric called Mindy over and pointed to Annabelle, Hugh, and Kingsley, the three writers who were still watching the action as if it were a world heavyweight boxing championship.

"Take those three to headquarters and put them in room 3A. Have someone keep an eye on them. I'll be in to question them later."

"You got it, Chief."

Mindy led the three over to her black-and-white and put them in the back seat. Then she jumped in the car and headed out to the highway.

Eric said something to Tommy, then he approached Mac and Chloe and me. "I'm going to try something here. I think if you ask him some questions, you might be able to get some answers. Let's see what happens."

"No problem," Mac said.

Eric walked over to Brian. "Anything you want to say to these people before I take you into custody?"

"Am I being arrested?" Brian asked, looking shocked.

"Not yet, but we're taking you in for questioning."

"Didn't you hear what I said?" Brian yelled. "Lewis is the one you should arrest."

"And I said I'm not arresting you. Yet."

If Eric was offering to give Brian an opportunity to talk, I wanted to help. "Why did you throw his phone away?" I asked loudly.

Eric's eyes narrowed in on me, and he nodded. Okay, that was a good sign that I was doing all right.

Brian stared at me but said nothing.

I asked, "Was he recording your conversations?"

Brian wrinkled his nose in disgust. "Who are you?"

"Watch it, Brian," Mac warned, his voice low and menacing. "You know who she is."

"Yeah," I said. "Remember me? I'm the person whose partition wall you sabotaged." I had known it was him from his reaction earlier. Or more precisely, from Lewis's reaction, which was a look of complete astonishment. Brian had been more cagey, his gaze unable to meet mine.

"That wasn't me," Brian insisted.

Mac joined in the Q&A. "Hey, Brian. What did you mean when you said that Lewis stole your life?"

Brian blinked several times, suddenly unsure of himself. After all, this was the great MacKintyre Sullivan questioning him. He looked away.

"Brian," Mac repeated. "What did you mean?"

His nostrils flared. He was angry at being confronted and having a hard time hiding it. Finally he said, "Lewis stole my book."

Mac cocked his head. "Which book is that?"

"The big one," he muttered.

"The bestseller?" Mac asked. "You wrote that?"

Brian chewed on his bottom lip and looked away.

Didn't he realize we could tell he was lying?

"Answer me, Brian," Mac persisted. "Did you write that book?"

"Um, yeah."

I glanced up at Mac. "You know he's lying."

"Oh, yeah." But Mac forged ahead. "Why didn't you tell anyone?"

"Because . . . it's nobody's business."

"So you were okay with him taking all the accolades for a book that you wrote? What about the money? The royalties?"

Brian sighed so heavily, it was as if he could no longer fight off our questions. "I arranged a payment plan."

"Ah. So did he pay you?"

Brian scowled. "Not enough."

"So he didn't actually steal the book," Mac reasoned. "You sold it to him."

"Yeah, but then it hit the bestseller list, and I wanted more money. He agreed to give me more, but I haven't seen it yet."

"Sorry to hear that," Mac said. "But I still don't understand why you didn't put your own name on the book."

"He wanted the book," Brian said, as if that made perfect sense. And maybe it did, given the odd nature of their relationship.

"Now what about Lewis's second book," Mac said. "The one he just turned in?"

I glanced at Eric, but he still didn't look inclined to stop the conversation.

"Oh, that one," Brian said. "It's um . . ."

"Did you write that book, too?"

His eyes darted back and forth. He was more nervous about the second book.

"Who wrote that book?" Mac asked.

"I don't know."

"So it wasn't you?"

His skinny shoulders were visibly shaking. "Uh. Hmm. No."

"It's Travis's book, isn't it?"

"I don't know. Maybe."

Mac persisted. "Did Lewis steal Travis's tablet?"

His eyes widened. "Yes."

"No!" Sheri shouted. "Brian stole it."

She was sitting on the running board now.

Eric turned to her. "You just can't stay put, can you?"

"I'm helping," she said.

Eric just shook his head at the whole bizarre scene. "Sheri, do you know for a fact that Brian stole Travis's tablet?"

"Yes."

"How do you know?" Mac asked.

She lifted one shoulder in a careless move. "Because I heard them arguing about it."

"There's no way you could hear us!" Brian cried. "We were all the way at the end of the breakwater."

Mac bit back a smile. The man had effectively confessed. "So Brian. You and Lewis did argue about stealing Travis's tablet."

Brian realized that he'd trapped himself. I almost laughed at his confused expression, but there was nothing funny about this deranged man who admitted to being a thief and who could quite possibly be a deadly killer as well.

His bottom lip quivered in a pout. "Maybe."

"Why were you arguing?"

He didn't want to answer, and it was obvious that he was trying really hard to come up with the perfect lie. The problem was, he just wasn't very good at this. He needed Lewis by his side. The two of them had been a devious and strangely capable duo, but alone, they couldn't seem to function very well. They each needed their wingman.

I glanced around and had to wonder what rabbit hole we'd all tumbled into: there was Brian in the center; Sheri on the running board, dangling her legs back and forth as if she didn't have a care in the world; Chloe and me together, both of us spellbound by Mac's cross-examination of this spoiled, immature man; and Eric and Tommy, who were strangely willing to let Mac take the lead, but alert and ready to pounce if Brian made one wrong move.

Finally, there was the spirit of Lewis hanging over it all, currently unable to tell his own story.

"Lewis wanted to steal everything Travis had on the tablet," Brian finally admitted. "I thought he was being piggish. I told him I'd only taken it for the one story about the raging river. I agreed that Lewis could send that one to his agent. I told him he should be grateful." He bared his teeth. "But he was never grateful."

"So let's go back to Lewis's first book," Mac said, taking a quick look at Eric, who still appeared to be perfectly happy to have Mac asking the questions. He and Brian were both writers, and they were talking about books and stories, which was Mac's field of expertise. And Brian was obviously cowed by Mac's presence, so that was helping to get some answers out of him.

"Okay," Brian said hesitantly.

"If you didn't write it and Lewis didn't write it, where did it come from?"

"I can help you here," Sheri said.

Mac extended his hand. "Please do."

She fluffed her hair back. She was now onstage, after all. "An obscure self-published author named Simon Marcello wrote the book under a different title. He has since died."

"Do you know how he died?"

"Oh, he was murdered," she said, matter-of-factly. "Blunt-force trauma."

"How do you know all this?" Mac asked.

"I'm a research librarian," Sheri said, smiling smugly. "I know a lot of things. And if there's anything I don't know, I look it up. For instance, if you google a particular line from Lewis's first book, you'll find out that it's actually a line from Simon Marcello's book."

"Wow," I whispered. Was it really that simple?

"And how do you know that Marcello was murdered?"

She glanced impatiently at Mac. "I looked it up. His murder is still unsolved. Maybe Brian can explain it."

"Shut up, Sheri," Brian grumbled.

Sheri held up one finger. "I do have a theory, though."

"What's your theory?" Mac asked, recognizing that Sheri was on a roll.

"I believe that Mr. Marcello was unaware that his book had been stolen. But then Lewis's book hit all the bestseller lists, and Brian was afraid that all of that publicity would ultimately attract the attention of Mr. Marcello, and he would put up a fuss. He'd probably try to sue Lewis, which would land Brian in hot water. So Brian killed him."

"Shut up!" Brian howled.

Sheri batted her eyelashes at Brian. "Did I strike a nerve?"

She definitely had. We all watched Brian's false bravado fizzling. His fists were bunched up, and his face was turning red.

"Why do you think it was Brian who killed him and not Lewis?" I asked.

Sheri studied her fingernails. "It's simple. Brian is a psychopath. Lewis is simply a self-centered narcissistic opportunist."

"Don't talk about Lewis!" Brian shouted.

I saw Eric take a few steps closer to Brian, whose neck muscles were straining with every word Sheri spoke.

Before he popped his cork, I hurried to ask a question. "Sheri, if you're aware that Lewis is a complete fraud who ripped his books off from other writers, why do you all still like him?"

Another shoulder shrug. "I don't hold it against him. I mean, I guess it's a little skeevy. But this book writing business is hard. People do what they have to do to get ahead. Besides, Lewis is cute. He's got great hair. And he's got money. So in case I haven't mentioned it before, I'm more than happy to ride his coattails."

Mac had told us that she'd mentioned it before, so I believed her. However, I wasn't about to bring up the fact that his money was quickly dwindling away.

"Lewis can get me into all the best publisher parties," Sheri continued. "He can invite me to book signings at all the top stores. And do you know how hard it is to get on a panel at the National Book Association convention? Lewis got that for me. They gave out two hundred of my books. You can't buy that kind of publicity."

Was anyone in this group a normal person? I was afraid not. I took a quick look at Mac and watched him shaking his head. He was over it.

Eric took a few casual steps closer to Brian. "Tell me about Linda Rutledge."

Brian was startled by the question. "Well, I saw her first. And she liked me."

"But Lewis was the one who was always coming around with her."

"He doesn't play fair." Brian sounded more like a fourth grader on the playground than a grown man.

"You know, I was at the writers' workshop that night," Eric said. "And I recall that you *did* see Linda first."

"I know!"

"But then Lewis made his move, and you were out of the running."

Brian glanced around, unable to meet Eric's gaze. Was he embarrassed? "It's okay. I still like her. She's really pretty and she was nice to me. Lewis thinks he's got all the right moves, but Linda wasn't going to fall in love with him or anything. Lewis didn't like that she was nice to everyone. He didn't like that she was so friendly with Travis." His smile was sly. "Lewis didn't like the competition. He decided to get Travis in trouble."

"How was he going to do that?" Eric wondered.

"By setting it up for Travis to take the blame for killing Linda."

I scoffed. "That makes no sense at all. So he gets rid of the competition for her affection by killing her. How does that get him what he wants?"

"Clearly he's not such a genius, after all," Brian snarled.

"Or you're lying," I said, staring the man down.

Eric walked back and forth in front of Brian, disconcerting him. "You know, Brian. Lewis was just taken to the hospital."

"I know. But how come?"

"He hit his head really hard, and he's probably still unconscious. He might not recover."

"Too bad," he muttered.

"So let me ask you this." Eric stopped pacing and looked at Brian. "Did Lewis kill Linda?"

His gaze darted from one side to the other. He was nervous again. "Yes."

Eric stared him down. "Are you sure?"

"Well, yeah."

"So if Lewis recovers and I ask him that same question, what will he tell me?"

"He killed her!" Brian insisted.

I took a step forward. "I thought you and Lewis were best friends. Why would you accuse him of killing anyone?"

"We are best friends," he insisted. "But even best friends have to get their butts kicked once in a while."

"What does that mean?" I asked.

He shrugged. "Lewis was getting cocky, and I knew he was about to throw me under the bus."

"So you thought you'd throw him first."

He shrugged but said nothing.

Eric resumed his casual pacing. "Were you wearing Lewis's suede jacket the other day?"

"He gave it to me!"

"It's a nice jacket," Eric said. "How much did you pay him for it?"

"Nothing."

"Did you offer to hide the bloody murder weapon for him?"

There went his eyes, darting every which way again. It was getting to be a habit with Brian. A definite tell. "What if I did? It doesn't mean I killed anybody."

Mac spoke up from the sidelines. "Sheri thinks you killed Simon Marcello."

Brian's chin jutted out defensively. "She's not as smart as she thinks she is."

"I am, too," Sheri drawled.

I sighed. Every one of these people needed a keeper. I was just glad that in a few days, I would never have to see them again.

"With the exception of Sheri," Eric explained later that evening, "the other writers weren't much help for anything other than peripheral character references."

"I assume you stuck Brian in a cell," Mac said.

"Oh, you bet. Even if he isn't guilty of killing Linda and attacking Parks, he's a thief and an accessory to murder."

"And there's the murder of Simon Marcello," I said.

"Yeah, I've already got Mindy looking into that case."

We were silent for a moment as we all considered what had happened over the past week. Then I asked, "Do you think Brian is actually a writer? Have you seen any of his work?"

"I haven't," Mac admitted. "But I can't believe the rest of the group would keep him around if he wasn't actually producing anything."

"Lewis might've insisted," Chloe said.

I nodded. "That's what I was thinking."

"It's a good question for Sheri," Eric said, and made a note in his pad.

"Any word on Lewis?" Mac asked.

Eric reached for his wineglass. "Still unconscious. We'll have to wait until he recovers before we can get his statement."

After a long day of talking to a psychopath and other assorted weirdos, we were sitting in my dining room drinking Barolo and eating excellent pasta and antipasti from Bella Rosso on the town square. Robbie, Tiger, and Luke were happily curled up under the table.

"I hope he recovers soon," I said. "But even if he does, who knows if he'll ever tell you the truth?"

"I'll play them against each other," Eric said. "Promise a lighter sentence to whoever spills first."

"That's so brilliant," Chloe said, and leaned over to kiss him.

"Isn't it?" Eric grinned and kissed her back. "I read about that technique in a police procedural."

Mac laughed.

"But Brian's goose is cooked," I said. "He's killed before. According to Sheri, anyway."

Mac swirled his wine. "In my estimation, she's the only reliable witness."

"Why do you think so?" Eric asked.

"She's whip smart," Mac explained. "She recognizes her own craven ambitions and is able to spot the same feature in others. Of all of them, she's the only one who's studied her craft to the nth degree. I wouldn't be surprised to hear that she's visited prisons and interviewed hardened criminals for research. And I've read her book. She's a good writer and a very scary woman. But she's not a killer."

"Are you sure?" Eric asked.

"What do you think?" Mac countered.

Eric leaned back in his chair. "I think you're right."

"I think so, too," I said. "And she's a valuable witness. Her vanity is so strong that she'll happily reveal the deepest darkest secrets about the others, just to prove that she's the smartest kid in class."

Chloe elbowed me. "Sounds like you're the smartest kid in class."

I had to laugh. "Hardly, but I did enjoy that spontaneous courtroom scene by the lighthouse this afternoon."

"Yeah, Mac." Chloe set down her wineglass. "You were like Perry Mason there for a while."

"Huh," Mac said. "I was trying to channel *Better Call Saul.*"

Eric laughed. "Either way, you did a good job."

"Thanks. I recognized that Brian might spill his guts if I was the one questioning him."

"I saw that, too," Eric said.

Mac grinned. "That's why you let me blather on and on."

"I wish we had thought to record it," I said.

"None of that is admissible," Eric explained. He paused, then smiled and held up his phone. "But I taped it anyway."

Chloe applauded. "Thank God. That was really smart."

"It sure was," I said.

In his honor, we helped ourselves to more pasta and antipasti.

"Your phone," I mused.

"What?" Mac asked, instantly alerted to my tone. "What're you thinking?"

I gazed at him. "I was just thinking about the way Lewis records everything on his phone."

"The phone that's sitting at the bottom of the ocean?"

"Are we sure it's at the bottom of the ocean?" I wondered.

"I saw the water splash where Brian threw it," Mac said.

I sighed. "Okay. Well, never mind trying to recover the phone. But I was thinking. Remember when Travis thought he'd lost his tablet, and he talked about retrieving his stories and documents from the cloud?"

"Sure," Mac said, sitting up straighter.

"Do you think the information on Lewis's phone could be on the cloud, too?"

They all stared at me, then Mac grabbed me and kissed me. "You are a genius."

"So you think the recordings can be accessed?" I asked.

He kissed me again. "Yes. Sheri told me he's a fanatic about backing up his data. And I know he uses a voice recorder app that I'm familiar with. The data can definitely be retrieved." Then he scratched his head. "Don't know why I didn't think of it."

"You've had a lot on your mind."

He sighed. "No kidding."

"We'll have to get a warrant," Eric mused, then smiled. "That won't be a problem, though, since I've already applied for it."

I smiled. "You're always two steps ahead."

Lewis had been transferred from the hospital emergency room to ICU and regained consciousness two days later. Eric questioned him at his hospital bedside, and later that night, he dropped by my house with Chloe and told us the story. "He denied everything that Brian claimed was true when we questioned him at the lighthouse."

"I'm not surprised," I said. For once, we weren't discussing all the sordid details while stuffing our faces with food. But we did have a good bottle of wine, and we were happy to share it with Eric and Chloe.

"Me, either," Eric said. "He maintained his innocence the whole time, but his story will collapse eventually. Although I must say, he's a much more skillful liar than Brian."

Mac studied the wineglass, thinking. "It might be because Lewis actually believes his own lies. Brian is more tentative, but he's sly. He's shifty. He'll change stories in midstream if he has to. I doubt he can even remember all the lies he's told."

"Still," I said, "I do believe they're equally evil."

"I don't often use the word *evil*," Eric admitted. "But in the case of these two men, I think it applies."

"I'm still interested in hearing those recordings from Lewis's phone."

"Yes, I think that'll tell the real story," Eric said.

Chloe took a sip of the deep red wine. "So when Lewis denied everything, what did you say?"

"I told him that even if he denied killing Linda, he was still going to prison."

"He must've balked at that," Mac said.

"Oh, strenuously," Eric said. "He cried real tears, claimed he was a victim in all of this. But he committed fraud when he took money from his publisher for the book he stole. And he probably did it for the second book, too. And he coerced Brian into doing all sorts of unlawful acts. They're both going to prison. How long they stay will depend on how good a lawyer they each get."

We all sipped our wine and considered the two men.

I wondered how they'd become friends. They must've recognized something in each other that would complement their own personality traits.

"Birds of a feather," I murmured.

Everyone nodded. They must've been thinking the same thing.

"By the way," Eric said, "I asked Sheri about Brian and his writing. She confirmed that he's never shown the group any of his work. All they had to go on was Lewis's insistence that Brian's work is brilliant. He's a genius, according to Lewis. Sheri just rolled her eyes at that."

"But they let him stay in the group anyway," I said. "What's up with that?"

"Sheri did say that Brian was very good at critiquing everyone else's work." Eric read from his notepad. "'Brian was especially helpful with murder scenes,' she said. 'He has a real keen eye for detail, and he knows the finer points of blood spatter and all sorts of ways to kill. He pushed all of them to get more graphic and more violent with their murder scenes.'"

"Wasn't she grossed out by that?"

"Actually, no," Eric said. "She admitted that it was really helpful. 'That's what sells,' Sheri said."

"Wow," Chloe said.

Mac shook his head. "The sad thing is, she's right."

Two days later, it all came out. Eric had recovered a whole series of recorded conversations between Lewis and Brian that were astounding. And so ugly. It made me sick.

Faced with the naked truth of those recordings, Brian and Lewis confessed to everything. Even though

Brian killed Linda and Simon Marcello himself, Lewis was charged as an accessory. Lewis was also charged with fraud for passing off Simon Marcello's work as his own. Lewis confessed to stealing Travis's work and doing the same thing.

The police had also confiscated all of the computers and electronics that belonged to the writers. Eric confirmed that Lewis had copied everything from Travis's tablet, and we all agreed that eventually, he would've claimed every one of Travis's stories as his own.

And if they were following their usual pattern, they would've eventually found it necessary to kill Travis.

"They've already confessed to their crimes," Eric explained the following night as we sat in his kitchen dining on Chloe's lasagna. "But their lawyers might insist that they recant, so we'll have to wait and see if there's going to be a trial in Lighthouse Cove."

"Exactly what are their crimes?" I asked.

Eric's gaze was steady. "Look, it's wrong of me to do this, but I'm trusting you guys."

I exchanged a quick glance with Mac. What was Eric going to do?

"Here's the thing," Eric continued. "You were both responsible for getting us to this point, so I'm going to let you hear the recordings. If you want to."

"Absolutely." I looked at Mac. "I know you want to hear them."

"Oh yeah, I do. I want to know what was in their gutless little brains that drove them to do what they did."

I nodded at Eric. "I want to hear what they say, even if it makes my stomach turn."

"It just might," Eric said tightly. He pressed the Play button, and we all sat and listened to everything.

The lasagna was delicious, but, sad to say, I lost my appetite within a few minutes of listening to Brian and Lewis.

"You can do it," Lewis coaxed. "You're good at that stuff."

The phone recordings revealed that it was at Lewis's urging that Brian had stolen Travis's tablet. Lewis was determined to undermine Travis to get him away from Linda. The kicker came when he saw the two of them together at the pub that night. He didn't like that at all.

But a secondary reason to grab the tablet was to read Travis's stories. Maybe there was something on there that he could use. Turned out, there was plenty. Lewis went ahead and sent his agent the best story. Then he told Brian how he planned to use the other stories eventually, too. Brian told him he was being selfish, and Lewis laughed hysterically.

He and Brian's arguments over Linda were the most revealing in terms of their bizarre dynamic. Lewis's point was that yes, they would only be in Lighthouse Cove for two weeks, but for those two weeks, Linda would belong to Lewis. It was clear that the man's main goal in life was to be seen as a winner.

Brian antagonized him constantly. "You're not a winner," he said on more than one occasion. "You're a cheater."

"I won Linda," he bragged.

"You cheated."

"Nobody cares," Lewis said. "All they know is that when we walk into a room, she's on my arm."

"You're pathetic," Brian said.

"I'm pathetic?" Lewis cackled. "You wanted her, but I won her. Who's pathetic now?"

As I listened, I realized it was all a game to the two of them. They would only be in Lighthouse Cove for two weeks, but they would do their best to screw with everyone they came into contact with. Their relationship was so bizarre. It seemed as if they always wanted the same thing: the same girl, the same dream of being a writer. But then it was as if Brian wanted that dream for Lewis, not for himself. However, when Lewis got what he wanted, it didn't make Brian happy, because even though he was the one who had helped Lewis achieve his dream, he would just as quickly and eagerly snatch it away.

It couldn't be said enough: their relationship was creepy and sick and twisted.

After Linda's body was found, Lewis recorded this short passage: "So you killed her."

"Who says I did?" Brian said.

"Why would you do that?" Lewis cried, simply accepting the fact that Brian had murdered Linda. "You knew I liked her."

"I liked her, too," Brian said easily. "But you had to go and tell her that you didn't have anything written, and that you didn't have any ideas. You only did it so she'd feel sorry for you. But seriously, don't you think she would've put two and two together when your new book was announced? Of course she would! She would've started asking questions, and everyone would've figured out that you stole Travis's story. I had to get rid of her, because you couldn't keep your mouth shut."

"You did it to hurt me," Lewis cried.

"That was just a bonus," Brian said.

"Bastard," Lewis said.

"Loser," Brian replied.

Their name-calling sounded almost rehearsed, as if they had been through it all before.

Suddenly Brian gave a quick, sly laugh. "Hey, remember Felicia Harding?"

Lewis snorted. "Dude, that was in high school."

"Do you remember her?"

"Of course. She was a really good kisser." There was a pause, then Lewis said, "I wonder what happened to her. I remember she disappeared after meeting me at the library one night."

"That's right." Brian laughed again.

There was a long pause. Finally Lewis whispered, "Wait. Are you kidding me? You did it?"

"I did what I had to do."

"Damn," Lewis muttered. "Why didn't you tell me? I'm your best friend."

"I'm telling you now." Brian giggled. "Because we're best friends."

"Man, you are fierce!" Lewis said, sounding impressed. "But . . . we were only fifteen years old."

"Got to start sometime," Brian said, his voice alarmingly calm. "And practice makes perfect."

Lewis laughed. "You are one sick puppy."

"Those are *two* sick puppies," Chloe said.

"Some of the sickest I've ever known," Mac admitted.

"I looked up the Felicia Harding case," Eric said. "She disappeared when she was fifteen. No trace of her since."

Something occurred to me. "Do you think there were other victims?"

"Someone starts killing when he's fifteen years old?" Eric pondered the question. "Chances are, he'll keep doing it until he's caught."

"Seriously sick." I had to take a breath. "As much as I hate to agree with Sheri, Brian really is a psychopath."

"Lewis isn't much better," Chloe said. "What do you call someone like that? A narcissist?"

"A 'narcissistic opportunist' is what Sheri called him," Mac said. "I'd add 'with sociopathic tendencies.'" He shook his head in disgust. "Makes me want to discontinue the writers' retreat."

"They were an anomaly," I argued. "Please don't worry. There'll never be another writers' group like theirs."

"We can only hope that's true."

I poured everyone a bit more wine. "I don't want to give one more minute of energy to those two, and the same goes for the rest of them. They were barely in town for ten days and caused nothing but chaos. It still disturbs me to think about it."

"It disturbs you because you can't look away," Eric said. "Those two are like that bloody car crash on the highway. Not only can you not look away, but then you continue to think about it for the next hundred miles."

Mac stared at him. "That's good. That's really good." He pulled out the small leather-bound notepad that he carried everywhere. "I'm writing that down."

It was just the right thing to say. We all laughed and sipped our wine and then went around the table talking about happier subjects. Like the fact that Parks was home from the hospital, and my dad and Belinda were going to visit Homefront next week. My vegetable garden was thriving, and Mac was more than halfway through his latest book. His darling niece Callie was coming to stay with us for the summer. Chloe's show was up for a Daytime Emmy. Eric won the office football pool. And life went on.

The next day, I went back to work at Homefront. Chloe and I were able to start applying mud to the drywall. It would take a day to dry before we could start sanding, so I went up to our latest group of houses and took out some aggression with my pneumatic staple gun.

I happened to look up and was pleased to see Parks walking toward the house. His head was wrapped in a bandage, but he looked great. I climbed down the ladder and greeted him with a light hug.

"How are you feeling?" I asked.

"Much better, thank you." His voice was softer and he seemed fragile. "I understand you found the person who killed our Linda."

"Yeah. We found him."

"Must've been the same crudball who conked me on the head."

I nodded. "So you saw who hit you."

"Sure did. It was that skinny writer with the dead eyes."

Brian, I thought. That description was way too close for comfort, and I felt chills creep up my spine. "Do you mind telling me what happened?"

"Don't mind at all. I saw him go into Travis's house, and when he came out, I confronted him." Parks folded his arms tightly across his chest. "He didn't like that, but he didn't do anything about it right then. Just called me an old snoop and walked away."

"What happened next?"

"About ten minutes later, someone knocked on my door. I opened it and there he was. I wasn't going to invite him in, so I walked out onto the stoop. He tried to look all contrite and apologize. Said he was always taught to respect veterans. I thought it was a load of bull and said so, then turned to go back inside. That's when he whacked me hard on the head, and I went down."

"I'm so sorry."

"Yeah." He touched his head gingerly. "Me, too."

"You'll be happy to know that he's in jail."

"Good. Glad to hear it. We don't need troublemakers like that around here."

I had to smile, but it wasn't because of a happy memory. No, his words reminded me of what Whitney had warned me about the other day. Troublemakers were showing up here, she'd claimed. She had been completely right about that. But also completely wrong, as usual.

Yes, troublemakers had shown up here, but they hadn't been a part of Homefront's community. They weren't veterans. Those troublemakers had come from the outside and had caused real pain and sadness for our town.

What Whitney didn't understand was that this veterans' village was a refuge for heroes. Sure, some of them had fallen on hard times in the past, but they were brave men and women who were welcomed here because of their service to our country. I just hoped

Whitney would figure that out someday. It would probably be about the same time she figured out that stiletto heels were not her friend. Which would happen sometime around . . . never.

I waved goodbye to Parks and climbed back onto the roof and once again worked out all the troubles of the world using my handy-dandy pneumatic staple gun.

When I was finished, I stood up on the roof and gazed around at the thriving little community I'd had a hand in building. And felt ridiculously proud and happy for all of us.

Epilogue

Two weeks later, Mac grudgingly prepared to welcome his next writers' retreat group to Lighthouse Cove. He had been close to deciding to cancel the rest of the groups and stop the retreats altogether, but he wanted to give it one last shot. Maybe a good healthy group would clean away the stench of that last one.

Mac had always been the cool, calm, and collected kind of guy who took care of business and didn't sweat the small stuff. He'd allowed the sick personalities of Brian and Lewis to invade his life, and he hated the feeling that they left him with. He didn't want or need that kind of energy surrounding him.

I couldn't blame him. And I was truly furious that the last group had left him with those feelings. Mac was an amazing man with a strong personality and a healthy outlook on life. It was painful to see him wrestle with the possibility that the whole writers' retreat experiment had been a failure. It hadn't been, but you couldn't prove it by the bad behavior of Brian and Lewis and the others.

"The new group will be here at two o'clock," Mac said, as we sat at the kitchen table eating breakfast.

I took a bite of my turkey bacon. "Tell me about this group."

"Okay." He sipped his coffee. "There are four women, all multipublished romance authors. Two of them have hit the bestseller lists, and all of them seem savvy and professional. Each of them publishes several books a year, so they're serious working writers. As always, I checked out their social media pages, and they're all strictly business."

"What does that mean?"

He rested his elbows on the table. "They use social media as a means of talking about their books and their writing. They recommend other books they're reading and other writers they like. They don't share their personal angst or their money problems or their diet secrets or their whacko conspiracy theories. And they don't rag on other authors. At least, not on social media."

"So far, so good," I said. "They don't sound like psychopaths."

He gave a short, dry laugh. "That's a pretty low bar."

"I know." I smiled. "Sorry about that."

"No, I appreciate it." He scratched his head, then sat back in his chair. "Damn. I'm not sure I'll ever recover from that last group."

"I'm not sure I will, either. They were all seriously nutso." I stood up, walked around the table, and leaned over to wrap my arms around him. "It's not fair that you should take the blame for their destructive stupidity."

"I brought them here," he said quietly.

"They brought themselves here. Nobody blames you."

"Linda Rutledge . . ."

"No," I said, rubbing his back. "Linda wouldn't blame you, either. She was a lovely, kind woman who never hurt anyone. They took advantage of her good nature."

"I could kill them for that alone," he muttered.

So could I, I thought. In that moment, I thought of Linda's quiet way of showing kindness, and felt a stab in my heart. I had only known her for a few days, but she had left an indelible impression on me. I had an almost ghostlike feeling that I had lost someone who would have become a lifelong friend.

So much had been destroyed in such a short period of time by those two awful men. I had shed enough tears to last a few years, but right now, I wanted to shed a few more for Linda. And for Travis. And for Mac, too. I wasn't sure any of us would ever get over the loss.

I stroked Mac's back, smoothed my hands over his head, and then rubbed his neck. "Do me a favor. Kill them in a book."

He was silent for a long moment until he finally chuckled. "You know, Irish. The day I met you was the luckiest day of my life."

My heart fluttered in my chest. "It was mine, too. I love you. And I hate to see you suffer because of them."

He stared at me for a long moment and ran his fingers along my cheek. "You're so good for me."

I smiled. "You're pretty good for me, too." I kissed

him, then stood up, and went back to my chair and my coffee.

"Thanks for that," he said. "I'm going to be okay."

"I know. But I'm happy to hear you say it."

After a minute, his eyes narrowed. "Yeah, this is good. I've already got it pictured in my head. I'm going to kill them all in a book, and that book will sell a gazillion copies."

Now I laughed. "It's the best revenge."

"And all the proceeds will go to Homefront."

"Oh, Mac." I sighed. "That's even better."

The four women arrived that afternoon. By the time I got home from work, Mac was standing at the stove cooking tomato sauce for spaghetti and meatballs. Cooking was one of the things he did when he'd had a particularly good day of writing.

I put my things down on the kitchen table, then walked over and kissed him. "You had a good day."

He pressed his forehead to mine. "Thanks to you, it started out perfect. Then it got even better. And now that you're home, it's the best."

"That's so nice to hear."

He went back to stirring the sauce, and I put my things away in my office. When I walked back into the kitchen, Robbie was frantic to get my attention. "Hello, lovey. Did you have a good day, too?" I bent down and picked him up, and he shivered in ecstasy. I sat at the kitchen table and gave him lots of scratches and rubs. "You're such a good boy. Yes, you are. Yes, you are."

Luke and Tiger wanted in on the action and skulked over to play with the laces of my work boots. After a few minutes, Robbie barked once and jumped down from my lap. The cats took that as a sign that they could relax their guard, so they circled around and curled up on the kitchen rug.

I pulled a bottle of red wine from the wine fridge. After opening it, I poured two glasses and set one of them on the counter near the stove. I was almost afraid to ask, but I forged ahead. "So, tell me about the writers."

"Okay." He gave the sauce one last stir and put the cover on the pot. "I met them at the mansion. Showed them around. Introduced them to Frank and Irma, who had set out a spread of cookies and munchies and coffee and sodas."

"That was nice."

He smiled. "Yeah, they're good people. So anyway, I told the writers to stay out of the lighthouse, and they assured me that they would. I walked them out to the beach, and they were delighted. They love the porch. They all agreed they can't wait to start writing out there." He took a sip of wine. "They call their writers' group the No-Drama Queens."

"Oh, I like that."

"Yeah, it kind of says it all. They're cool, they're calm, they're smart, they're funny, and they're no drama. They like to have a good time. They like to hang out with one another. They like to read and write."

"Are they properly respectful of your great talent and abilities?"

He laughed. "Absolutely. They each brought one of my books with them and asked me to sign it."

"That's an excellent sign."

"Yeah. Seriously." He shook his head in awe and relief. "They've got a totally different vibe from the previous knuckleheads."

I let go of a breath I must've been holding. "I'm so glad."

"You and me both. I asked them if they wanted me to set up a book signing at Lizzie's for them. They said they'd already contacted her a few weeks ago, and they'll be signing on Friday."

"So along with everything else, they're self-sufficient."

"Yeah. No drama." Then he grinned. "So it was a good day."

A few weeks later, Chloe and Eric drove from Los Angeles to Lighthouse Cove on a sunny weekend. When they reached Eric's house, there were thirty people hanging out on the front lawn and up on the porch, drinking Mac's famous margaritas and munching on chips and salsa. All of our girlfriends were there with their guys, and Uncle Pete, Dad, and Belinda had driven into town for the occasion. Most of my crew and a few of the vets, including Travis and Parks, had shown up as well.

As soon as Eric parked the car, we shouted, "Surprise."

"Welcome home!"

"Chloe, Chloe!" we all chanted.

The expression on her face was priceless. She said hello to everyone and thanked them for the nice surprise. Then she whispered, "I don't know who half of these people are."

"But they know who you are," I said. "And they're your new friends."

She burst into tears and I couldn't have been happier.

One week later, Chloe and Eric came over for dinner. Mac grilled salmon, and Chloe helped me put together a big salad with veggies from the garden.

"So I was thinking," Chloe began, after we were seated in the dining room. "I want you to come down and be a guest star on my show next month."

"Are you kidding?" I said. "I can't just fly off to Hollywood for a week."

"Yes, you can," she said.

"What if I go with you?" Mac said casually.

I stared at him. "You would go with me?"

He ran his hand up and down my arm. "I know you've been really busy lately."

"Yeah, I guess I have been. The lighthouse is almost finished, though, so I'll finally be able to take a day or two off."

"Good," he said, exchanging a quick look with Chloe.

I stared at him, then turned to look at Chloe and frowned. "Are you two in cahoots about something? What's going on?"

"Nothing," Chloe said. "So will you come and do my show?"

"And will you come with me to the Hollywood premiere of Jake Slater's new film?" Mac asked.

"So you *are* in cahoots," I said. But I wasn't about to complain. The last time one of Mac's books was turned into a film, he had been on an extended book tour that happened to end in New York City just in time for the premiere.

He held my hand and smiled at me. "What do you say, Irish?"

I didn't need to think about it. "I would love to."

"Hey, what about my show?" Chloe demanded.

I grinned. "Yes, yes. Thank you. I would love to do it." But I held up my hand to stop her. "You have to promise me, though. No dead bodies."

She smirked. "Oh, sure. That's easy. I promise."

"Oh man, you just jinxed the whole trip." Eric rolled his eyes at the two of us. "That settles it. I'm coming with you."

A few weeks later, I was able to move the location of my construction class from the meeting room at the community center to the last row of five homes that still remained to be built at Homefront.

There were only five women left in the class, but they were stalwart in their determination to make it through. And all of them were so proficient with tools and procedures by now that I felt completely at ease allowing them to work on the houses. Wade, Sean, and Johnny were right there with me to supervise and help teach each of them how to pour a foundation, frame a house, insulate walls, build a roof, and so on.

Julia was one of the five still remaining. "I have my job and I love it, so I'm not looking for a new career. But finishing this class is a matter of pride at this point. And in my heart, I'm doing it for Linda." Her eyes filled up, and she waved her hands in front of her face. "I didn't want to do that."

"It still hits me sometimes, too," I admitted. "I was looking at a backsplash the other day, and I had to sit down, the sadness was so overwhelming."

"I get angry, too," she confessed. "Linda's father was not very helpful when I asked if he wanted to keep her collection of mallets and all of her glass and stone pieces."

"What did he say?"

"He told me to throw everything away."

I closed my eyes for a moment. "I hope you didn't."

"No way. I still have everything. And by the way, I'd like you to have one of her mallets. Your choice."

Not for the first time that day, I had to blink away the tears. "I would love that."

The women watched me hammer the OSB board to the exterior wall and listened to me explain the differences between OSB and plywood. "Both will do the job for you, whether you're installing it on your outer walls or your roof. OSB is made up of wood fibers and resins that some say will disintegrate faster than plywood. But others say the resins will help it last longer. OSB is more waterproof than plywood. There are pros and cons on both sides, it just depends on your experience, along with the local weather, and stuff like that. My guys and I are currently on Team OSB, but check back in a year or two. We might've switched."

Within three weeks, the last five houses of Homefront were finished. My construction students worked on parts of all five, but they mainly concentrated on house number fifty.

One day Julia brought Linda's tools and her bits of glass and pottery and marble to the site. And between the two of us, we managed to turn the materials into a sweet, colorful backsplash for the kitchen.

On the day we finished the last house, all of the women and most of my crew gathered around the small front lawn. Many of the vets wandered over to celebrate with us. I was happy to see Parks and Travis in the crowd.

Travis had been an essential part of the crew that had helped me and the women finish the last five houses. At one point, he'd pulled me aside and told me that he felt Linda's presence when he worked with the other women, hammering and painting and turning these materials into homes for other veterans. It was helping him get through some difficult moments.

"She's still here with us," he said, and it reminded me of what he'd said at the memorial service. I caught a glimmer of tears in his eyes. "I planted a gardenia bush next to my front door, and when I smell that beautiful fragrance, it reminds me of her. I can make it through the day knowing that she's here, watching out for me, just like she did that day the glass shattered."

Julia spoke to the crowd first, telling everyone what the class had meant to her and what we'd all learned. "This class is incredibly important and close to my heart. I can verify that women feel empowered when they know how to build things. Our trip to the hardware store was an amazing experience. It's nice to walk into a place like that and know what you're looking for. Seriously, I'm no longer intimidated by all those choices I have to make. And most of all, this class was fun."

I spoke next. "It was such an honor and a real challenge to teach this class. I learned a lot, too, and I'm excited to announce that I'm offering all four of my students a job with my crew."

There was an audible gasp, and then a huge cheer went up. That's when I noticed that the audience had grown to at least fifty people. And I noticed that Eric and Chloe and Mac were standing out there. Travis moved a little closer and flashed me an encouraging smile, and I felt better for it. I hoped he did, too.

I took a deep breath. "So Amy, Heather, Sari, and Becca. Welcome to the team."

Everyone applauded.

"Where do we sign up?" Heather shouted.

I laughed. "We'll talk later."

After the applause and cheers died down, I said, "I just have two more things to say. First, there are three new picnic tables at this end of the park, all made by the women in this class. Check them out. They're really well constructed and should provide you all with years of happy picnic memories."

There were laughs and a lot of applause. It was a good crowd.

"And second." I held up a small brass plaque and gazed with appreciation at this crowd that had been so spirited and attentive. "This will be mounted next to the front door of house number fifty. It's a plaque that reads, 'This house is dedicated to the memory of Linda Rutledge. May whoever dwells here live a full and happy life with many kind and generous friends.'"

And once again, despite the enthusiastic cheers of the crowd, there wasn't a dry eye in the place.

ACKNOWLEDGMENTS

While researching the subject of veterans' housing for this book, I came across an organization called the Veterans Community Project in Kansas City, Missouri. They build communities of tiny houses for veterans in need, and since Shannon Hammer and her construction crew also build tiny homes, I thought, how perfect! So Shannon and her crew joined with Mac Sullivan to design and build Homefront, a new veterans' village in Lighthouse Cove, and that's how the idea of *Absence of Mallets* was born! Please check out the good work of the Veterans Community Project at veteranscommunity project.org.

Ready to find
your next great read?

Let us help.

Visit prh.com/nextread